About

Tim Standish grew up in England, Scotland and Egypt. Following a degree in Psychology, his career has included teaching English in Spain, working as a researcher on an early computer games project, and working with groups and individuals on business planning, teamworking and personal development.

He has travelled extensively throughout his life and has always valued the importance of a good book to get through long waits in airports and longer flights between them. With a personal preference for historical and science fiction as well as the occasional thriller, he had an idea for a book that would blend all three and *The Sterling Directive* was created. Tim sees this as the first in a series of novels featuring Agents Sterling and Church (and almost certainly Patience). He is already working on the second book, which will be set in America and reveal more of the alternative history of Sterling's world.

When not working or writing, Tim enjoys long walks under big skies and is never one to pass up a jaunt across a field in search of an obscure historic site. He has recently discovered the more-exciting-than-you-would-think world of overly-complicated boardgames.

The Sterling Directive

Tim Standish

unbound

This edition first published in 2020

Unbound

T C Group, Level 1 Devonshire House, One Mayfair Place, London W1J
8AJ

www.unbound.com

ISBN (eBook): 978-1-78965-086-0
ISBN (Paperback): 978-1-78965-085-3

Cover design by Mecob

Printed and bound in Great Britain by Clays Ltd, Elcograf S.p.A.

For my parents

Super Patrons

Sian Lang
Pete Langman
Mary Ann le Lean
Donna Lelean
Elizabeth LeLean
Hannah LeLean
Jeremy LeLean
Joseph LeLean
Les LeLean
Maureen Lelean
Paula LeLean
Terry Lelean
Chris Limb
Ethan Maltby
Jonathan Massey
Janice McGuinness
Megan Meredith
Alan Mitchell
Sean Moore
Kate Newton
Mike Nugent
Mark O'Neill
Andrew Park
Dan Porter
Jason Reid
Martin Roche
Richard Ryan
Les Sharman
Louise Sheridan
Dan Shlepakov
Dan Simpson
Naomi Simpson
Cindy Vallance

Sonja van Amelsfort
Edwina Waddy
James Whittingham
Steve Wilinsky
Stephen Wren
Anita Wyatt

Prologue

The early engines were huge, cumbersome warehouses of rods and cogs, too complex and expensive for any but states to own and operate. Hence their operations largely consisted of the collection, codification and analysis of data, with the overall aim of protecting and sustaining the longstanding status quo. Government agencies such as Britain's Bureau of Engine Security closely guarded the secrets of engine technology, keenly punishing its illegal use.

It was not until the final decades of the century that engine technology became cheaper to produce, more portable and more accessible to a wider marketplace of inventors, manufacturers, researchers and, inevitably, the criminal classes. From this seething pot of experimentation bubbled not just technological, but societal and even political changes as old mores and certainties were challenged and disordered.

In Britain, Gordon of Khartoum swept to power at the head of a new political movement whose continental sloganeering of equality and brotherhood unfortunately proved unbeatable. Despite its reduced circumstances, France's pre-eminence in the new battleground of on-wire engine warfare cemented its place as a player in the great game; and Paris's reputation as an infamous haven for tappers and data brokers is well deserved. Even the Confederate States of America, long shunned because of President Jackson's actions in the Second Civil War, found its way slowly back into world affairs, the commercial possibilities of new, connective technologies breaching the walls of political isolation.

The 1880s then, and even more so the 1890s, proved to be the beginning of a new era: the Age of the Engine.

– Maria Corelli, *A Young Woman's History of the Modern Age* (1908)

LONDON. 1896.

1. Smoke

'Gentlemen. Before we proceed I must ask you both whether you are willing to resolve this dispute by any other means?'

The fog that clung to the concrete surface of the platform was given a pale glow by the first light of an early dawn; Burns, my second, could barely be seen where he stood, scarf wrapped across his face, in the shadow of a black iron pillar some way beyond me, a little further than the distance I would have to walk. It said much about the length of my absence from London society that the only support I could command in such a venture was the man known about the club as 'Secondary' Burns, a man who had, to my knowledge, offered his services as duelling assistant to eight of our fellow members, each and every one of whom had subsequently been unsuccessful in their aim.

No wordplay intended.

'Very well. On the count of one, you will each take a step in the direction you are facing. At each subsequent count, you should take an additional step until the count of ten is reached. At that time each of you will turn and fire a single shot at his opponent. If as a result either of you has been mortally wounded, or if honour is otherwise deemed to have been satisfied, the exchange is complete. If, however, these conditions are not met, you will reload and continue to fire until that is the case. Do either of you not understand these instructions?'

Somewhere between where Burns was standing and where my final pace would take me there was an empty cigarette packet on the ground, but from where I was I couldn't tell the brand and, for some reason, this suddenly seemed oddly vexing.

The station official waited a sensible amount of time for either second to voice a concern or query. Both remained resolutely silent. The official nodded to the doctor who stood off to one side and, after one last enquiring glance to each party, continued.

'Very well. ONE.'

The thought occurred to me as I set off that, if I stretched my strides slightly, I would be able to reach a point where I would be able to make out the lettering on the cigarette packet. I adjusted my pace accordingly, but stepped carefully; a heavy frost still lay, unmelted, on the platform's surface.

'TWO.'

The trouble was that the few brands available prior to my departure had, since I had been away, been joined by a proliferation of new cigarette brands which, in an attempt to win favour with the short-sighted purchaser, had based their design on those of the established manufacturers. Somewhere on one of Waterloo's other, functioning platforms, an early service from Paris hissed to a halt, whistling its arrival cheerily. I imagined newspapers being folded, cases grasped, coats donned, hats carefully seated on heads.

'THREE.'

The industrialisation of London seemed to have grown apace, with smaller engines appearing to be more commonplace than they were when I left for America. The military had of course retained the monopoly on the more complicated engines, the specifications of which were still secret. However, partial declassification of the technology involved had led to many smaller companies being able to compete beyond their natural reach and had instigated a commercial revolution. At least that was what it had said in the in-flight magazine that I had glanced at on the way over from Canada. From what I had seen of London so far it seemed mainly to mean: more smoke.

'FOUR.'

The name was Victoria… Or perhaps victory. Either would make an obvious title for a patriotic brand of tobacco.

It made me think of one of the first patrols I had undertaken in my posting; my section had come across a little village, barely more than a collection of shacks and lean-tos and almost certainly inhabited by the French speakers who populated that area of the Canadian Provinces.

'FIVE.'

Given what we'd been told about local sentiments I had been astounded to discover an almost life-sized picture of Her Majesty adorning the largest hut. I mentioned this symbol of heartening patriotism to my sergeant, a veteran of the region who responded to my question with a short laugh. 'Bless you sir,' he said 'that's the name of the gin they make round here.'

'SIX.'

Some weeks afterwards I was informed by a fellow officer that I had acquired the nickname 'Ginny' Maddox. It was the last time that I had hazarded an opinion about the locals in earshot of my sergeant.

Something buzzed sharply past me and I was puzzling over its source when the sound of a shot echoed through the platform. Pausing in my stride I cautiously put a hand to my shoulder and it was only when I saw it covered in a bright smear of blood that I realised what had happened. I was about to turn when another sound distracted me. I looked ahead and saw Burns collapse, gasping, to his knees. I turned to the official who had begun proceedings.

'If you will continue counting, sir.'

'But... I mean... I—'

'Continue the count, if you please.'

'SEVEN,' the official continued, more uncertainly than before.

I recommenced my pacing, feeling the pain and warmth spread out across my neck and shoulder as blood began to slowly seep into the cloth of my jacket.

'EIGHT.'

Over the years an increasing number of rituals and restrictions had been crafted to differentiate what happened at the Waterloo duelling grounds from the more common act of murder as practised by grubbier protagonists in the rest of the capital. One of these, the embargo against weapons produced after 1815, lent a confidence to my careful pacing that I might not have felt had we been using modern pistols.

Even so, the percussion pistols deemed 'quite the thing' by fashionable society this season were one of the most sophisticated styles available and, though still fiddly, were relatively quick to load. As I stepped out the remaining two yards I ran through the reloading actions in my head, estimating that my opponent's nerves would provide enough time for my remaining two strides.

It occurred to me that, while being shot once from behind said something about the baseness of the shooter, being shot twice from the same direction spoke more badly of me.

'NINE.'

Burns was on all fours, pawing the ground, trying to lift himself up; his breath spouted in steaming gasps from his mouth. His face, as far as I could make out, seemed more puzzled than in pain.

I was close enough to see the packet clearly now. Victoria. The engine-stippled design rendered her majestic and unsmiling in a pose long since unrepresentative of her ailing health.

'TEN.'

I turned. Edgar had his back to me, struggling along with his second to reload the pistol. 'Edgar!' I called down the platform.

The Honourable Edgar Theodore Huntingdon looked round, his face white against the black of his second's hat brim and time slowed, sound faded. I remembered him in our staircase at college, loudly confident, dismayed at our lack of enthusiasm for midnight carolling. And in London, determinedly the bon vivant of our set, dragging us all to the latest and brightest places. And in Cooper's. Always back to Cooper's.

I raised my arm and sighted, my breath clouding in the freezing air, held the gun steady, gently pulled the trigger and felt that guiltily reassuring kick of the gun's blast. The cloud of smoke obscured my view and the gun's blast froze my hearing but I knew instinctively that I had hit.

I sidestepped for a clear view and I saw not only Edgar, but also his second seeming to hang for a moment as a faint red mist clouded the air around them both.

Hearing returned, breathing began and my senses quickened. The two men collapsed to the floor.

The first time I killed a man was in Canada; our camp had been attacked one night by a small force of outlaws from across the border. Awakened by the sound I raced to the perimeter and began shooting into the darkness, aiming at nothing, just wanting to show my men that I was no stand-off officer.

We had fought the attack off and at first light I went out with my sergeant to check the bodies. We came across one lying not far from the section of the stockade I had helped defend. He had been shot in the stomach and was barely alive. Sergeant Jones had bent down to him and looked up at me. 'The poor bastard's got his lights hanging out, sir. He's done for.' He had told me, 'Best finish him off.' He had smiled at me and nodded in what he had probably thought was an encouraging manner.

I had looked down at the man's face. He was a thuggish-looking fellow with a bristled, coarse face. One of the criminals periodically set free to harass us at a long and deniable arm's length by the Confederate States. I had drawn my pistol and pointed it at the man's face then pulled the trigger with my eyes half shut. Jones had clapped me on my shoulder and had walked towards where another body lay with me in tow, a chick to his mother hen.

I had managed a few yards before doubling over and vomiting. The sergeant had tugged me to my feet, muttering 'better out than in' and suggesting that perhaps I might like to leave the rest of the perimeter to him. I had wiped off my mouth, drawn in a breath and replied that I was happy to continue; stern faced and with a semblance of composure I had done just that, enduring Jones' gruesome commentary as we were touring the ground. By the end of the circuit I had even managed a laugh or two that had seemed to result in a grudging few points being added by him to my meagre tally of respect.

That night I had lain under cold, stiff canvas, curled in my cot like a child, and prayed for sleep.

Now, eight years later, as I stood looking at the body of a man I had once counted my closest friend, I watched a dark stain spread from a hole in his chest and I felt nothing.

The man who had acted as our official walked towards me even as the attendant doctor rushed to confirm the inevitable.

'I really must congratulate you sir, not only on your bravery but moreover most deservedly on your marksmanship. Really,

I am quite astounded to have witnessed such an exemplar of gentlemanly conduct. Next time I hear someone say that there are no old-fashioned officers left in the army I'll be sure to point out their error. I dare say that here's one pair of overprivileged layabouts that have been persuaded of that.' He barked a little laugh and beamed at me as if waiting for applause.

I looked at him. Handed him the gun without a word and stared at him in silence until uncertainty began to creep across his face.

'Make sure someone attends to him,' I said tersely. 'I would take any ill feeling toward him as if it were directed to my own person and consider myself obliged to act accordingly.'

'Please... I meant no disrespect... of course I shall ensure all arrangements are conducted most carefully,' he stammered out, fear competing with obsequiousness for prominence on his face. He would no doubt be in the offices of some Fleet Street hack before Edgar was lying cold in the mortuary.

He reset his face to 'respectfully solemn' and waited for me to commend him on his show of respect. When no such affirmation was forthcoming he haltingly broached the main reason for his approach.

'Captain. The matter is... er... the second of the deceased gentleman on such an occasion usually vouchsafes any... er... monetary transfer that should prove necessary. As the young man in question is sadly... er, I wondered if... er... that is to say—'

'See that any expenses incurred are forwarded to me.'

'And, er, Captain if you don't mind me asking, the other, er, gentlemen? Should I include them on your account?'

I looked down at Edgar's second, whose face had been smashed into bloody ruin by the pistol's ball. 'By all means add this one, but,' I turned back to where Burns was lying face down on the stones of the platform, 'I feel disinclined to pay for a second who doesn't have the decency to shout a warning. Here.' I fished a card from my tunic pocket and handed it to him.

He took the card. 'Quite understandable, Captain, many thanks. I just need to check the available funds, if you wouldn't mind waiting here. I'm sure you understand. Thank you so much.'

He walked as quickly as decorum would allow to his office at the far side of the platform where through the window I saw him bend to insert my card into an old-fashioned-looking reader on his desk. Face pressed close to the display, he impatiently drummed his fingers while he waited for the message to travel to and from the bank's engine house. He glanced up, saw me looking at him and returned his gaze to the machine, probably unbelieving that a mere Captain, no matter how gentlemanly, could afford the services of the London Necropolis Company. I reached up to my head, which had begun to throb and found the blood already sticky. Not deep but hurt like the devil.

I heard something behind me and turned. Edgar was still alive, trying to raise his head. I stepped to where he lay, and knelt. The ground behind him was soaked with half-frozen blood. His eyes tried to focus on me; his lips moved almost silently. I bent to hear the words he was hoarsely forcing out between gritted teeth.

'Charl. Char. Charles.' He took a ragged breath. I'd seen men like this, desperate to cling on to the breath even as it leaked from them. 'Luh. Lucky. Lucky ba... bastard.' He tried to smile but it was beyond him. His eyes changed, the light leaving them as he tried one more time. 'So. Sorry. Charles. Not my fault. Fuh. Fuh.' He choked and coughed a thick lump of blood onto his chest. A tear started its slow way down his cheek. 'Less.' He grunted with effort to form the word, and I realised he was saying Alice. A flash, then, of wet, red memory. The taste of bile in my mouth. I swallowed both away.

And watched as Edgar stopped talking, and then, simply, stopped.

Oddly, though this very moment was one I had imagined and wished for, especially in the early years of my exile, I found myself curiously devoid of sorrow or anger or vindication or any other emotion. Just empty and tired, standing in the cold on the International Platform at Waterloo, and very suddenly aware of the dull but persistent ache in my shoulder.

I stood, straightened my tunic and turned to where the official was returning with an odd look on his face.

'Sir, my Lord, I had no idea of course or I would never have assumed, that is to say of course there is no issue of credit insofar as your lordship is concerned. Most humbly pleased to be of service of course sir, that is, er, my Lord.' He proffered a clipboard with a printed form and handed me a pen.

As I read it my breath caught in my throat. The name that I should have been reading was the name I had travelled here from Canada under, the name of a humble captain in an unfashionable regiment. In fact, my real name was printed out as plain as day: The Hon. Charles Arthur Maddox. In haste I had given him the wrong card. Suddenly nervous I looked about the platform that was, of course, still deserted at this time in the morning.

'The London Necropolis Company thanks you for your patronage my Lord and hopes that you use us again for any funerary needs you may have in the future.'

I smiled uncertainly, signed the form. He handed back my card and I tucked it away in a pocket. In my mind I imagined engines turning their gears, my name appearing with a click, lighting a light on somebody's desk. I took one last look round the platform, nodded curtly to the official and to the doctor bent over the bodies of Edgar and his second.

'Gentlemen.'

I hurried towards the platform exit where a Metropolitan Police sergeant and a *garde impériale* waited to check my pass. I took it from the same pocket that held the card I should have used and handed it to the sergeant, whose three stripes were brightly picked out in silver thread upon the collar of his overcoat.

He unfolded the pass and studied the printed likeness carefully, concentration furrowing his brow, before glancing at the rest of the paper.

'A monthly, sir?' he observed as he looked up, the surprise in his tone causing his colleague to take more of an interest. 'You're not expecting to be back here again are you?'

'I had no expectation of being here in the first place, sergeant and I sincerely hope that the business is now concluded, but I always remember something I was told by an officer I once met.'

'Really sir?'

'Yes, we were at dinner one evening and he was asked to say what, in his opinion, was the single most important skill for a soldier to have.'

'And what did he say that was, sir?'

'To be prepared, sergeant, to be prepared.'

He laughed indulgently, his French colleague joining in after a moment's delay. 'Very good, sir. A very sound piece of advice I've no doubt. Well, this all seems to be in order.' He refolded the paper and handed it back. 'And may I say a fine piece of shooting on your part.' He smiled for a moment and then seemed to remember his role. 'Just make sure you keep that sort of thing in here on the platform.'

'But of course.'

'If I may point out, sir, you really ought to have that injury seen to. Might just be a lucky graze, but you can never tell with these old pistols. If you will allow me to call you an ambulance…'

I nodded and he led me into the station proper. We had reached the stairs leading down from the entrance to the road where a few ambulances, guessing a duel was on or, more likely having been tipped off for a few shillings, waited for fares.

'Ask one of those chaps to take me to the hospital at Charing Cross would you?'

'Right you are, sir.' He smiled, a customer of Charing Cross could be expected to furnish an appropriately large gratuity.

'Oh, and sergeant!'

He looked up from mid-negotiation. 'Sir?'

'Tell him he'll be waiting for me there and then taking me on to an hotel.'

'Right-o, sir.' I felt in my pocket for a coin.

From the main entrance to the station the earliest of the day's commuters bustled on their way to work. London was beginning to stir.

2. Rendezvous

The room's kinetographic screen was mechanical, and every time an image changed it did so with a cascade of minute ripples from the top to the bottom of its ornate silver frame. I had only found one channel that wasn't pornographic; a short, repeating visual summary of the day's headlines. A parade of Indian troops receiving medals, Salisbury leaning tiredly at the dispatch box, Gordon at a rally, the crowd festooned with placards, a well-dressed young couple hugging in front of a set of steps, Vice-President Custer and his wife arriving at Croydon Aerodrome; each image fluttered into being for a short time, the bottom half of the screen showing the relevant headlines. A dozen or so others went past and then, just as I was beginning to feel relieved, the screen showed an image of Waterloo Station with the words 'Mystery Toff Tops Two!' emblazoned beneath.

I silently cursed my stupidity and pressed the buttons that switched off the screen, causing it to ripple for one last time, the pictures vanishing from top to bottom, leaving the surface within the frame a dull grey.

'You don't like the girls, Milord?'

I turned to face her. 'Of course I do.'

'You like Marie?'

'But of course.'

'I think the Madame will be here soon, but maybe we have time for a little game?' She turned to lie half back on the bed, the heavy velvet robe slipping as she did so to 'accidentally' expose a most non-demure expanse of pale skin. She cocked her head invitingly and settled back into the silk pillows, shrugging the unfastened hems of the robe further apart as she did so.

I watched this perfectly rehearsed routine and, despite myself, felt it beginning to have an effect on me, despite the fact that I had seen it, with subtle variations on countless previous occasions with the other Maries I had met here in this room.

She was, I thought to myself, ever so slightly shorter than the last Marie I had known. In all other respects, though, they were identical; the same pale golden skin, long raven hair and slightly angular features framed by the same clothing, make-up and setting. I had known three different Maries here, with this version a fourth and there may well have been others while I was away in Canada. However, everything was engineered to exaggerate the effect so that one could, with very little effort, imagine that on every visit, the same, unchanging girl was to be found waiting, alluring in her red velvet robe.

It was the same in every room in Cooper's, the same process of illusion repeated, though with different themes in each. I had never chosen an Emily or a Pilar, a Mariko or a Heidi, but if I had done so, I would have known precisely what to expect. Mrs Cooper prided herself on her ability to consistently provide for her clients' expectations, an intention echoed by the portraits that hung above the staircase at the front of the house, each in the style of a different artist and each portraying one of the girls *au costume*. This gallery acted as a sort of catalogue for visitors to the house, an artistic promise of what lay in store. Some customers cycled through the rooms as the whim took them, but I had always remained loyal to Marie from the very first time I saw her. And, as I watched her now, it was reassuringly easy to suspend my disbelief and believe that this was my dear sweet Marie, waiting through the long, lonely years for my return.

But nostalgia was only a small part of why I was waiting here at Cooper's, rather than sensibly staying in my hotel room until it was time to head to Paddington to catch the sleeper. Killing Edgar had been foolish and with him dead the only person who might give me the answers I needed was Mrs Cooper. I looked at my watch; almost five o'clock. Another thirty minutes before I would have to leave.

Perhaps taking my clock-watching as indifference, Marie chose that moment to roll entirely out of the robe and to lie, nude, on the bed, with her arms above her head, legs drawn up and turned to one side, her head gazing upwards as if unaware of the effect she might be having. Unhampered by the velvet, her perfume drifted languorously across the room. I could not think of a single soldier who I had served with in the last eight years who would not have thought this a dream come true.

And then, unbidden, that long-submerged image pressed itself briefly into my mind again and for slightly longer than an incoherent flash this time: another room here in Cooper's, with another girl lying on a bed of scarlet. Any thoughts of taking up Marie's offer drained from me in a moment. I forced the memory back down and mustered a thin smile.

Puzzled and not a little irate at my failure to respond to her invitation, Marie tried another pose, lying face down with one leg bent up and head turned to with a playfully beckoning glance. I intervened before I was treated to a series of staged variations on the theme of 'coquette'.

'I say, Marie, why not order some champagne for us?'

She paused, giving the appearance of deep pondering. 'And per'aps some *chocolat,* Milord?'

'Some *chocolat* would be perfect, Marie.'

She wrapped herself back up in her robe, jumped up from the bed with girlish glee and skipped to the panel of buttons set next to the door. 'Just the drink?'

'A little to eat, perhaps; you choose.'

She gasped (just a little too) excitedly and opened the book; started punching in combinations of numbers.

'Careful now, m'dear,' I called, 'I'll have nothing left to pay you with!'

She half turned to me, eyebrows raised, clearly unconvinced by this assertion and continued to tap a series of numbers into the controls. Before she had finished, a gentle chime sounded and a small blue light went on over a discreet panel set into the wall near to where she stood. She slid it up and reached in to gather up the tray of drinks that had appeared. She brought it over to the table near the window and set it down before settling down in one of the armchairs, feet drawn up and red velvet gathered around her, waiting expectantly for me to finish filling the glasses.

I tugged the already opened bottle from the ice bucket and began to pour. She seemed genuinely excited to be about to drink champagne and I idly surmised that she must have only recently arrived at Mrs Cooper's if champagne was still such a treat for her.

And smiled to myself at how easily I had been taken in with what was a part of the act, the story that went with Marie. I handed her a glass, which was rewarded with a gasp, a smile and a 'Merci beaucoup, milord'. As I watched her sip prettily, her story came back to me.

A recent arrival from Paris, Marie had always 'just arrived by train the night before' in flight from French Imperial agents who had arrested her parents. She was always hungry and always thirsty and always ever so grateful to a kind gentleman who would buy her a glass of champagne and a cup of hot *chocolat*. Her command of English was moderately poor, always spoken with a sweetly continental accent and she was especially keen to learn any new words she might be taught. I picked up a flute of champagne and toasted Mrs Cooper in silence.

'Madame will be 'ere soon, Milord.'

It was the first thing that Marie had said to me when I had arrived to find her waiting for me downstairs and was a phrase that she had repeated several times in the hour since. 'I hope so,' I said, and sipped the champagne which was, of course, as fine as the surroundings.

I decided to wait it out a while longer. Mrs Cooper was someone I had thought about long and hard during my time away as I tried to fathom why she had acted as she had that night eight years ago. Edgar's motive was plain; he wanted me to take the blame for what he had done, but why had Cooper helped him rather than me?

'You like some music, per'aps?'

I nodded and Marie went across to the phonogram, plucked a cylinder seemingly at random and dropped it in. A tune of arabesque origin began to drift about the room, and I lay back in my chair, and tried to relax. Not an easy task; although I wasn't named as the 'Mystery Toff' in the headline, I was unconvinced that my anonymity would last for long and wanted to get out of the capital as soon as possible. But I needed to speak to Cooper, to hear her version of our last meeting here.

There was another low chime, the light came on again and Marie skipped across to the panel to retrieve a tray of what turned out to be pastries and fine chocolates.

This tray went on to the bed, while she brought a plate of pastries across and sat, with them, on my lap.

'Milord?' she offered me a pastry and, finding myself hungry, I nodded. My stomach agreed, gurgling as I swallowed the first bite, an easy cue for a hands-in-the-air gasp and shriek of laughter from Marie. 'You must have all of these, I think, you are so 'ungry. I will get some more for us.' She left me the plate and went back to order more food.

'You are a soldier, Milord?' she called back over her shoulder.

'What makes you say that?'

She looked up from the panel of buttons and shrugged her shoulders.

'I was.'

She came back and sat on the edge of the bed nearest me. Her legs swung slightly. 'Did you ever kill a man, Milord?'

I looked at her and adopted what I hoped was a serious expression and shook my head.

'Never.'

She frowned. 'You must be a bad soldier, Milord.'

'The worst that there is. I couldn't hit a barn door if my nose was touching it.'

She thought about this for a moment, either working out what this meant or doing a good show of working it out and a smile slowly appeared. She tilted her head and narrowed her eyes. 'I think you are joking me, n'est-ce pas?'

I laughed. 'Un peu.'

Her eyes widened, delighted. 'Vous parlez le Francais! Très bien!'

I assured her that this was not the case, that I only spoke a little French and that badly but she insisted on continuing the conversation in French, by turns complimenting me on my grammar and mocking my accent which, like the language itself, had been picked up in Canada. Then she wanted to know about Canada and I told her about the cold, the wilderness and the sporadic fighting. We drank champagne as we talked. Were there any women there, she wondered. None as pretty as she, I assured her.

Again the laughter and this time she came to sit in my lap again and rewarded me for my compliment with a gentle kiss on the forehead, and on the nose and on the lips, and then it was no longer gentle and her hands were round my neck and, suddenly light-headed, it took every effort on my part to lever her away. She looked at me calculatingly.

'Some more champagne, Milord.' It was not a request and this time she paced languidly to the door, the red robe trailing behind her so that when she turned to order another bottle, the curves of her profile were alluringly visible. I exhaled slowly and took a deep breath in, shaking my head, and got up, sliding the window upwards to let in some fresh air.

And paused.

'Milord?' Marie was behind me; I heard the robe fall to the floor and felt her hands on the back of my neck.

'Hush.' I shrugged her hands off, ignoring her, and moved so that I could see out of the window, down into the square outside. It was empty; a street sweeper walked across the small park in the middle, a small white dog trotting after him.

'Qu'est-ce que c'est?'

I turned to face her. 'I don't know. Put out the candles and stay back from the window.'

Patrolling in Canada, I learnt, along with my troops, to pay attention when one of us felt something was out of kilter, even if they couldn't say why. We would stop, stock still in the landscape, and open our senses to identify the sound, or smell, or pattern that shouldn't be there, or the familiar something that was missing. More than once we avoided an ambush because one of us sensed the smallest of incongruities.

So I froze in place, waiting until the room was totally dark and my eyes had adjusted. Then I heard it. A close to inaudible whining, intermittent and almost lost in the hubbub that drifted in the early evening air from Regent Street.

I moved towards the window and looked out again. The square was completely empty now; the walker and his dog had gone on their way and there was not a soul in sight.

Again, I heard the noise, this time louder, and its direction suddenly crystallised in my mind so that slowly, ever so slowly, I crouched down by the window and looked up. And knew, then, that I really shouldn't have come to Cooper's.

3. Mesh

The airship filled the sky.

It was small, not much more than an aerial cutter or light sloop, but in those first few moments that I saw it, its gossamer bulk dominating the sky above the square, it seemed impossibly massive. Within the craft a host of technologies would be whirring away in productive harmony: a small computational engine would be calculating height, measuring wind and adjusting each small propeller individually to maintain a steady position; other sensors would be monitoring weight and height and adjusting gas mixtures accordingly while finely tuned instruments were ready to respond to the instructions of the pilot. All this I understood but somewhere deep inside the un-evolved recesses of my mind an ancestral instinct still cowered and shook in fear at the marvellous impossibility of it all.

I stood stock still as a series of new sounds broke into the night air; the clank of catches, whirr of gears and the smooth rush of pulleys as the bay doors opened and several lines unfurled in unison to the pavement below. From the underside of the airship men emerged and dropped down the ropes, steadied themselves and raced to take up positions facing the club. I watched for a moment and then turned to Marie, who had huddled against me as I studied the scene below.

'Is there a back way from the club?'

'Oui. Through the kitchen.'

'They will have thought of that.' I held her shoulders. 'Is there another way? A window perhaps or a side door?' She gave a nervous shrug, her eyes wide in fear and this time it was no act. I held her hands, squeezed them briefly. 'You will be safe as long as you stay here, Marie. Do you understand?' She nodded. 'Stay here. Leave the door open but stay out of sight. All will be well.' I smiled at her in as reassuringly a manner as I could manage.

I had no idea how truthful my words were. I had never known the club to be raided before and in fact certain members of the local judiciary were encouraged to return regularly for an evening of free entertainment to ensure that that remained the case. But this was different. I doubted that the doormen employed by Mrs Cooper would be a match for this particular raid; my last glimpse down had told me that much as I watched the armed men take up their positions. I had seen that very arrangement once before, in a training session at HQ back in Canada, laid out on a plan of a street under the legend 'Assault, urban (search and retrieval)' or, as the lecturer had described it, 'Kidnap and robbery, gentlemen, kidnap and robbery.'

Staying away from the window I stood and walked to the door. I probably had a few seconds before the last one was in position, then a few more before their officer checked all was ready and gave his signal. A fleeting thought that I might be the object to be retrieved was quashed as quickly as it arose: no one knew I was in the country, there was no record of my arrival and any attention caused by the morning's events would surely be focused on my hotel. I had deliberately come out without my own card so that now I was simply Captain Brown of the North American Volunteer Rifles, back in London on leave and keen to purchase some pleasure. My main hope was that the intruders would be fixated on a rapid retrieval and exit and uninterested in me or anyone else in the club, though what their fixation might be had me baffled.

I opened the door and turned back to look at the girl where she knelt. She looked up at me and nodded quickly. I left her and moved down the corridor as stealthily as I could. From behind one of the other doors I heard a giggle followed by a braying guffaw. I crept onwards towards the head of the main staircase but before I reached it they started.

First the crash, startlingly loud in the stillness of the house, as the door was forced in; then the thump of boots and shouted orders as they manhandled the protesting doormen out of the way and spread into the house. I walked into plain sight, a startled client wanting to know what the blazes was going on.

'Armed officers! Lie down. Do not move!'

I raised my arms, still radiating shock, surprise and not a little outrage.

'Are you deaf? Get down! Now!' One of them started towards me; he was wearing what looked like army fatigues but instead of the usual khaki these were dark blue, almost black. The bulky, high-necked waistcoat he wore over them was a similar colour as was the kit belt that hung heavily laden about his waist. His face was blackened and barely visible above the waistcoat that I now realised must be some sort of anti-ballistic protector. The gun that he raised to shoulder height and aimed at me looked like a short-nosed machine carbine; notoriously inaccurate over anything above thirty yards but more than capable of hitting me over the short distance that separated us.

I knelt slowly as he walked up the stairs towards me, lowering the gun but keeping it pointed steadily towards me. I con-

tinued, dropped to the floor and lay flat with my fingers joined
behind my head. Moments later I felt the muzzle jab into my
back between my shoulders.

'And stay there if you want to live.'

He was not quite the professional that his equipment proclaimed; getting so close to me was the mistake of a novice and
likely because my slow compliance had riled him somewhat.
Even so, armed as he was, I rated my chances of any sudden
movement on my part resulting in long-term survival as 'poor
to non-existent'.

The rest of the squad sounded as though they had split up,
with the majority moving into the rest of the ground floor and
the remainder coming up the stairs, some going to the girls'
rooms and a few to the opposite end of the second floor where,
I knew, Mrs Cooper had her office.

'Who have you got there?' This voice carried authority;
came from near the front door.

The response was another nudge of the gun's barrel into
the nape of my neck and a shout from my captor: 'Some nob;
caught 'im wandering around when we came in. Here with
one of the tarts I shouldn't wonder.'

'Fascinating.' The tone was bored, scornful of this piece of
conjecture. 'Is he armed?'

'Don't think so, sir.'

'You don't think so? That is tremendous news. Well, bring
him down and let's take a look at him.'

I was pulled to my feet and marched down the stairs to
where a slim, fashionably dressed man waited. He had none of
the military accoutrements of his subordinates and though he
carried a sizeable revolver it hung loose in his hand as though
he had forgotten what it was. In his well-cut overcoat, fine
woollen scarf and bowler hat he seemed more like a client of

the club than an officer of the law, not that those two categories had ever been mutually exclusive.

'And who, sir, are you?' His stance, voice and face betrayed not a shred of urgency or interest but his eyes were a cold, startling blue with a focus and intelligence that gave the lie to the carelessness he was so keen on portraying.

'Captain Brown, North American Volunteer Rifles.'

'Well, Captain Brown, North American Volunteer Rifles, where are your papers?

I fished my card out of my pocket, conscious as I did so of the nervous carbine-wielder who was still behind me. I held it out to him and, after tucking his pistol away in a coat pocket, he took the card and looked it over. 'Back for a spot of leave, Captain?'

'That's right.'

'Expensive place, Cooper's. I'm surprised a captain can afford it.'

'I've been abroad. Nowhere really to spend it over there.'

'Far East?'

'Canada. Frontier duty.'

'Really?' His interest seemed piqued by that. 'When did you get back?'

'Yesterday.'

'And came straight round here, no doubt to renew an old acquaintance?' He seemed amused. As he thought of his next question two of his men came up from the cellar of the house carrying a strongbox between them. He glanced at them and motioned for them to set it down on the floor. The larger of the two saluted.

'Sir. Found this in the cellar.' He opened the box, the lock of which looked like it had already been forced. Inside was a layer of oblongs, shaped like pats of butter and wrapped in waxed paper.

'You have tested one, I presume?'

'Yes, sir. It's opium. There's another box just like it down there.'

'That's ridiculous, Cooper's is licensed.' I was surprised at my own interjection but I felt I had to say something.

The officer bent down to look at the box while the others stood to almost attention. He stared at the contents for a moment and then started tugging the blocks of opium out by the armful and throwing them onto the floor. He gave a gentle grunt of satisfaction and stood, holding a long brown paper package the length of a man's arm. Silently he unwrapped the loose covering and let it drop to the ground.

'As you say. But tell me, Captain, do you think that Mrs Cooper has a licence for these?' What he was holding toward me was very similar to the weapons that armed his squad, though with no magazine and still gleaming from the protective oil applied in the factory.

'That's not all, sir.' The taller of the box-bearers spoke up. 'We found a false wall down there. There's a wireless transmitter and some sort of engine. It looks milit'ry.'

'Now then, Captain. Tell me again, what were you doing here?'

'Seeing a girl.'

He smiled. Dropped the carbine back onto the packets of opium. 'I don't think so.' He waved a hand at me. 'You seem a trifle overdressed for a customer. I think that you were meeting someone.'

'I wouldn't call it a meeting exactly. Conversation wasn't really on the menu.'

'So, you aren't here to sort out problems with your supplier? Perhaps Cooper was asking for more money? Perhaps the rebels were asking for more money?' All pretence to casual disinterest was gone from the man as he took a step towards me and brought his face to within an inch or two of mine. His eyes sparkled with insight. 'I have hit upon it, have I not? You came here to meet Mrs Cooper, your criminal partner in some treasonous scheme?'

I kept my tone matter of fact. 'I've been out in North America for a few years. I got myself injured, came back to recuperate and thought this would be a good place to start. If taking a girl to bed counts as treason, things have changed since I was last here.'

We stood toe to toe for a moment while he stared closely at my face; searching for nerves or a sign that I was lying. I controlled my breathing and let him find nothing but inside my mind was racing. Was this why Mrs Cooper hadn't been here as promised? Was she in some sort of trouble?

He was smaller than me by a good few inches and thinly built but more importantly he didn't know how to spread his weight and a quick push would have had him over. I could have easily followed up with an arm lock or something more painful and I considered it for a second but I still hadn't heard the safety catch of the carbine behind me go on so thought better of it.

Suddenly he smiled and turned away, walking slowly away from me and spoke, almost to himself, 'Taking a girl to bed.' He paused and stared down into the box then lifted one of his arms to point back at me as if conceding a point in a debate. 'You are, of course, quite right. There is nothing wrong with that at all. Supplying Continental Army rebels with weapons to use against the Confederate States Government; now that's more than a harmless bit of fun. I will grant you though that, strictly speaking, it's not a betrayal of our nation. And who knows what else your Mrs Cooper has been plotting with her wireless transmitter? And possessing illegal engine technology? Well, that's a capital offence on its own.'

I stood my ground. 'This is ridiculous. Utterly ridiculous. I am sure that Mrs Cooper will tell you the same thing when she arrives.'

'A hypothesis, I fear to say, that we shan't be putting to the test.' He looked pleased with himself in a way that made me want to punch him. Several times. 'Mrs Cooper was shot earlier this evening while attempting to escape police custody.' He pointed to one of the others: 'Wilkins. Keep things locked down. No one in or out. And see what else you can find.' He turned at the clatter of boots on the staircase; another of his men returning from the upper floor. 'Anything?'

'A promising-looking safe in the office.'

'Good. Sergeant Wilkins will be taking charge; make sure that the others know.'

'Sir.'

'Now then, Captain. I think we have done enough standing in the hallway, wouldn't you say? Probably best if we take our conversation elsewhere.' He indicated the open front door. 'Shall we?'

'Shall we not?' I replied. 'This is a licensed establishment. I have done nothing wrong so I don't see why we shouldn't wait here for one of the more well to do guests upstairs to call their lawyer and explain to you the error of your ways.'

'Well, Captain, while that sort of bluster might intimidate the average constable, we are the Bureau of Engine Security and you must have been away for quite a while if you don't know what that means. So, I think we'll just move along.'

The prod in the small of my back pre-empted my reply and I followed him out into the square where the ship was waiting, at almost ground level now, with a short, brass-framed ladder reaching down from it.

'After you, Captain.'

I climbed up the ladder, clambered through a wide hatch

in the floor of the cabin and emerged into the rear space and under the watching eyes of another of the men in uniform. He gestured with his gun to a seat. I sat and waited while the grey-coated man entered and took a seat for himself. As he did so, electric motors whirred into action and the ladder concertina'd up into a storage space in the wall; short moments later the hatch doors swung up and clicked into place, sealing the cabin.

'All comfortable? Excellent. Then we'll be off I think.' He reached behind him and tugged down a robust-looking micro-phone from a hook on the wall and said one word. 'Millbank.'

We rose surprisingly quickly, the ship turning as we did, before we headed on our way. There must have been some sort of built-in sound system because, as we started to move, music started playing.

It sounded like Schubert.

4. Panopticon

The cell embodied the atmosphere of all English prisons: an unsettling combination of old stone and fresh detergent. The metal grille that formed the whole of the wall facing the courtyard was open to the night air and the narrow windows set high on the opposite side were mostly broken. It was damnably cold. Thinly whitewashed walls formed a space that slanted slightly outwards from window to door. The only source of artificial light was a pair of weak electric bulbs mounted on the ceiling that lit the room with a subdued yellowish glow. Through the grille I could see out into the darkness of the courtyard and, here and there, a few other similarly lit cells dotted the vast, curving circumference of the prison.

The airship that had brought me here was just visible, tethered and netted in the main yard where we had landed, its distinctive silhouette shielded by sheets of unevenly dappled material. The lights at the yard's perimeter that had briefly flared as we descended were dormant now, adding to the deserted air of the place. Occasionally I'd seen a dim figure patrolling across the expanse of flagstones that floored the central area. Aside from that, and the squad that had travelled with me, I had seen very little signs of life on the way to my cell.

I assumed that the majority of whatever force garrisoned the prison were holed up in the dark, truncated spire that rose up from the centre of the yard like a squat, black lighthouse.

They had Bertie'd me in a room there when we arrived using a portable machine: forty-four minutes ago, by the watch they had thoughtfully allowed me to retain when they locked me in here. More than enough time to run my head measurements through the Whitehall engines and find out who I was. And at that point, I assumed, they would be straight back up here with a more focused line of enquiry than 'we know you were up to something'.

I'd paced the room and quickly looked it over, expecting a brief wait before the interviewing began but it seemed that they were in no hurry. So I'd settled in as best I could, pulling the worn wooden chair that was the room's only furniture to the centre and sitting in a gently smothering silence. Faded letters were still visible beneath the cheap whitewash on one of the walls and I passed the time by trying to make out what they said. I assumed that it was some sort of morally uplifting verse and tried to fit the few I remembered from my youth to the barely discernible lettering, though without success. As a pastime it was dull but at least it kept me from dwelling on my idiocy to date and the fact that even at his most pessimistic and patronising, my elder brother Julius would never have imagined that my return would have gone so catastrophically wrong as it had.

Up in one corner a kinetograph gently clicked and whirred as it intermittently recorded and transmitted its pictures of the scene. In contrast to the rest of the cell, its brass housing looked fresh and new, as did the thick iron bolts that clasped its cables to the wall as they snaked away through the floor of the cell and down into the dark below. Somewhere in the bowels of the building a screen like the one in Marie's room would be relaying a staccato series of images as an ongoing register of my incarceration. I hoped that whoever was tasked with viewing them was finding the entertainment as tedious to watch as I was to be its subject.

My thoughts were jolted back to the reality of my present predicament as, after a brief clicking of bolts and with the soft grate of subdued friction, the iron bars forming the whole front of the cell slid gently to one side leaving a wide doorway for me to exit through.

Two of them stood there, faces half obscured by nocturnoscopes. In contrast to the single guard who had walked me up here the two of them looked alert, and both were well armed. Whatever was in the file had apparently levitated my status from 'awkward coincidence' to 'interesting individual'. One stood at the edge of the strained light pooling out from the cell while his companion waited on the landing, gesturing with his carbine for me to move outside. These two knew their distances well, keeping me between them but not close enough to take on both at the same time. I followed their steady pace along the walkway, passing empty cell after empty cell on our left and nothing but the vast space of the courtyard on our right. Along that inner edge ran a safety rail consisting of a rope strung between rusted iron posts that leaned uncertainly at regular intervals along the landing. Based on the obvious age of the rest of building and given their obvious state of rust and decay, I made a point of treading carefully as we made our way along to the stairwell.

We trudged our way down dark stone steps in careful convoy, our little group passing faint white numbers on the wall that counted off the floors and sections. We had come up the same way and I had assumed then that there were stairwells equidistant around the various blocks of cells contained within the walls. In keeping with the overall design the stairwell was open sided, giving any guards stationed in the yard or its spire ample opportunity to monitor our descent. We reached the ground floor and started off across the courtyard floor to the central spire where a plain and heavy iron-faced door was set into the base.

'Wait here,' the guard behind me ordered as the one in front walked up to door and bent forward to talk into a brass box fixed to the wall. The conversation was brief. The door opened onto a room that, as far as I could see, was pitch black and the guard stood to one side; again a gentle carbine prod let me know my role in the matter and I walked through the door and into the tower.

The door closed behind me, and I was left in disorientating pitch blackness for a moment before the room's lights glowed into life and quickly brightened to reveal a space in marked contrast to the abandoned decay of the rest of the prison. The brickwork looked recently and professionally painted and, about twenty feet from where I stood, the heavy wooden table in the centre of the room looked new, its surface unmarked. Either side of the table were two matching, iron-framed folding chairs. The only other furniture in the room was a series of iron coat hooks on the opposite wall, though the filled-in screw holes that dotted the wall around them spoke of an earlier and more cluttered configuration.

The wall behind me arced round to meet the flat wall on the other side of the table, creating a D-shaped room that was slightly less than half the ground floor of the tower and it was through a door set into this far wall that the grey inspector from Cooper's now entered.

He had discarded his suit jacket and rolled up his shirt sleeves, giving him the look of an engineer or factory foreman; the sleeves had been turned up neatly in a way suggesting that, although he acknowledged the necessity of dirty hands, it was something he would have rather avoided. A pair of drab, grey folders under his arm completed the persona; the worn cardboard edges of one sandwiching a thick sheaf of papers, the other slim and seemingly empty.

He dropped both folders onto the table as he sat down, then straightened their edges, and settled himself in his chair. He placed his hands flat in front of him, then spread his fingers and drummed them briefly before looking up at me. Behind him a less heavily armoured but still well-armed guard closed the door and stood at ease in front of it.

'Do sit down, please, Captain Brown.' A smile crept to the corners of his mouth for a brief moment and faded. I did as I was told, walking to the chair on my side of the table. He winced as the iron legs of the chair scraped loudly on the floor and I made the most of it, generating a few more moments of unsettling cacophony as I settled myself into position.

He waited till I had finished, allowing the silence that followed to lengthen for several seconds before declaiming in the slow style of a church reader: 'For the wages of sin is death; but the gift of God is eternal life.'

I was momentarily nonplussed before I realised he was talking about the writing on my cell wall. He was starting as he no doubt meant to continue by emphasising the apparent powerlessness of my position, telling me that there was nowhere to hide; they were watching my every move. He wanted me to know that he already had all the answers, there was no point hiding the truth because he already knew what I was thinking and so on. I threw a question back at him to let him know that I was keeping up: 'An attempt to induce piety?'

He smiled. 'Actually it was a bold experiment in social reform, put into place by the institution's penultimate governor. His idea was to ban all communication between prisoners, keep them in isolation where possible and provide no stimulus other than carefully-selected bible verses that he had painted in each of the cells.'

'Was it successful?'

'It depends on your viewpoint. Certainly the level of recidivism amongst inmates was seriously and, in some cases, permanently reduced.'

Something in his tone told me that this was another game that I could join in with if I wanted to. I hazarded a guess. 'They killed themselves.'

'In ever more ingenious ways. It seemed that solitude and constant contemplation of an unvarying line of scripture sent them demented, with the result that a fair few either ended up in Bedlam or victims of what the ensuing report termed self-inflicted deaths.' He paused. 'Nowadays there's hardly any need to imprison violent criminals; they're simply shipped off to the colonies, to stand guard against various sets of angry natives. But of course, you know that from personal experience.'

It was a good opening shot and it caught me slightly by surprise, but I managed to keep calm. 'Our company had its fair share of men who chose the army as an alternative to gaol, yes.'

'Ah yes, your company. Remind me?'

'D company, First regiment, North American Volunteer Rifles.'

'And when did you join?'

'88.'

'And when were you posted overseas?'

'A few days later.'

'That's much quicker than normal. Were you in some sort of hurry to get away from London?'

'The Rifles were in a hurry to have me out there. There was a shortage of officers at the time.'

'I see.' He paused. 'And you haven't been back to England since?'

'No.'

'And your military career to date has solely consisted of manning the Inner American Border? No postings elsewhere?'

'No.'

'And in,' he paused briefly, 'just over eight years you took no leave, made no effort to return to Britain until now. Why was that, I wonder?'

'Canada is a lovely place, once you get used to the weather. People there are terribly friendly. Very welcoming.' I smiled, helpfully.

He paused, reached for the thinner of the two folders and placed it, open, on the table in front of him. Inside was a single sheet of typed paper. He glanced down the page and then looked up.

'And yet now you have left that lovely place and come back here to London. Why, I wonder?' He left the question hanging with a small tilt of the head and a raised eyebrow. I declined this obvious invitation to respond and he continued. 'I can only imagine that you had vital business here which caused you to take such a long and,' here he glanced down and opened the thinner of the two folders, 'expensive journey and I must say that based on the evidence we have to hand it seems clear to me that the vital business was your meeting with Mrs Cooper.'

'I told you, I went to see a girl.'

'Why?'

'Why do you imagine?'

'She was another contact perhaps, part of the same operation being run by Cooper to smuggle illegal arms to rebels seeking to overthrow the American government. We know that the last shipment was intercepted near Boston. Perhaps, as the mastermind behind all this, you had to risk a trip home to make sure that the failure wasn't repeated?'

'I was overdue some leave. I took it. I was in need of female company. I found it. I can give you the details if you want and I will draw you a diagram if you find it helpful but I can't tell you anything about meetings, smuggling or lost shipments because I haven't the faintest idea what you are talking about.' I could feel myself getting angry as I spoke, and I tried to stop it coming through in my voice. He heard it though and decided to prod me a bit more.

'So you expect me to believe that you, a captain on frontier duty in a down-at-heel regiment had managed to "put a few bob by" which enabled you to purchase a first class airship ticket, pay for the Savile Row tailoring we found you wearing and the company of a whore at one of the West End's most expensive brothels? Where did all this money come from, Captain?'

'I was lucky at cards.'

'You are lying!' He slapped a hand against the table as he spat this at me and looked for a moment as if he would have gladly fetched me a similar blow. He mastered his temper, busying himself with the two folders on the table before continuing more calmly; 'And this is no card game, Captain, I assure you. Bluff and finesse are no match for facts and data, both of which we have in copious supply. I am afraid, Captain, that you may have misinterpreted the purpose of this conversation. The mystery here is not one of innocence versus guilt; it is rather that I am keen to decide which particular crime, of the many possibilities on offer, we try you for. For example,' he continued, warming to his subject, 'when we ran your Bertillon and cross-referenced the army identification you provided, what do you think we discovered?'

'I'm overdue for promotion?'

He was unimpressed. 'They don't match. You are not Captain Brown. I would even go so far as to say that there is no such person as Captain Brown, given that his sole action whilst serving in Her Majesty's Armed Forces has been to purchase an airship ticket. So we have you quite clearly impersonating an army officer and, by extension, lying to a police officer and forging official documents. To these charges we can add associating with a known fugitive, procuring controlled technologies, supplying Enemies of the Crown and latterly, of course, corrupting a minor.'

'Actually, we'd only just opened the champagne when your own set of military impersonators turned up. There was barely time for conversation, let alone corruption. Besides,' I added, 'she was no minor. I know the difference, even if you might not.'

A cheap shot but it seemed to irk him nicely. He stared directly at me, seemed about to lose his temper again but managed to calm himself and continue. 'As I was saying. You are not Captain Brown, which leads us to the question of who you really are.' He closed the thin folder, put it to one side and started to unwind the red cord holding the other folder closed. 'And indeed, when we ran a more detailed archive enquiry things became much more interesting.'

'I have no idea whose file you have there, Inspector, but it's not mine.'

He ignored me. 'Our data are comprehensive and the engines we use to interrogate those data are amongst the most finely calibrated in the Empire. We are the Bureau of Engine Security, Captain. When we search, we find what we are looking for.' The cord unwound, he carefully lifted the folder open. 'We find the truth.'

The paper inside the folder looked newly printed. They had been busy while I was up in the cell. If, as he was boasting, they had found out everything about me then I had a feeling that a tight spot was about to become tighter still.

'We find, for example, that you are indeed a company cap-

tain in the North American Volunteer Rifles, that you are
stationed in Canada and that you have been there for approximately eight years. Unlike your fictitious counterpart, however, your military record makes for the most gripping reading;
tales of derring-do abound within its pages. A rush of promo-
tions, even a medal or two. In fact, given the speed with which
the War Office habitually rushes to publicise this kind of thing
it makes one wonder why we haven't heard of you sooner. It is
as if, rather, the reverse was occurring; that someone was making a concerted effort to keep you out of the limelight. Now,
why would that be?'

He knew, but he wanted me to tell him. Straight out of the
beginner's guide to interrogation: establish rapport, encourage
compliance and so forth. He flipped forward to chapter three,
'Use of silence', and waited for me to answer him. Unfortunately for him I'd read the other half of the guide and knew
that my best option was sticking to my original story, no matter how threadbare, and no matter how much he claimed to
know different.

I shrugged. 'Army heroes are old hat. No one wants to hear
about frozen mud and border skirmishes. It's all about airships
nowadays.'

'Your story is too ordinary?'

'Precisely.'

He spread out some of the papers in front of him. 'The
Honourable Tiberius Charles Arthur Maddox. Son of a viscount. One brother a commodore, the other one of the nation's
leading industrialists and managing director of Maddox Global
Maritime. Both title and family wealth derived from priva-
teering and prizes of war but, more recently, insurance and
overseas investments.' He tapped the papers. 'I would call that
interesting, wouldn't you Captain? I can see the headlines
now: "Plucky Toff pitches in with Courageous Tommies."' He

smiled. 'Of course, they would have to leave out the part where you joined an infantry regiment as an alternative to standing trial for the crime of murder. And assured the authorities of your exiled obscurity and non-return for,' he picked one paper out of the pile and read from it, 'ten years for which period of time the proceedings would be held in abeyance. This paper, signed by you, is dated 12 November 1888. The fine print makes clear that refusal to comply with the agreement renders it null and void with an immediate resumption of criminal proceedings. Which, given that you still have just under two years remaining of those ten, leaves you, Captain Maddox, up to your neck in the latrine, if you will permit me to coin a military phrase.'

'Actually, Inspector, I believe the term is shit-house.' He smiled. 'And no doubt you can extend a helping hand if I give you the information that you want.'

'You understand me precisely, Captain.' He leaned back confidently in his chair and steepled his hands, happy in the knowledge that I was about to throw in the towel. I took a small pleasure in seeing his face change as I disabused him of that notion.

'Then I'm sorry to say that we will both end this conversation as disappointed men, Inspector, because, as I have already told you, I haven't the slightest clue what those boxes were doing at Cooper's or where they were bound. I know nothing of gun smuggling or American rebels, though God knows anyone opposing President Jackson and his lunatic cabal of petty dictators deserves all the help available. I was at Cooper's because I wanted a girl. That's all. Now you can ask questions all night, but I won't be able to answer a single one of them so do us both a favour, put me back on the next airship to Canada.'

He looked like he was gathering himself for another threat

when there was a knock at the door and, obviously irritated, he stood up and squared the papers back into the folder, then walked over to the door and half-opened it to speak to whoever was on the other side. A short, murmured conversation ensued before he stepped out of the way and an older man walked into the room. He was dressed for a night out, a silk scarf over his evening wear, top hat and gloves in one hand. He walked over and stood behind the chair, the inspector a few paces behind and to one side of him. He dropped the hat on the table and the gloves inside it. I noticed as he did that his skin was smooth, his long pale fingers neatly manicured. He took a silver cigarette case out of his jacket, took out a thick, oval cigarette and lit it carefully, all the while watching me for a sign of reaction.

'Would you like one?' he offered me the case.

I shook my head. 'What is this then? Good constable, bad constable?' I said. 'You're wasting your time. I've seen it done before, and not by amateurs either.'

His eyes narrowed slightly at that, then he smiled. 'You don't recognise me, do you Maddox?'

'As I told your mistaken colleague, my name is Brown.'

'And as my well informed and absolutely accurate colleague told you, Captain Maddox, the majority of what you may or may not have done in Canada is immaterial given your return to these shores before the end of a hard-won agreement to commute a capital sentence to a decade in exile. Or have you forgotten that as well, hmm?'

And I recognised him. He had been there that night in Cooper's, arguing strenuously for a private but swift trial. Some sort of plain-clothes policeman. He had moved up in the world judging by his clothes.

He saw the recognition and smiled. 'Ah. I see that you haven't forgotten, Captain. Though we were never formally introduced. My name is Fuller. Deputy Director Fuller if we are being formal.' He offered me a handshake, which I ignored. 'My, my, what an awful habit of impoliteness you seem to have picked up in the army, Charles. And your brother argued so convincingly that it would set you on the straight and narrow.'

'I am afraid you really do have me confused for some other poor fellow.' It was coming back to me now; his over-friendly tone and know-it-all manner. The way he made jokes with Julius in the corridor outside Cooper's office while they bartered for my life. Julius had never told me the details of the deal he had made but I had always assumed it was some sort of combination of money and influence. I didn't imagine that there would be an opportunity for another deal second time around.

He smoked his cigarette in silence for a few moments, then dropped it to the floor and stubbed it out under his foot. 'As my colleague has already said, by returning before the end of the agreed period, you have forfeited your freedom and, regrettably, your life.' He pulled on his gloves picked up his hat. 'The only question remaining is whether we merely have you hanged for murder or make the case to have you shot for treason. Do give that some thought this evening, won't you?' And then, turning to my first interrogator: 'The Captain has some weighty thinking to do. Let's put him somewhere where he won't be disturbed.' He put on his hat. 'Good night, Captain. We'll talk again tomorrow.' He walked through the door and I heard his footsteps recede and another door close before the Inspector spoke, calling the guards in and telling them to take me to the secure wing.

When they did, I was surprised to be directed not back out into the courtyard but through the door opposite and along a corridor to another spiral staircase which, at the guards' direction, I walked down.

As we walked, I thought back to the idea of Cooper being

a gun-runner, somehow involved in treason. It seemed fanciful, but if it was true that might explain why she cooked up a story with Edgar to have me blamed for the death. They would have known that my family had enough influence to hush things up, and to avoid any undue publicity. But if that was the case, why call the police, why not just call Julius first? My head ached under the bandage. I couldn't make sense of it. I wondered whether, if I was careful, I could use the interrogation, the questions Fuller asked me, to try and work out more of the background before he got bored of the whole thing and had me shot for treason. Or just shot.

We passed two doors on the way down before reaching a third where the staircase ended, and which began to slowly open inwards as we reached the bottom step. Through the doorway I could see a small room.

Curved whitewashed walls stretched either side of a folding table behind which sat a uniformed guard. Arrayed in front of him was a series of riveted brass cubes and what looked like some sort of control panel. The guard looked up as we entered and pointed to our right with a curt 'Number three.' A shove to my shoulder encouraged me in that direction and, as we moved away from the desk, I could see that the rest of the room's wall was punctuated by a series of rounded metal doors that were set tight into the brickwork and that, unsettlingly, put me in mind of the kind of thing one would expect to see subdividing the lower compartments of a ship. The doors had numbers stencilled on them and, at the one labelled '3', my guards stood either side of me and indicated that I should wait. After a few moments there was a motorised rumble from behind the door followed by the sound of rushing water. A minute or so later the noise stopped, and the door opened to reveal a low-ceilinged corridor with an identical door at the other end. The floor, walls and ceiling, I couldn't help noticing, were all dripping wet.

'In you go.'

I had to stoop to go through the doorway and into the corridor. When I was halfway along it the door closed itself again behind me. Thick, rubberised cables ran along the ceiling, held in place by metal staples. In the delay before the next door opened, I had a short moment of fear as I imagined that this was no cell, merely a cheap method of execution, and I spent what seemed like an age with only this thought and the sour, nose-wrinkling tang of the Thames for company before the door in front opened and I completed my journey, stepping through the iron door frame and down into a metal chamber.

It was small and an almost perfect sphere; not quite big enough for a man to stand up or to lie down in. Behind me the door swung shut with a dull metallic thud and from beyond it I heard the rush and gurgle of the corridor refilling. I sighed heavily and slumped against the door, finally acknowledging what I should have admitted the moment I landed: I really should not have come back.

5. Sound

We were at the Pickwick's in Montreal airport.

It was a cold and bright October afternoon, a month or so before my planned trip to London. Gus was having what he insisted on calling a 'run ashore' and we had agreed to contact our brother Julius so that he could have one last attempt at persuading us to give up the idea of me returning. Through the window behind Gus an airliner was tying up to one of the mooring posts. He sighed and took a deep breath. Breathed out contentedly. 'That,' he declared at a cheery volume, 'was bloody marvellous.'

The waiter paused as he cleared the last fragments of our not-quite-finished Basket Lunch from the table. 'Would you gentlemen have room for dessert?'

Before I could say no, Gus jumped in with a swift 'Pair of brandies, there's a good chap. Large ones. And coffee. Charlie do you want coffee?' I shook my head. 'Well bring me two anyway, the tiny ones, and plenty of sugar.' Gus sighed again and burped loudly. 'I love this place. Good food for a chain, bloody good service and a bloody good view of things.'

He shifted round with a grunt to look at where the liner was now moored; metal gangways were being wheeled out fore and aft by men in red overalls, white maple leaves printed on their backs. Dots of colour against black tarmac and the vast grey bulk of the liner. 'Just in from Frankfurt. One of the latest models, very light, they get an extra three knots out of it, apparently.' He beckoned me forward. 'See those bulges on the underside of the fins?' He glanced back at me, waited till I nodded then continued. 'Counter-rocket munitions. Flares, shrapnel clusters, that kind of thing. After Frankfurt they started fitting them to all their civilian 'ships. Not much help against aerial attack of course but keeps them safe from anything from the ground.' He shook his head, turned back as the waiter arrived with our drinks. 'They're idiots if they think Bismarck will ever back down. Old or not, next year, mark my words, he'll find the ringleaders, beat them bloody and go looking for a war to keep the people's mind off the price of bread.'

The waiter came back with our drinks, darkly golden liquid in small French-style glasses. He placed them carefully down, added two espressos down by my brother's. Gus reached for his brandy, raised his glass. 'Absent friends.' I raised my own, nodded at him and took a sip. Gus knocked his back, squinted disappointedly at the empty glass and waved it in the direction of the waiter. Outside, passengers were starting to emerge, heads down and hats held firm against the wind as they walked across the gangways to the terminal.

The waiter came over with the brandy. 'Anything else gentlemen? Are you sure I can't tempt you to a pudding? We have a very fine trifle?'

I shook my head. 'That's fine, thank you. But if you could bring us a teleprint. We've booked a connection.'

'Of course, sir.' He walked across to the other side of the restaurant and disappeared through a door.

My brother squinted at his watch.

'What time were we supposed to be on, can you remember?'

I thought for a moment. 'Three.'

Gus grunted. 'Bet the first thing he types is that we're late.'

A minute or so later the waiter came back with a machine and plugged it into the socket set in the centre of table. It was relatively modern, a single unit with a keyboard, a small mechanical display a few lines tall and a built-in printer. We waited for a few moments while it ticked and tapped itself into life. A red light came on next to the display which rippled across from dark to light grey, to show a short a string of letters:

```
Pickw_mtl>
```

Gus's hand landed on my back. 'You do it old boy. I've got no idea how this stuff works.'

I flicked the printer switch to 'off' and typed in the command to connect us, hit the return key and waited. The letters disappeared and a single black dot strobed across the display.

The machine clattered to life, turning incoming dots and dashes into letters then a short line of words that appeared on the display.

```
Mdx1_ldn>U R LATE.
```

Gus barked triumphantly. 'Tell him the clocks have changed here for farming time or something.'

I started typing.

```
Pickw_mtl>APOLOGIES. NAVY ALWAYS LATE. RUM.
```

```
Mdx1_ldn>DRUNK?
```

```
Pickw_mtl>MERRY.
```

'Ha! I'm obviously not drinking quickly enough. Waiter! A mug of your finest ale if you please.'

```
Mdx1_ldn>IMPERATIVE CEASE VISIT.
```

```
Pickw_mtl>IMPOSSIBLE. ALL IN PROGRESS.
```

```
Mdx1_ldn>MOST IMPERATIVE CEASE VISIT.
```

'Not very eloquent is he? I thought he could come up with better than that, given all the time he spends hanging around with politicians.'

'It's cost-saving. They charge per character.'

'Do they?' Gus thought for a moment. 'And who's paying, us or him?'

'Julius is.'

'Hmph.' Gus leaned over me, exuding brandy like a closely worn cologne. 'Let me have a go.' The keyboard shook as his hands hammered down.

```
Pickw_mtl>TEH THING IS BLOOOOOODY WELL ONM
WHATEVER YOU SAY JC ALL SORTED DONOT WORRY
NO PRONLEMS AL WILL B WELL LA LA LA LA LA
DHIATENSORPWFULCMYZXKGBVQJ!!!!!!!!!!!
```

Julius's response was unsurprisingly brief:

```
Mdx1_ldn>MOST IMPERATIVE CEASE VISIT.
```

'Bloody bean counter.'

The words held on the display as Julius Clarence Maddox, our younger brother (and current Executive Director of Maddox Maritime Global) waited for our response. I knew what was going through his head – he'd already had this conversation with Gus in person earlier that year. Elections were looming, the Tories were looking very beatable now that Gordon had thrown his hat into the ring and the last thing Julius (and the company's highly lucrative state contracts) needed was a potential scandal involving one of his brothers. Therefore, though he regretted the necessity for caution, he could not in any way permit me to travel back to see our father, regardless of the seriousness of his illness. Gus's repeated insistence that the trip would be short, and that our scheme to render me undetectable would be foolproof, had fallen on stony ground.

```
Mdx1_ldn>ELECTIONS. VISIT UNTENABLE.
```

Gus reached over again, more calmly this time and typing well enough despite his earlier claims.

```
Pickw_mtl>VISIT ON. ALL ARRANGED. ALL WILL
BE WELL.
```

```
Mdx1_ldn>UTMOST. REPEAT. STRESS UTMOST
IMPORTANCE NOT COME.
```

```
Pickw_mtl>MADDOX OR MOUSE?
```

Gus's final sally: a teasing challenge from our childhood.

```
Mdx1_ldn>M
```

The screen froze. The machine's transmission hung, cycling dah dah, dah dah, dah dah over and over again.

```
M.
```

```
M.
```

M.

I woke in the cell, twisted into the curve of the riveted metal floor, ill-taken sleep clamming my eyelids. Shoulders stiff and limbs aching, I tried to sit up. There was no camera here, though two lights clung to its ceiling in closely wired cages and a small loudspeaker was installed just above the door that I had stooped in through.

I had discovered earlier, by thumping my way up the walls, that, though submerged, only a small section of the roof was actually in contact with the river, with the majority of the cell buried below the mud of the Thames. It was damnably cold, cramped and insufferably uncomfortable: ideal for helping traitors recover their memory. Escape was unthinkable.

M.

I squeezed my eyes shut and rubbed my hands across them to rub away the last few grains of sleep.

M.

It took a second for me to realise that the sound was real.

I listened carefully: two long taps, M in Morse code. I stood, hunched in the centre of the cell, and focused on the sound. I waited for a few moments and the sound, the pace, the time never varied. I realised that it was being caused by something tapping sharply against the cell's roof. Someone was out there, underwater and trying to communicate.

I tapped out a reply against the roof: long, short, long. R. Roger. Ready to receive. The M stopped.

Q...R...K...?

A Q code. And one I recognised. I said a silent thank you to my first CO in Canada, whose insistence that all officers spend time learning to man the wire had driven the mess up the wall at the time. QRK: how well could I hear them? I rapped out a five against the roof. I didn't get their response at first, had to ask them to repeat it a few times before I understood what they were saying.

S...T...A...N...D...C...L...E...A...R...R...O...O...F

I paused before responding. There was only one reason they would tell me to get clear of the roof. Whoever was out there was planning to come in and join me. I tapped back RCD, received and pressed myself into the scant cover provided by the door frame.

Q...R...V...?

Was I ready? My signals knowledge wasn't up to the task of translating the immediate responses that came to mind, with the exception perhaps of the most direct one and I wasn't sure that that would have been particularly helpful. So, instead, I rapped the QRV code back to them on the roof near the door to confirm my readiness.

I was halfway through the dots of the V when a bright beam of sparks lanced in through the roof, sending a circle of molten metal drops hissing to the floor. I tried not to think about the heat, closed my eyes, pressed myself as far into the door as I could and waited for it to stop. It took less than a minute before the hissing ended with a terrific, deafening clang and a rush of water that poured in and filled the floor to just above my ankles. I opened my eyes cautiously to see that an opening slightly larger than a manhole had been cut through the inches-thick chamber roof, steam rising from the edges. Hanging down the middle of this hole was a rope ladder and stretched between two of the rungs was a sign, stencilled with luminescent paint:

'Ne paniquez pas. Vous êtes sauvés.'

And underneath, in smaller letters:

'Ascendez-vous.'

I stepped round to face the ladder and climbed up carefully and looked through the hole into a squat, domed cylinder, little more than an oversized and elongated diving helmet. Pulling myself up, I rested on the edge of the hole and saw that there was more luminescent writing near the top of the chamber.

'Suivez les instructions numérotées.' There were indeed three numbered instructions, accompanied by simplistic pictures of the activity they described.

1. Apposer la masque.
2. Maintenez fermement les poignées.
3. Appuyez sur le bouton rouge.

I tugged at what I now realised was a mask, set between the two handles that protruded from the roof of the cylinder and pulled it down towards me. It seemed to be some sort of simple aqualung, attached to the metal with a thick rubber tube, and I put it on, checking for a flow of air before tightening the straps that held it in place. I grasped the handles and steeled myself for step three, staring at 'le bouton rouge' in front of me.

Below me, in the cell I heard the sound of pumps starting up. My captors coming to investigate the noise. I had a choice, stay here and hang or take my chances with my, apparently French, rescuers.

I pushed the button.

Nothing happened.

I stood, gripping tight knuckled to the handles as I stared at the writing in front of me. I let go with my left hand and pushed the button again, holding it down this time and a rapid circle of explosive snaps rattled around the joint between cylinder and cell. I just had time to disentangle my legs from the ladder before I was wrenched away from the cell and dragged up, body and legs buffeted violently by the dark green torrent that rushed into the cell below. I closed my eyes and cursed my ineptitude, lunacy and bloody-mindedness as I was dragged clear of the cell and through the rage of river water like a sounding lead, legs dragging behind me as I bumped through the murky darkness of the Thames.

Inside the pitch blackness of the rescue helmet I tried to breathe slowly, heart hammering and fingers cramping as I held on for grim death. Something weighty clanged against the outside and I held my breath, deafened, expecting a crack and wondering how watertight the breathing mask was. The apparatus held and ten seconds or so later I felt the pull lessen and my pace slow before the angle changed and realised I was being winched upwards, out of the water. A faint red light from above just allowed me to just make out the surface of the water below and, off to either side, the concave slopes of a pair of ships' hulls. Then I was moving up through a square trapdoor into a red-lit chamber loud with the hum of winding gears and finally, thankfully, came to a halt. Hands grasped my shoulders and pulled me to one side.

'It's alright, you can let go.' A man's voice.

With some difficulty I managed to unfasten my fingers and, hands numb, forced the mask off and dropped the few feet to the floor, almost collapsing. I staggered, limbs shaking, but managed to stay standing. Thames water dripped from my clothes onto what I now saw was some sort of parqueted flooring.

'Here.' A thick white towel was pushed into my chest and I started to dry myself off as best as I could while my rescuer stood in silence.

Tall and broad shouldered, with a pugnaciously blunt face, he looked like he could more than hold his own in a fight and wore a scowl that suggested he was ready for one. At the same time there was a sharpness about his eyes that hinted at something more than a bruiser and I made a mental note not to underestimate him. He wore the waistcoat and trousers from a tweed three-piece, the sleeves of his shirt rolled to his elbows, exposing skin long tanned by warmer climes and a coloured, serpentine tattoo that curled its way down the underside of his right arm. A boxy, large-calibre automatic pistol was clearly visible in a shoulder holster under his left. 'You all right?' he asked.

'You're not French?'

'French?' He paused, looked puzzled for a second. 'Oh, the gear. No, all we could get at short notice. Plus a little red herring for our friends over in Millbank. Are you okay?' Just a little sharpness of the East End in an accent that would have been harder and rougher once, but that something – time, travel, practice – had worn almost smooth over the years. Almost.

I checked myself over. 'Good enough.' I wrapped the towel around my shoulders, took a breath of air, coughed. There had almost certainly been occasions in Canada when I had felt colder and more bedraggled than this but, in the moment, they escaped me. I folded my arms across my chest, stuffed my hands in my armpits and shivered.

He nodded. 'Take it steady. You're on board a ship called the Maiden Lucy. At a party. Don't worry, we'll get you sorted.'

'A party?' I thought I had misheard him. If not, I had clearly been rescued by some sort of madman.

'That's right. All part of a cunning plan apparently. Come on, let's get you sat down.' He walked me over to where a small jumble of furniture was stacked on a black lacquered chaise longue at one side of the room. He up-righted a chair and set it down on the floor. 'There you go, take the weight off.'

I didn't feel in any condition to argue, and sat down on the chair while my new gaoler, if that's what he was, took another chair over to the trapdoor, then disconnected a thick cord that curled down from the ceiling to a Morse encoder on the floor. 'Help yourself to a drink,' he shouted over his shoulder as he stepped up on the chair and, balancing well for such a large fellow, went back to work on some sort of apparatus that was held fast to the ceiling.

Next to me, on a small side table, was a red enamel mug and matching flask from which I poured a mugful of what turned out to be a thin beef broth. I sat, shivering, and took a few welcome sips. I looked around the room; it was ornately decorated, with floral wallpaper and lamps styled to look like Japanese lanterns. A large rug almost the width of the room was rolled up along the opposite wall. At least this cell would be slightly better furnished, I thought, and if there was one thing the army had taught me over and over again it was this: never question an opportunity to sit down with a mug of something hot in your hand.

On the chair my rescuer-cum-gaoler laboured for a few more moments, swearing loudly at the fastenings in front of him until, with a final, satisfied oath, the cylinder dropped straight down through the hole in the floor with a splash. He stepped down from the chair, moved it to one side and folded first one then the other of the two metal doors down into place. Their upper surfaces were panelled with the same wood as the floor and, with both in place, almost invisibly disguised the hatch below.

He pressed a switch on the wall and the lamps around the room changed from dull red to a low yellow glow.

'Name's Church. Shouldn't be long but if anyone does wander in while I'm away, your name is Alistair Sterling, you're a banker and you're here for a party. You fell overboard and you're trying to warm up.' He walked towards the door. 'Wait here and I'll get you some clothes.'

I nodded, not really seeing what other response I could make.

The man called Church spun the door's circular handle and stepped out through it, closing it behind him. I sat and waited, sipping warmth from the mug, enjoying the marked improvement in the style of my incarceration. With the trapdoor closed the noise of the river faded, and I became aware of other sounds: the low and steady vibration of engines below us and from somewhere above the faint sounds of a party in full swing. I wondered about Fuller and whether they had interrupted his evening again to let him know that I had escaped from his unescapable cell. I smiled at the thought of him hearing the news. But the smile faded at the thought of his Bureau teams combing London for me. Would they guess I was here on board and, if they did, what could the man called Church do to stop them? I took a breath, calmed myself. Whatever was about to happen, warmth and fuel were a priority, so I put those thoughts to one side and focused on the broth, drinking it down sip by slow slip.

I was on my second mugful when the locking mechanism spun again, the door opened, and Church came back into the room, carrying a large, flat cardboard box that he put down on the pile of furniture my chair had come from. In behind him walked a woman in dark grey paramilitary uniform, perhaps six feet tall, with a mannish build, a wide, sharp-cheeked face and dark brown hair tied tightly in a bun behind her head. Her eyes stayed on me as she walked into the room and stood by the wall to the right of the door, feet apart, hands loose by her side. She didn't seem to be carrying a weapon. She didn't look like she needed one.

'So, this is Agent Sterling!' said a voice. 'How fabulous.' I looked back to the door as a second woman strode into the room. Shorter and undeniably more feminine than her companion, she was slim rather than slight, her head covered by an oversized bronze helmet from beneath which long tresses of dark hair cascaded to just below her shoulders. She carried with her a charm and confidence undiminished by the flowing, ankle-length toga that she wore, and I stood as she strode across to me and stretched out the hand that wasn't holding a trident. She was Indian, with large, dark brown eyes, high cheeks and a small mouth that broke into a beaming smile as we shook hands. Something about the way she did it put me in mind of a family trip to Bombay as a boy, and the drinks party to celebrate our arrival where my over-serious ten-year-old self had delighted a gaggle of ornately dressed women with my solemn handshakes and laboriously enunciated greetings.

When this woman spoke, though, her accent was pure essence of Mayfair, with a cheerfully exclaimed 'What an absolute delight to meet you!' as if we had run into each other by surprise at a tea party.

'Britannia, I presume.'

She laughed loudly, still shaking my hand and treating me to another wide and cheerful smile. 'Well done, Sterling. How lucky we are that you made it across in one piece. I do hope you weren't too banged around? Everything, as they say, hunky dory?' She tapped my chest with the trident for emphasis.

'Indeed.'

Her tone, smiles and flapping hands were of a county hostess meeting a late arrival from the station. Finally letting go of my hand, she glanced around at the room.

'Oh that is good news! Well, welcome aboard! Kitty and I will head back up. Do join us as soon as you can. Oh and Church, do sort this out,' she pointed the trident at the furniture, 'and let's be on our way.'

'I am grateful, madam, for you bringing me here but I rather think that you have me mistaken for someone else, I'm not –'

And she stopped, and for a second the smile dropped, her lips thinned, and there was nothing in her eyes but intellect: deep and razor sharp. She stepped towards me, her cheery bluster vanished, and a focused, quietly confident tone in its place. This close to her I could see flecks of amber in the brown that made me think of cat's eyes.

'We know who you are, Captain, and who you are pretending to be. We know why you are here and exactly why you shouldn't be. Millbank will have their brightest and fastest out looking for you, so, all in all, it's probably best if we look after you for now and probably best if you use a different name, wouldn't you say? By the time we reach Westminster, you will have been here all evening, indistinguishable from all the other guests at a rather exclusive and wonderful party. So do humour me, Captain, let's call you Sterling for now and let the explanations catch up with us later. As far as I am concerned Milady or Ma'am should see us through the evening.'

'Yes, Ma'am.'

She smiled again, a beaming grin that made the world a brighter place and the steel of her mind slipped back beneath a cloak of amiable jollification. She turned on her heel to leave, then froze halfway. 'And do hurry up, we really should be on deck. I think it's almost time for the fireworks! And don't forget the costume.' This last shouted over her shoulder as she strode out and down the corridor, her dark-haired aide pausing for a moment and then moving out through the door after her, rubber-soled shoes squeaking slightly as she walked along after her mistress.

'A bit like being in a typhoon, isn't it?' said Church after they had both left. 'Even when you know what's coming, it doesn't make it any easier.'

'If I'm honest all of this is a bit like being in a typhoon. Where am I? And who the blazes are you people?'

'Well,' said Church, 'if I stopped to tell you all that we'd miss the fireworks. And you don't want to miss the fireworks, do you Mr Sterling?'

And something in the way he shifted his stance brought a polite threat of injury into the room in a way I would have been wary of even if I hadn't just been nearly drowned. Whoever they were, it seemed as though playing along with them for now was my best option.

Church nodded, made a satisfied sound. He picked up the box he had brought with him and passed it over to me. I looked down at the large label on it: printed in a large theatrical script was 'Debenham and Freebody' and then, handwritten underneath in purple ink, 'Fawkes.'

'Right,' he said, pulling a folding chair away from the wall and sitting down. 'Let's get you dressed, get upstairs and get this bollocks over with.'

6. Ghosts

The briefing room was at the rear of the house. Large, lighter squares showed where pictures had hung on pale green wallpaper in what must have been a drawing room at some stage. French windows stretched from floor to ceiling providing a glimpse of a neat garden, bare of leaves beneath a dull, clouded sky. A projection screen was set up on a decorator's trestle table in front of the windows; a short arc of unmatched chairs faced it.

I stood next to a marble-topped sideboard, sipping thick Arabic coffee from a porcelain coffee cup decorated with small, pink roses. The coffee was wonderfully dark; precisely foamed and gently perfumed in a way that very nearly, but not quite, managed to erase the lingering memory of absinthe.

I was washed, clean shaven and wearing a new, perfectly tailored suit that had been waiting for me in the room where I had slept. I felt oddly as if I was attending an interview by mistake.

From the outside this looked like every other house in the terrace; a private residence, infrequently occupied by its county-dwelling owners. In fact, according to Church's brief and grudging explanation as we had travelled back here from the boat this morning, it was the headquarters of a quasi-governmental organisation that he called 'The Map Room'. What this had to do with me, he hadn't told me. I assumed that, like my erstwhile captors the Bureau of Engine Security, this 'Map Room' thought I knew something of value in relation to Cooper, or Canada, or both.

The door opened and Church came in, leaving it ajar. He walked over to the sideboard and stood staring at it for a moment or to, then looked at me. 'No tea?' I shook my head gently. He gave a disappointed grunt, then carefully poured himself a cup of coffee from the pot and took a sip. Grimacing slightly, he reached for the sugar and used the tongs to deftly drop several cubes into his cup. Once again, the normality of the situation left me feeling slightly bewildered. Somewhere Fuller was marshalling a search to recapture me and here was what looked like some sort of secret policeman from the decidedly dubious end of the scale offering me tea.

'You sleep alright on the boat?'

'Just fine.'

'There's a cot set up in one of the rooms upstairs that you can use till we get you some digs sorted. I'll show you later.' He stirred his coffee and tasted it. 'Well,' he said thoughtfully, 'It's not horrible.' He took another mouthful. 'So. Did your new friends buy the switch?'

I thought back to night before, ran through my first encounter with the other guests on the boat. I nodded. 'As far as I could tell.'

'That's good. What did you talk about?'

'Diamonds. Horses. America. Advice on investments.'

'What advice did you give them?'

'Never play cards with a Frenchman. Quite well received. Who was the other Fawkes?' We'd met him in the corridor on the way up to the party wearing a costume identical to mine. At Church's nod, his mask still on, the other Fawkes had briefed me succinctly and expertly, providing me a potted history of his experience so far. The final part of his handover, before I joined the party, was to give me the bottle that he'd 'popped out to fetch'. Taking his place, still, it seemed, in role as Alistair Sterling the banker I slotted back into a gaggle of raucous partygoers with a comfort dually born of his briefing and my own memories of similar parties from my younger days in London. Wide eyes. Arch exchanges. Loud laughter. 'Too much drinking and very little sense,' as my father had described it once. Getting the sense that, short of diving off the boat or shouting for help, I was being left to my own devices, I had taken the opportunity at face value and set out to try and forget that I was still, to all intents and purposes, a prisoner.

'Just a bloke. No one that you'll meet again anytime soon.'

'And who I am supposed to be today?' I asked. 'Still a banker or am I something else?'

'That depends on you, old son,' he said, draining his coffee. He put his cup down as the door was pushed open and a man wearing a butler's uniform walked in carrying another chair. 'Morning, March.'

'Mr Church.' He put his chair to the left of the projector and stood to face us. 'Good to see you back, sir. The others will be here momentarily.'

'No chance of tea is there, March?' asked Church.

'Mr Collier did specify coffee, sir, but there will be tea arriving later.'

'Fine,' said Church in a tone of voice that conveyed very clearly the opposite. 'Who else is coming for this?'

'Mr Collier will be briefing, Miss Green assisting and I think one of the Jays will be joining you.'

'Any news from Regal?'

'Nothing overnight, Mr Church. If you'll excuse me, I ought

to finish.' Church nodded and the butler walked over to the table, flicked a switch on the projector then went behind the screen and started pulling the curtains across.

I suffered another absinthe-induced twinge as they were talking, and it made me think of Edgar. He used to love the filthy stuff. And I saw the flash of pistol again, Edgar falling to the platform again. Choking on his own blood, struggling to speak. Eyes dulling as he died.

'Sterling.' Church's voice brought me gratefully back to the room. Mostly back. 'Do you want some more coffee?' I shook my head. 'You sure, you look like you need it.'

'No thank you, I'm fine as I am.'

I watched Church refill his cup, and add another small pile of sugar cubes to it. A quick stir and he went to sit down on one of the chairs. I followed him over there, putting the image of Edgar out of my mind with a tight swallow and sat next to Church. I leaned towards him as March bustled about the room. 'Jay?'

'J as in J Company.'

I thought for a second. Found myself frowning. 'There is no such thing as a J Company.'

Church leaned toward me and winked slowly. 'Stick around, son. You'll go far.'

'Church.' The voice came from the doorway where a tall, slightly stooped man stood, dressed in a slightly old-fashioned looking grey suit, hands in pockets and perfectly still. 'And, this must be Sterling, I presume?'

'It is,' said Church before I had a chance to reply.

'Collier.' He smiled a thin, fleeting smile and stepped across the room with a precise, unhurried stride. We both stood. 'How do you do?' His handshake was the only part of him that moved.

'How do you do?'

'Good to have you with us, Sterling.'

'I'm sure it is, Mr Collier, but no one has explained to me what "being with you" might actually mean.'

'All in good time, Sterling, all in good time.' Collier turned away from me, spying the butler as he stood over the projector, mild puzzlement furrowing his brow as he stared at it, brass cartridge of slides held uncertainly in one hand. 'Don't worry, March,' Collier instructed him, 'You can leave that for Green to sort out.' He glanced at a flat, grey metal wristwatch. 'When she arrives.'

March murmured a grateful 'Thank you, sir', carefully placed the cartridge down on the table next to the projector and, with a precisely brief bow, left the room, closing the door behind him with the care of a man for whom smooth transitions have become a point of pride. Collier walked two careful paces to the chair facing us, turned, sat and folded one leg over the other then, hands in pockets, he stared up at the ceiling. His socks, I noticed, were a dark shade of purple.

The door opened and a woman strode in purposefully, folder under one arm: dark woollen suit, shirtwaist and tie, auburn hair piled high. Collier seemed oblivious as she dropped her folder on the table, picked up the slides where March had left them and deftly slotted them into the projector. She clicked a switch that lit up the screen with the first slide: a plain white background with a simple title: 'Directive 74' and, underneath, 'Sterling/Church'.

She turned round. 'All set, Mr Collier.'

Collier's head tilted down from its examination of the ceiling. He acknowledged Miss Green without turning round, words gently ambling out into the room: 'Thank you Miss Green. And this is Executive Sterling.'

'Sterling, of course! Hello Mr Sterling, sorry!' Her manner and enthusiasm might have marked her out as American; her accent unmistakably did. Northern. New England I thought, so perhaps she had got out before the worst of the war reached them. She picked up her folder and came to sit down on the other side of Church. She flicked through the papers, then suddenly stopped and threw her hand across Church with a 'Pleased to meet you, by the way.' We shook hands.

'Likewise.'

She turned back to her papers and, finding the place she was looking for, looked up at Collier.

'Thank you, Miss Green.' Collier had settled in the chair, projector control in one hand. 'And thank you, Mac, for joining us.'

'Sir.'

I turned in surprise at the new voice to see that, seemingly appeared from nowhere, a man in labourer's clothes now sat at the opposite end of the row, chair slightly back from the empty seat next to him. He slouched, unshaven and, at first glance, unremarkable but, on closer inspection, masking an alertness, a readiness for action. He caught my eye and nodded, one professional to another. He took out a crumpled packet of cigarettes and lit one while Collier continued.

'And so, as we are all here, I suggest that we begin.' I raised my hand. 'Yes, Mr Sterling?'

'Would it be terribly discourteous of me to ask for a little more explanation before you carry on?'

'Explanation?' Collier asked. 'About what, in particular?' He had the look of a master teaching a Latin class suddenly presented with a question about trigonometry; amiable but slightly bemused.

'Oh, nothing much,' I replied, feeling myself begin to anger as I did, 'just a few trivial matters: why I am here, who you all are and what we do when the real Executive Sterling asks for his seat back.'

Collier thought for a moment before he spoke. 'You are here, Mr Sterling, for the same reason as the rest of us; a briefing on the directive that you and Mr Church will be taking on. As a new field executive, we have allocated you a relatively simple task and one that, with your own undoubted talents and Mr Church's able support, we are sure you will make a resounding success of.' He smiled. 'As for the question of chairs, there is only one Executive Sterling and you, I am pleased to say, are he. So we need not worry ourselves about that.'

'And if I decide that I am not, in fact, he?' I asked.

'Well now, Mr Sterling, I'm really not sure why on earth you would. After all, it's a perfectly pleasant morning, we are well supplied with coffee and, it would seem to me, enjoying, to all intents and purposes, a life of freedom.' He paused meaningfully. 'But I know that Milady will speak to you after this briefing so perhaps you will have a chance to explore that possibility with her then. In the meantime, though, shall we proceed as if you are, so to speak, in the right chair?' He paused and raised his eyebrows.

And, suddenly and bone-wearily tired, I concluded that, as long as they weren't going to arrest me, shoot me or try and drown me again, I might as well go along with it. I nodded.

'Excellent,' said Collier, 'and so, to business.' He clicked the slide.

Five photographs of women's faces. Police file photos. Dates underneath each of them, from August to November 1888. I vaguely remembered the furore about the murders that autumn, providing as they had done a seemingly inexhaustible supply of gore and mystery for the capital's newspaper editors. The date of the last murder was only a few days before I was shipped to Canada, I noticed.

'Nichols, Chapman, Stride...' Collier paused and looked around like a schoolmaster who had stopped at '*amat*'.

'Eddowes and Kelly.' It was the American woman.

'Thank you, Miss Green,' said Collier. 'Top marks as always. Five victims, one killer, vile murder, police baffled, et cetera et cetera.' Collier was about to click on to the next slide when Church interrupted him, the gravel of his voice harsh against the polished calm of Collier's delivery.

'You are having a laugh, aren't you?'

'Mr Church?' Collier stared at him with a look of mild interest.

Church jerked his head at the screen behind Collier as he replied: 'This. The Ripper. Is it a joke? Bit of jolly for the new lad? So, good one, now put the real directive up and let's get on with it.'

There was a bleak stillness in Collier's tone as he responded: 'No joke, Mr Church.'

'All right, so say it's actually serious. We're not police,' Church went on, 'and even if we were we wouldn't be touching this with a bargepole. It's a blind alley.'

Collier shifted his gaze to me. 'Mr Sterling, what is your view?'

I thought for a moment. 'You, that is we, do seem like a particularly sophisticated hammer to swing at what might not turn out to be a nut at all,' I replied.

Collier made a dry noise. It took me a moment to register it as laughter.

'Very droll, Mr Sterling. We are indeed fashioned for situations more imperial in scope. However, one condition of not officially existing is that, from time to time, we must carry out a favour for those that do. This is one such favour.'

'Look,' Church responded, 'if the Ripper ever existed, he's in the ground or good and gone and there's nothing left but mud and dead ends. It's a rainbow hunt.' To his right, Green shook her head.

'Miss Green?' Collier asked. 'You are not of that opinion?'

'Mr Church is right about the mud but wrong about the Ripper.' she replied. 'He did exist.' Church shook his head, muttered something under his breath. 'Would you put the next slide up, please, Mr Collier?' Collier clicked the device again and Green got up and walked over to stand next to the other side of the screen. The new slide showed an aerial photo of a cobbled street. Striding down the street was a single black-clad and hatted figure, carrying some sort of bag and looking back over his right shoulder.

Green pointed to the image. 'The so-called Ripper photo. Taken from the static dirigible the Met had set up over Whitechapel after the third murder. This was taken in the early morning of the Miller's Court murder, just after 4am. Matched the description of a man seen by a witness close to one of the earlier murders, though no one on the ground saw him on this occasion. The papers ran it for a week, but it didn't amount to much beyond mobs setting upon the occasional surgeon.

'And, if he was the Ripper, he is walking away from the last and the most brutal of the murders generally ascribed to him. In this case the girl, Kelly, was severely, horribly mutilated in an extended and concerted attack that the coroner surmised would have taken place over several hours. There are pictures in the background files I've prepared for you, but I wouldn't advise looking at them on a full stomach. In any case general opinion agrees with Mr Church and, given that there were no further murders, presumes the Ripper dead, fled or insti-tutionalised shortly thereafter. The latter seems likely, not just because of what happened in Miller's Court but judging by this, one of the few letters received by the police that might be genuine.'

Click.

Green went on, confident in her material; it was obviously a subject she knew well: 'This letter was sent to George Lusk, chair of the Whitechapel vigilance committee two weeks after the third and fourth murders. Known by people who care about these things as the 'From Hell' letter because of the sender's address.'

The note was short, letters sprawling across the paper in what looked like faded, brown ink.

'Note the writer doesn't identify as "The Ripper" though the name was well used in the press by the time it was sent and that he mentions a kidney, which was enclosed, and a knife, which was not. There is some speculation that, although it seems to be written by an illiterate, it was actually written that way deliberately to disguise the intelligence and class of the sender. In the end it was written off as a prank by a medical student.'

'I wonder why.' From Church.

'Then there is also this card.' She clicked on to the next slide; a facsimile of a postcard, simply addressed 'Hell' and continued 'Dear comissonor. My cincer apologes for no kidne nor knife as promsd but you will hav them soon.' The writing was identical in colour and style to the other letter. Addressed and signed in the same way.

'I don't remember seeing that one at the time,' I said.

Green waited a moment before she answered. 'You won't have done. It was sent a week ago.'

Collier interrupted the silence that followed that announcement with a courteous 'Thank you Miss Green.' He waited until she had retaken her seat and then clicked on to the next slide. 'And this photograph is from two nights ago.'

The slide showed a woman's face, eyes closed, obviously a morgue photo.

'Polly Ann Shaw, a sometime prostitute.' Collier spoke neutrally. His voice toneless, unexcited. 'Her throat was cut. Her chest and abdomen were mutilated, and organs roughly excised. Indications are this was carried out by either the Ripper or someone intimately associated with the crimes. This morning Sir Edward Bradford, the Metropolitan Police Commissioner, received a package containing a worn surgeon's knife and a freshly removed kidney. There was a note inside that said "From hell, your servant".'

Silence again. Then Church spoke, his tone still disbelieving.

'Alright, so let's say that this isn't just some crackpot who has got it into his head to try for a bit of reflected glory. Let's say, however ridiculous that is, that this is true and, after an extended absence, the Ripper is real and back murdering whores in the East End. Fine. If that's the case, I can see why Bradford might be pissing himself about it but what I don't see is why any of this makes it a favour we want to get involved in?'

The door opened and March walked in with a tray. 'Tea, Mr Collier.'

'Thank you, March, just pop it down, we'll serve ourselves.'

'Very well, sir.' March replied as he deposited the tray on the sideboard next to the coffee. 'Would you like me to clear the other away, Mr Collier?'

'No need, March. Thank you.' Collier smiled the same thin smile as before. March stood briefly to attention, gave the same curt nod that he had before and left the room, drawing the door closed silently behind him.

'At last,' said Church to himself, getting up and going across to the tray to help himself.

Collier waited for him to finish, to walk back across the room and to sit down before he clicked the slide control again. It was another version of the aerial photo of Miller's Court, showing the same striding figure but with more of the street in the frame. 'The press were never given access to this. In fact neither were the police. This is the uncropped photograph that shows Miller's Court and, if you magnify that section of the photo, you can see the murder scene itself.'

He clicked again. The next image was zoomed in, blurred and grainy. 'So we can see the yard that Kelly's room opened onto, and we can even, if we look carefully, make out her door and there, in the open door we can see—'

We all recognised what Collier was describing at the same time, but I was the first to speak: 'There is someone else there.'

'Exactly, Mr Sterling.' Collier responded, a glimmer of acknowledgement in his voice. 'Two people, not one. It's a stretch of the imagination but the one in the doorway seems to be looking at the one in the street just as that figure is looking back.' He paused to let that sink in. 'So one could make the jump that the two were acting in concert. Two people working together to commit murder, neither of whom have ever been caught or broken silence and whose joint existence is only proved by a photo which was only ever released in a deliberately doctored format.'

Collier paused, walking over to where March had left the tea tray. He opened the silver teapot, glanced inside and, seemingly satisfied, dropped the lid back down again.

'And so, this begins to me to have the whiff of conspiracy about it. And a conspiracy that had direct or indirect influence on the investigation, could suppress evidence at will and did so to enable the perpetration of a series of public and brutal murders.'

Collier turned back to the tray and began the business of filling his cup as he spoke. He added neither milk nor sugar but instead a small slither of lemon peel.

'This photograph isn't the only indication. We have also had evidence from another source about information from the cases being systematically controlled and withheld. We have judged it a high possibility that the conspiracy is real and, moreover, could involve a group within law enforcement or even state security. Which is why we have been asked to look into it.'

He took a sip of tea.

'The forerunner of this office was formed to ensure cartographic accuracy, to fill in the blanks and, where necessary, amend any errors. We continue in this tradition. Part of our brief is to look out for things that shouldn't be there and make corrections. Mr Church is absolutely right; we are not police, and therefore the identification and capture of the Ripper is none of our concern. Our aim, by which I mean both of your aims, Mr Church, Mr Sterling,' he looked at each of us in turn, 'is to ascertain the extent of the conspiracy, identify its personnel and remove it in a way that causes no embarrassment or unwelcome publicity to the Government.'

He looked round at us brightly. 'Now I do believe that March has been good enough to provide biscuits, so may I suggest we take a break?'

Church moved first, then Green. I glanced across to see what the scruffily dressed Mac thought of all this, but he had departed as imperceptibly as he had arrived.

I stood and stared at the picture on the screen where the figure was leaning out of the doorway to 13 Miller's Court. One arm, slightly blurred, seemed to be holding on to the edge of the door and it was difficult to tell from this angle if he was opening it to leave or pulling it closed behind him.

7. Patience

The break was brief, and we moved quickly on. Green handed out manila files thick with paper as Collier outlined our first steps. Church had been tasked with interviewing Sir Anthony Willard, a surgeon who had played a prominent part in the original investigation, while I was off to Whitechapel to, in Collier's words, 'sound out a few of the locals'.

I was looking through my file of paper, trying to avoid the worst of the photographs and still not really sure what on earth I was doing there when March came back into the briefing room with a second pot of tea and the news that Milady wanted to see me.

March led me out of the room, back towards the front door and up the sweep of the main stairs, striding ahead of me with a conversation-discouraging demeanour. I followed along in silence to a room at the front of the first floor. March knocked on the door and waited. A few moments passed before it was opened by a tall woman whom I recognised as Britannia's companion from the night before. She wore the same chauffeur-cum-bodyguard uniform and the same air of grim watchfulness; she opened the door and stood to one side as we walked in.

A large mahogany dining table occupied the centre of the room. The same wood panelled the lower part of the room's walls while their upper halves were darkly painted and thickly arrayed with rugged landscapes. Fully one half of the table was covered with stacks of letters and documents arranged around a teletype terminal, the wiring for which snaked to a comparatively new-looking socket in the wall. The room was bright, lit by a large bay window running for most of its width, where a chaise longue and low table sat, framed by heavily patterned and slightly faded velvet curtains. An ornate gas chandelier hung from the ceiling, aflame despite the daylight.

But it was the room's main occupant that drew the eye. She was flamboyantly costumed in dark green velvet, sleeves fashionably puffed and picked out in patterned silk. A feathered hat lay behind her on a side chair, gloves draped carefully next to it. Her dark hair was set in ornate waves, her make-up perfect and face serene: a marked contrast to the last I had seen of her the night before, standing on a table and conducting the National Anthem.

She looked up from what looked like a lengthy teletype message and smiled. 'Ah, Sterling, do join me. Kitty, you can leave us.' The girl paused for a moment before she moved. March opened the door for her and followed her out. A clock struck the hour somewhere, back in the house, its insistent chimes echoing through the marble floor of the entrance hall below.

Milady waited until the door closed, then leaned back from the table and looked me over for a moment before speaking. In sober daylight she looked older than she had appeared at the previous night's revels, though no less striking; her features unmarred by fatigue, the ghost of a smile hovering.

'Agent Sterling. Do take a seat.'

I pulled out the chair nearest to me and sat down. 'Is that who I am now?'

She reached into a silver box by her elbow, took out a thin, black cigarillo and tamped it into a dull ivory holder. 'It would seem the most attractive identity of the options available, wouldn't you say? Captain Brown won't stand up to more than the most superficial scrutiny and Charles Maddox is wanted for murder and treason. Spending some time here with us would seem to be highly convenient, even desirable, at this juncture.' She lit the end of the cigarillo from a lighter set into a large malachite block that was weighing down a particularly thick sheaf of paperwork. She smoked in a leisurely way, blowing the strong-smelling smoke over her shoulder in the general direction of the windows. 'Unless you care to test your mettle against the efforts of the Bureau of Engine Security? They do seem awfully keen to find you.' The smile half-materialised then, the edges of her mouth twitching ever so slightly upwards.

I couldn't fault her logic, but I didn't intend to give her the satisfaction of capitulating too quickly. 'I'm not sure I would be too worried if their search methods are as lackadaisical as their detective work.'

The smile began to fade again. 'What do you mean?'

'Well they seemed to be labouring under the impression that I was a sort of smuggler and that Mrs Cooper was a spy.'

'Well I can't speak for the former but the latter,' Milady drew on the cigarillo again and another wave of smoke followed the first, 'is undoubtedly the truth.'

Suddenly the room seemed like a very still and real and vivid place. I felt myself shiver in a way that I wasn't able to entirely blame on the night before. 'What?'

A wide smile beamed across her face. 'Oh, I assumed you'd know, being on such good terms?' She watched me as she drew on her cigarillo again. I could smell the tobacco now: dark but somehow floral. 'Mrs Cooper, dearly and recently departed owner of her eponymous establishment, was a spy for the American rebels, and probably since long before you knew her. We suspect that they funded her enterprise in the first place as a sort of listening station. Did you know that the Confederate States Ambassador was a frequent visitor? No doubt Cooper had listening devices in the rooms and reported everything back to her superiors.'

'Superiors?' I was still struggling to believe that Mrs Cooper was a spy. We had been quite close, I thought. I had never even suspected that she was anything other than a shrewdly genial club owner.

'The Continental Intelligence Agency they seem to be intent on calling themselves. What's left over from the old Union army intelligence. Little more than three men and a dog huddled round a stove in New Hampshire, but a proper name goes a long way to advertising the seriousness of one's endeavour, don't you agree?'

'Like the Map Room for instance?'

'Ha!' She exploded with a short bark of a laugh, the rounded point of her chin jerking upwards. 'Very good, Sterling. Of course, the thing about us is that we don't need to advertise; in fact we're terribly keen on doing the very opposite.' She drew on the cigarillo one last time before resting it on the edge of a small silver tray where it continued to burn, sending thin tendrils of smoke towards me across the table. 'Now, the thing is, earlier this year your friend Fuller from the Bureau somehow found out about Cooper and saw it as an opportunity. You see he is desperately keen to persuade the Prime Minister to expand their purview into counterintelligence. But arresting a brothel madam for passing on gossip wouldn't have fitted the bill, so he persuaded her to get into the gun-smuggling game. One of Fuller's men pretended he was a corrupt customs official who could be bribed to provide the right paperwork. The idea was to ensure some samples of ageing, semi-functional weapons arrived in America safe and sound, before arranging a significant shipment of something more modern, engine technology or something similar, tipping off the Confederate States Government and using the success to stake a claim for the Bureau's expansion.'

'Then why have they just raided their own smuggling operation? It makes no sense.'

'Well, unluckily for our friends at Millbank, it turns out that Cooper was a lot smarter than they gave her credit for and used the Bureau's sanctioned and carefully curated pipeline to transport up-to-date and operational weaponry along with the duds supplied by the Bureau. The Northerners were smart enough not to start using them immediately, waited till they had a good few safely stowed away. Then a detachment of Confederate States cavalry was ambushed near Concord by a rebel group using Maxim guns and wiped out almost to a man. Even the Bureau twigged that something was amiss and when they had the latest shipment checked they realised they had been had.' That raucous bark of a laugh again. 'Priceless! No medals, no budget increase, no wider brief to fight the Empire's enemies abroad. They were fairly incandescent I can tell you.' She smiled. 'And then you turn up, on the very night they are about to reel Cooper in, and turn out to be a British soldier recently returned from Canada. You can see how they may have jumped to conclusions.' She removed the cigarillo from its holder and stubbed it out.

'What happened to Cooper? They said she was shot trying to escape?'

'Typical Bureau, even trying to get credit for that. No, they caught her at Croydon trying to board an airship for Canada and when they tried to arrest her, she managed to get hold of one of their pistols and shoot herself. Terribly passionate people when riled, Americans.' She must have seen something in my face. 'I'm sorry, you must have been close.'

I shook my head. 'Not really, just a good customer.' In my head I was thinking back over my conversations with Mrs Cooper. Had she seen me as more? As another source of information? I could remember nothing more than gossip about other patrons or her asking my opinion on where to hang a picture or to taste a new dish for the menu. None of it seemed particularly spy-worthy. At the same time I realised that I had been hoping that Cooper's death had been a lie, that there was hope that she was still alive and that I could have asked her why she betrayed me.

'You could not have known.' Milady's words brought me back to the room. 'Sadly, an opinion not shared by the Bureau, who seem to have got it into their heads that your clandestine visit was motivated by either murderous revenge or rebellious espionage or both.' She slid a set of papers across to me. 'Which, incidentally, would be perfectly explicable and eminently forgivable behaviour if you were an agent of our organisation.'

I took the papers and flicked through them, glancing at the contents; two copies of an agreement that declared that I was gainfully employed by the Royal Office of Topography & Survey and in fact that I had been for the last three years. It also mentioned that the nature of my duties empowered me to adopt false identities and 'conduct certain actions that would otherwise be outside the law'. The final page contained a date and my details with a space for a signature.

'You're saying that if I sign this and become your agent, then I can't be arrested?'

'Well you can be, but you would be released very quickly afterwards, and whichever poor uniform had brought you in would be given a stern talking to by Church, which by the way, is not something I would recommend.'

I looked away from her to the window, staring through it at the buildings outside. I should have been home with my father, having had the satisfaction of making Edgar confess to what he had done and having persuaded Mrs Cooper to change her testimony. Sentence annulled, I was to have become a free man, leaving the army and the bitter cold of the border garrison behind for good and rebuilding a life here in London. But Edgar had challenged me in front of witnesses, and I had been angry enough to accept. In the moment, killing him had seemed like justice. Now it seemed like folly. I looked back at Milady who was observing me with a steady, calm gaze.

'Why me?' I asked.

She smiled. 'You interest me. I see potential in you. And, of course it's a chance to tweak the Bureau's tail which is always amusing.'

In other words, I wasn't to be told. Not that I expected to be and in a sense that didn't matter as, short of bursting through the door and testing my close-quarter combat skills against those of Milady's Amazonian companion, I saw that I had very little choice. I stared at the papers.

Seeming to take my silence for indecision, she spoke again: 'If you choose to join us, you will of course be able to resign once the current directive has concluded.'

I looked up into those unreadable eyes. 'This is not permanent, then?'

'Heavens, no!' She seemed amused. 'In fact, it almost certainly will not be. However, we are in need of new talent at the moment, and talent is something you seem to possess. Look on it as a mutually beneficial exchange, to be extended if agreeable to both parties. If you want to leave once things have died down, then that's up to you. If, on the other hand, you decide to stay on board, well, I for one would be delighted.' She paused for a moment, watching the effect of her words. 'You should understand, though, that where we work there is no rule book, no guide, no terms of engagement. There is only the field executive, what he senses and what he decides. What you decide, Sterling. Your skills, your experience, your judgement will aid you but in the end you will need to rely on your instinct as much as your intellect.' She paused. 'There will be hazard.'

'So,' she smiled, the hostess once again, and stood up to offer me a pen. 'What do you say?'

What could I say? See me out at the front door, I'll take my chances against the secret police who control all the Empire's data. And don't worry, I certainly won't tell anyone about your secret spy operation. That didn't feel like an option that was genuinely on the table. All the same I waited for a few seconds later than was comfortable just for the look of the thing. Then I signed.

'Marvellous! Now I think that there are a few more details that Church will iron out with you before we pop you out onto the street but otherwise, we are, as they say, "all squared away".' She stood up and I followed suit, standing as she donned her gloves. 'By the by,' she said, wrestling the second one on, 'I thought that you should know that there seems to have been a temporary improvement in your father's condition so, providing this business is wrapped in a timely manner, you will still be able to pay your filial duty. Assuming that is the main reason you came back?'

I stared at her.

She laughed. 'Really Sterling, it isn't so very hard to make the connection once you know what you're looking for.'

The door opened and the bodyguard strode back in with

long, impatient steps. 'The train leaves in less than 30 minutes, ma'am.'

'Excellent. Thank you, Kitty. I am pleased you decided to join us, Sterling. I shall see you anon.'

'Just one last question, Milady.'

'Of course.' All smiles and attention.

'How on earth did someone like Mrs Cooper manage to get hold of Maxim guns?'

'Oh you know, Sterling. Criminal connections no doubt,' she said casually, 'Not really our worry. Now, I really must dash or Kitty here will be terribly cross with me and, Lord knows, we wouldn't want that.'

And after a flurry of activity in which she took another sip of her drink, retrieved her hat and gloves and rushed out before striding back briefly to retrieve her cigarette holder, Milady finally left the room. Kitty waited patiently throughout before following her, after a brief pause for a glance that left me in no doubt as to where blame would be apportioned should any problems ensue from their delayed departure.

And I was left alone in a room that suddenly felt very empty, with the sense of being no longer the centre of things and the lingering smell of tobacco in the air.

Now that I'd decided to go along with the idea, being here didn't seem so bad. I would be safe from Fuller's retribution and clear my name. Perhaps, I mused, just as Maddox the soldier had helped me leave Charles the scandal-in-exile behind me, Agent Sterling could do the same for me now and be a clean slate to start again.

'Are you staying?'

I looked up. Church stood in the open doorway.

I nodded. 'It seems that I am.'

Church walked over and reached out his arm and we shook

hands. 'Welcome aboard,' he said. 'First things first. Let's head downstairs and get your Bertie sorted.'

Church closed Milady's office door behind us and took me back downstairs to the front hall, back along to the briefing room then down a tight set of turning steps. These led down to a narrow and dimly lit, flagstoned corridor. Church set off towards the rear, past a grimy window looking onto a small courtyard, then to an open doorway from which light spilt into the corridor. Church stood to one side and ushered me in ahead of him.

The room was square, the floor paved with the same stones as the hallway, the walls whitewashed. By contrast to the corridor it was quite warm and brightly lit by a variety of electric lamps positioned on a tall set of metal shelves against the back wall. Against the left-hand wall was a rough trestle table, its surface crammed with cylinders, punch cards, wiring and assorted bits of semi-identifiable technology. Taking up most of the rest of the room, so that there was barely space to walk between it and the table, was a relatively new-looking analytical engine, wires and cables draped away from it in every direction.

Bracketed to the wall in the centre of the table was a larger and more modern version of the kinetic display I had seen in Cooper's and sitting in front of it was a slight figure in shirt sleeves and braces, engrossed in soldering something to the side of a telegraph encoder. His long white hair was archaically ribboned tight at the nape of his neck, and at first I thought him decrepitly old, then, as he stopped what he was doing and pushed himself back from the desk on a wheeled chair, I realised he was much younger.

And then she turned around, and I realised that it was a young woman, no more than twenty years old, and my first thought was to wonder where her parents had got to. Tilting back in the chair, she shifted a set of bug-eyed goggles up onto her head and regarded us both with a look that gave the impression that, on a list of things she would rather be doing, engaging with us would not have featured highly. She had a slim face and the kind of dainty, girlish features more in keeping with a society salon than a cellar full of technological odds and ends.

'What do you want?' Her voice was high, her tone exasperated, her accent pure deb.

'Patience. This is Sterling. Needs his Bertie sorting.'

'Pleased to meet you.' I held out my hand.

Rolling her eyes, she gave my hand a perfunctory shake and dug out a wire-festooned helmet from amongst the clutter scattered across the desk. She flicked switches on the engine which spun into life and the familiar clatter of a teletype started up. 'Grab a chair from somewhere.' She pointed over her shoulder towards the back of the room. I waited until she was back at the desk before I attempted to squeeze past. I found a folding canvas stool, one of several stacked by the shelves, and sat down at the desk on the side nearest the door. The screen in front of Patience flickered, strings of words and numbers rippling upwards. She leaned over and settled the helmet on my head then, seemingly satisfied, returned to the keyboard. 'Be two minutes to mount it.'

'Getting slow, Patience, used to be quicker.'

'Shag a dog, Church, why don't you?' Patience said in an uninterested voice, still staring intently at the screen in front of her. 'Everything's so shuttered up now even connecting takes a genius. Too many tappers trying to steal stuff. Apparently.' She shook her head, her eyes and mouth wide in exaggerated horror. 'Shocking.' She leaned forward to inspect the screen, one hand hovering over the keyboard in front of her, the other on a black dial set into a small box. 'Which is why...' She clicked the dial round, tapped keys, paused, tapped some more. 'We have to make a slight detour to get to where we want to be.'

'And where is that?' I asked.

For the first time since we had entered the room the frown vanished, and a grin darted across her pale, elfin face. 'At this very moment ... a census branch office in Tenby transmitting a batch of regular updates to the central records depot in Neath, where we are pausing briefly to indulge in some diabolical evildoing!' She ended her explanation with a passable imitation of a pantomime villain's laugh, then flicked the dial to a different position. I felt dots of pressure across my head as the helmet took its measurements. She watched the screen carefully, typing a series of entries.

'What kind of evildoing, exactly?' I asked her.

She didn't look round. 'One. We are removing every descriptor or distinguishing feature of you from your public record so that it is impossible to identify you. Two. I am replacing all of that information with new values that in no way resemble you. Three. I am keeping a copy of your real data here so that I can produce an endless stream of false but highly believable identities for you.' She pressed the keyboard one last time and swivelled in the chair. 'And, voila, you are now invisible. Thank you. Thank you very much.' She raised her hands and nodded gently, a modest conjuror accustomed to the roar of her audience.

'Time, Patience. We don't have it.' Church's voice behind me in the doorway.

Another roll of the eyes. Then to me: 'You can take it off.'

I pulled the helmet off and dropped it on the desk. 'Won't they know that the information has been changed?'

'They might if anyone ever bothers to cross check with paper-file copies but they won't because they are morons. And I mean that in the literal sense. We're using Tenby because that's the home of a lazy senior clerk who had an unofficial connection added so that he doesn't have to go all the way to Neath for minor changes and who was vain enough to brag about it to an on-wire girlfriend who, as it turned out,' she continued with a smirk, 'wasn't that interested in meeting after all.'

I stood up. 'Thanks. I know where to come for all of my nefarious telegraphic needs.'

Patience looked at me, brow furrowing slightly at this poor attempt at humour. 'Fine.'

Church stood to one side as I came out then leaned into the room. 'Thanks, Patience. Oh, and I've told you before, tidy this place up. It's a right state.' Her reply, imploring Church not to be an arse, followed us out of the room as we headed back to the stairs.

I laughed, slightly shocked. 'Is she always like that?'

'Always. Best tapper I know though. She really is a magician. And bloody knows it.'

I followed him upstairs and through to the hallway where Miss Green was talking to someone I didn't recognise. He broke off from the conversation and came across to the two of us.

'Excuse me Mr Church. Mr Collier would like a word. He's in operations.'

"Ta Wallis. Sterling, I'll see you later when you're back.'

'Back from where?'

'Back from taking your fiancée for a romantic tour round Whitechapel.'

'My fiancée?'

He pointed at Miss Green, who stretched out a hand on which was a ring that more than made up for in sparkle what it lacked in size. 'Shall we?'

8. Whitechapel

The bus was old but recently repainted and well cared for, in marked contrast to the grim and narrow lanes we trundled along. Refuse-strewn alleys led away between the hulks of narrow, variously degenerating tenements. The only sign of their residents was the occasional pale-faced glance from an upper window as we passed by. Light and warmth seemed sparse here; it was early afternoon, yet patches of frost still lay unmelted in the shadows of dreary, grey doorways. And down the middle of it we drove, a gaudy reminder of the other world. I wondered if those pale faces hated us or if they had simply learnt not to see us as we stared out at their poverty. I wasn't surprised that the driver had a pistol holstered next to his seat.

There were six other people on the tour, apart from Green and myself. In the front seats, nearest our guide, two Home Counties matriarchs sat side by side, thin faces bunched in concentration as they peered out through the window. They spoke little. Just behind them were a family of Germans, dressed in precisely tailored and emphatically British clothing; he in tweeds, she in a pale blue naval-themed tailor-made with the boy and girl in brass-buttoned uniforms. They were largely silent, though the younger child would, after conferring and much at his father's insistence, occasionally ask the guide a question. Whenever he did so his English was flawless, with just a trace of accent and I could hear my father's voice ringing out over breakfast, explaining how the Prussians would take over the world one day and that learning our language was only the first step.

I pictured my father then, lying in his room in the house at Falmouth, telescope to hand, tyrannising the staff and, from what Milady said, lingering bloody-mindedly against his body's best efforts. Maybe, I thought, if I played Agent Sterling to the hilt just long enough to prove Church's prediction of a goose chase accurate, I could satisfy the terms of the agreement, resign with a pardon firmly in place and get back to the family home in time to see him.

Our guide was called Evan, ruddy faced and heavy set with a wide, toothy smile that flashed on and off as the moment required. He wore a dark blue bus conductor's uniform with a badge that showed the route number as 666, the same being shown at the front of the bus next to its destination: To Hell. I had expected him to have, or to affect, an East End accent but instead, when he spoke, it was with a gentle Welsh lilt.

I hadn't known what to expect when Collier had said he was sending me out for some local colour, but it certainly wasn't this. I had been vaguely aware of the Ripper murders when they were happening but hadn't really cared much, even though Edgar, myself and the set we hung out with would sometimes pop down to the East End for larks. Thinking back to those days, we had been so oblivious to anything but ourselves that even as brutal murders as these didn't hold our attention for long. Before the briefing that morning, I wouldn't have known how many murders there were, let alone the dates and names and, despite the penny dreadful aura that clung to the proceedings, I found myself quite interested in the tour, though not as much as Green, sitting excitedly beside me.

At first I had thought she was putting on an act, but as the tour progressed it seemed that her enthusiasm was genuine. She had only joined the Map Room recently herself and, as she had told me earlier, was keen to prove her worth, earn what she called her 'agent name' and get out into the field. To me, she certainly seemed to know what she was talking about.

'Excuse me?' From the seat beside me Miss Green's hand shot up for what I conservatively put as the seventh time since the start of the tour.

'Yes, miss?' His tone was still jocular, but the brow furrowed nervously as he waited for what was to follow. I got the distinct impression that our guide was beginning to regret his earlier humouring of the young lady's keenness. The German children had obviously formed the same impression and glanced round whenever Green spoke.

'Are we going to be stopping at Goulston Street?' she asked.

The guide looked slightly puzzled for a moment before responding. 'Goulston Street, ma'am?'

'Yes, to look at where they found the writing.'

'Ahh,' he said, nodding wisely, and broadened his focus to the rest of our small company. 'Ladies and gentlemen, what the young lady is referring to is an incident that occurred after the fourth murder where a young constable found a woman's apron stained with blood and discarded in a passageway.'

'And some writing, Mr Evan!'

'Indeed,' he said, 'some writing was found nearby—'

'Exactly above it,' she interrupted.

Raising his hands defensively, he carried doggedly on. 'Well, certainly in a close proximity. The thing is though, miss, ladies and gentlemen, that this discovery did cause some consternation at the time, particularly as the writing mentioned Jews.

Nowadays those of us who study the case professionally,' with a meaningful glance at Green, 'and with the benefit of modern research methods, tend to discount this as a coincidence or at best an attempt by a local resident to stir up trouble. So, not really worth a visit on this tour... where our next stop will be to explore the night of the "double event" where the Ripper was uniquely witnessed in the act of his brutal work and almost caught! Alas the citizens of Whitechapel were to have no such luck and he went on to commit the most foul and depraved of his atrocities. So, think on that as we turn now,' a quick look over his shoulder, 'into the cheerful bustle of Commercial Street.'

The bus edged steadily out into the street, in between a dray piled high with beer barrels and a horseless carriage disgorging a set of bankers on their way to an early lunch. The centre of the street was dominated by trams, pedestrians chancing their luck between them whenever they slowed. Hawkers shouted their way along the edge of the road shadowed by small clumps of children hoping for charity, whether deliberate or accidental. To the south I spotted a couple of airships, smaller than the one that carried me across the Atlantic, probably domestic flights headed north to Manchester or Glasgow. The traffic noise was cacophonous; the smells of market, trade and transport thick about us as the driver skilfully nosed us into the traffic flowing south. As he did, the German boy asked, 'Please sir, if you can say, why the road is named this way?'

Back on familiar territory, the guide relaxed into his explanation of the City, markets, exchanges and industries excluded from the Square Mile. Green sat back against the chair looking thoughtful.

'What do you think of the show so far?' I asked.

She turned to me. 'Actually pretty good. He seems to know his stuff. What about you?'

'Enjoying it more than I thought I would. What did the writing say?'

Green looked pleased that I had asked. 'The Jews are the men who will not be blamed for nothing.'

'And what does it mean?'

'Well, there are some fanciful interpretations, Masonic proclamations and whatnot, but those of us who study the case professionally,' she said wryly, 'see it as just your everyday anti-Semitic graffiti. There's plenty of it around here. The apron did come from Eddowes and the Ripper dropped it there. There were lots of rumours at that stage that the killer was Jewish so it might have been an attempt at a smokescreen.'

'And what do you think?'

'I think it was thoughtfully and deliberately done to confuse the police. Not that they needed much help with that at the time. But not by Jack, by his partner or by whoever was looking after him.'

'Looking after him?'

'Look around you,' she said, as the bus arrived at the junction with Whitechapel High Street where the raised arms and red light of the traffic signal had brought the traffic to a temporary halt. 'Most of these roads are packed all day and don't get much quieter at night, and yet a lone man, unhinged enough to perpetrate some pretty foul atrocities, managed to evade capture night after night. I've been looking at some profiles the Pinkertons have been developing. Killers who work on the spot tend to be careless and make mistakes. They get caught. The ones who plan coldly tend to kidnap their victims and murder at a place of their choosing; they prepare everything, including their escape, so carefully. Jack looks like the first type, a spur-of-the-moment killer. I don't think someone like that is careful or smart enough to stay free without help. Now maybe that help was police incompetence or indifference, but I think it was more than that. Partner or the full-blown conspiracy that Mr Collier seems in favour of, I don't know. But something.' The signal changed and, with a gentle lurch, we set off again.

'You could well be right, but I think you should give our poor host some time off.'

'The guide?' she looked slightly aghast that I would suggest such a thing. 'But that's half the fun. I think it must make a change for him from ploughing through the same dull script every day. Besides, when I asked Mr Church how I was supposed to act he just told me to be myself.'

'Did he?'

'He did.'

'Well then, carry on Miss Green, I mean Rose.'

'Whatever you say Albert.' Green winked at me and leaned forward in her seat attentively. Bert Norris was one of the soldiers from my company in Canada and it seemed as good a name as any to masquerade under for this outing. I leaned back in my seat and took in the scenery, letting the drone and chirp of guide and audience fade into the background.

It was a strange feeling to be back here after being in Canada for so many years. We'd often been told by the CO and the occasional visiting dignitary how valuable our work was and how the folks back in Blighty appreciated our sacrifice. Certainly, they did in Canada; by and large the populace was grateful to see us, and it wasn't uncommon for officers and NCOs to be given a drink or a meal on the house in some places. But back here in London I could see how forgotten that particular frontier was and how little interest shown in what was happening there.

Of course, there were no exotic native celebrations to photograph or foods to taste, no glamorous cavalry charges or airship battles, just grinding days of watching and patrolling and hoping for something to happen, then wishing it hadn't when it did. It was a familiar complaint in the officers' mess back in Canada that resurfaced whenever a newspaper arrived from home. It was over 10 years since the Second Civil War and the Confederate States of America was slowly being allowed back onto the world stage. The British image of President Jackson had shifted from the evil tyrant who had carpet-bombed Washington to the remorseful elder statesmen keen to make reparations, and, with nothing to fear from our new friend, the money that was spent on troops in Canada would be far better used at home.

That wasn't my experience. If anything, the unofficial incursions on the Canadian border had become more frequent and bolder in the last year, certainly for our garrison. The CO had promised to take it up the line just before I left but with little optimism that anyone in HQ would pay attention.

'You look serious! What were you thinking about?' said Green, next to me. The bus had stopped.

'Lunch.'

'Well, we've three more stops to put you off your appetite!' I stood to one side to let her off the bus and followed her out to the pavement. The others followed us out and last of all came the guide, who jumped down from steps and clapped his hands together.

'Ladies and gentlemen. Welcome to the scene of the third murder or should I say the third and fourth murders, Jack's "double event", an evening of horrific and audacious crimes!' He reached into his pocket for his notebook. 'We'll be walking for now and Ronald there will pick us up again at Mitre Square. But for now we'll bid him "addoo" and make our way to the first of the two, the murder of Elizabeth Stride.'

The guide walked us down a narrow street of low, somewhat dilapidated buildings, mostly made up of workshops and traders. It was less dirt ridden than some of the streets we had been down earlier in the bus but only marginally so and a marked difference from the bright awnings of the taller buildings we had left behind with the bus. We walked a little way down the street to where a higher, three-storey building stood, tables and a bar visible through the windows at the front. A faded sign over the door read 'International Working Men's Club'. The guide nodded to one of the men standing outside who lifted a pipe away from his thick black beard to return the greeting and beckoned us towards a narrow passageway next to the building. I saw the father of the family hesitate as he saw the men, before shepherding his wife and children protectively past them as they followed our guide into the rear, which opened out into a small, dingy yard, barely big enough to turn a cart with one door leading off it into the kitchen of the club.

'Imagine if you will, ladies and gentlemen, the scene. A hard-working and loving husband returning late is driving his pony and cart into this very yard when suddenly the pony shies and throws him backwards! Looking down he sees a body on the ground. Shocked he runs into the club and returns with two colleagues and the three of them discover that it is a woman with her throat cut most horribly, blood pooling on the ground beside her. Unlike the other victims, though, there were no other injuries. But why, you ask? Because the killer was disturbed in the act! Forced to flee, his dreadful urges unsated, he roamed the night looking for his next victim and we will be following his path on foot as we travel to the site of the next murder and the dreadful mutilations of Mitre Square!'

'Excuse me, Mr Evan.' One of the old ladies raised a finger as she spoke.

'Just Evan is fine, ma'am. What can I do for you?'

'We weren't told there was going to be walking on this tour. How long do you expect this part to take and, could you please tell me, will there be any steps?'

Our guide smiled politely and replied, 'It won't be more than fifteen minutes or so, ma'am, and if you're fatigued at any stage I'm sure our group won't mind resting for a moment.'

She and her companion seemed mollified by this response and they moved off along the street, led by Evan. The German family fell in behind them while I waited to bring up the rear, Green walking alongside me. 'Do you think,' she asked in a low voice, 'whether it is exhaustion they are concerned about or contamination?'

'Both?' I hazarded with a small smile that I forced into a laugh as I remembered we were supposed to be a couple.

The walk was a little over the quarter of an hour promised, particularly with the few pauses introduced by Evan, ostensibly to point out a sight or two along the way but rather, I think, with our two older companions in mind. Out of the bus, at ground level, the blare of the street was even louder and little conversation was possible as we walked along.

I remembered Mitre Square from the briefing file: a quiet spot right at the edge of the city; mostly commercial storage with a few empty houses. A constable's beat passed through the square and that night he came through twice: the first time it was peaceful and empty without a soul in sight, the second time a woman lay half naked and eviscerated in the south-west corner. Green looked bored as the guide explained all this to the group. Her mood wasn't improved when, having said his piece, Evan asked if the gentlemen would like to view photographs of the scene, making it clear that, for reasons of delicacy, children and ladies would not be permitted to see them. Despite vociferous protests from Green, however, our guide refused to budge from his position. I declined to look at them myself, which Green took as solidarity with her but, really, I just didn't want to see them. I'd seen enough of the ones in the briefing pack that morning.

Back aboard our transport, most thankfully in at least two cases, we turned out of the square into a busy road then almost immediately left it to dive into a warren of narrow streets that were, if anything, worse than those we had passed during the early parts of the tour.

'Before we arrive, ladies and gentlemen, I'm afraid I must let you know that we will be unable to alight from the bus at Miller's Court.' He held his hands up at the mild outrage that arose at his statement, mainly, it has to be said, from Green. 'I'm very sorry about that but it's for your own safety. I'm sorry to say that there has been an increase in criminal activity in recent weeks, added to which there are extensive building works going on in the area and I'm afraid we don't want any of you good people to come to any harm. However, I do have such photographs and plans of the dwelling as to make it almost as if we were there.' Agreeable nods from all but Green whose hand shot up.

'What building works?'

'Ah, yes miss, of course. It's one of the Models, I do believe the Peabody's. Rentable housing to raise the quality of living and aspiration of the common man, as it were.' He smiled. 'A most laudable aim, as I'm sure we would all agree.'

When we arrived we saw that what he said was true; the side of the road where Miller's Court was had been demolished in its entirety and in its place stood a building site and a large hoarding proclaiming the arrival of 'improved housing and workspaces for the poor as may combine in the utmost possible degree the essentials of healthfulness, comfort, social enjoyment and economy'.

'As he says, it seems laudable,' I ventured at Green.

'Hmm. Convenient though, wouldn't you say?'

Evan talked us through the murder, explaining that he would be leaving out some of the more gruesome details in deference to the weakly constituted of the company. I heard Green snort audibly as he said that.

'A question, miss?'

She shook her head and smiled sweetly. 'Not at all Mr Evan, you carry on. You're doing a fantastic job!'

I remembered the photos from the file of material we'd been given and thought it was a sensible decision. The room in the pictures that I'd seen was a charnel house, the victim subjected to a series of frenzied, inhuman mutilations and even the guide's toned-down version was gruesome enough and a reminder of how fitting the destination on the front of the bus was. And lingering on that thought for just too long, that other room from my own memory jerked into view in my mind's eyes, sharper now, and her name came with it this time. The name that had shaped Edgar's last breath. Alice. I desperately riveted my attention to the guide's closing pitch, focusing fiercely on his words till she left me again.

'Thank you, ladies and gentlemen. And that is the end of our tour today. I hope you have found it illuminating, educational and not a little unsettling. Don't forget, Jack was never caught so be wary if you walk these streets again, he might be waiting. And if people ask you where you have been today, you can truly tell them you have been to Hell... and back!' He finished with a flourish and was rewarded with applause, most loudly from the two children, until a glance from their father settled them down.

And the tour was over, except of course, we were told, if we had more questions we could repair with the amenable Evan to the nearby Ten Bells public house to share a drink 'at the very tables where the Ripper's victims imbibed their nightly tipple' and ask him any further questions that we may have.

'And don't forget,' he continued, 'to keep hold of your tickets and you will be afforded a generous discount on all tickets for the Gaiety Theatre at the Aldwych. Thank you all so much and, of course, I would be more than happy to accept any further appreciation you felt appropriate.'

The old ladies tutted at this, but he seemed to strike a vein with the father of the family who furnished Evan with what could have been half a sovereign. Palming it deftly, he turned to Green and myself. 'Hello miss. I'm sure you will have some more questions for me? Perhaps you and your gentleman would like to join me for an ale?'

'We'd be delighted,' I said, deciding that, if I was going to do the job, I might as well do it properly. I offered my arm to Green, who took it, and we walked after Evan; spying an apt moment in the traffic, we darted across Commercial Street and into the pub.

Lunchtime was over now, and the pub was quiet; a few late diners finishing off their drinks, a couple of women clutching glasses of gin at a table nearest the door. Darkly decorated but with enough light let in from the street outside, the bar was not quite warm enough to be welcoming. A vase of slowly wilting flowers on the countertop did something to add a little cheer to the place but this was a place for drinking and forgetting, a refuge for workers of all trades, including the oldest one. We followed our guide through to the lounge bar where the landlord looked up from his *Sporting Times* with a half-cheery 'Usual, Evan?'

He nodded. 'That's it, Teddy. And something for my guests.'

'Please,' I said, stepping next to him at the bar, 'let me pay for these.'

'Well that's so very kind of you!' he beamed back at me, as if pleasantly surprised by the notion that he wouldn't be paying.

'Not at all. We thought the tour was a good afternoon out, didn't we Rose?'

'Oh so much!' chimed in Green. 'And I have a few more

things I would be interested to discuss with you, conspiracies for example.'

The landlord put Evan's drinks down on the bar – a pint of brown ale and a large whisky – then waited for my order.

'Pint of pale for me, a small glass of mild for the lady.'

The landlord nodded and pulled the drinks.

'Conspiracies?' Evan shook his head. 'I've never seen much evidence for them,' he said, taking a sip of beer. 'Stupidity is much more likely if you ask me, or panic, or the left hand not knowing what the right hand is doing. When it was going on you had Metropolitans, the City, the CID, and the Branch all sticking their oar in. Everyone wanted the credit of catching him then suddenly no one wanted to be on the end of a battering from the press when anything went wrong. I think you'll find chaos, not conspiracy, a pretty convincing explanation. Other than that, it all seems pretty straightforward to me: the man was a bloody lunatic, pardon the phrase ma'am, killed for a spell and probably ended up in Bedlam or dead. And all that talk of Masons or the Royals being involved. Fanciful at best, kept alive by people who should know better. Thanks, Ted.'

The landlord set our drinks on the bar. I paid, measuring the amount from a handful of coins, and tried the ale. It was surprisingly good and much better than what I had been used to in Canada.

Green took a sip of mild and made a slight face at the taste. 'Well I have read several articles to the contrary.'

'On the wire? Who was it – Richardson?' Evan laughed, took another sip of beer and chased it with most of the whisky.

'I'm afraid I can't remember.' Green said.

'Probably Richardson. He's a lunatic himself. Ran a little tour of his own for a few months after the murders but the police moved him on after some trouble with some of the locals. For his own good more than anything. Now he was your man for conspiracies, saw them everywhere. The nuts on the wire loved him. He was here when the murders were happening, wrote endless letters to the police suggesting how they could catch the Ripper. Even offered to dress up as a prostitute to try and catch him. Well meaning but some odd ideas!' He took a large gulp of beer and knocked back the remainder of the whisky.

'He sounds like fun,' said Green. 'I feel like I should meet him! Is he still around?'

'Richardson?' replied Evan. 'No, not any more. Moved away somewhere I heard. You wouldn't want to listen to him for more than five minutes anyway. Totally barmy.' He tapped his head to illustrate the point.

'Another drink, Mr Evan?' I asked.

'Don't mind if I do, Mr...'

'Norris. But call me Albert,' I replied.

'Well Albert, that's very kind, just a pint this time I think.'

I nodded to the landlord who was polishing glasses further along the bar. He put down his cloth and went to pour Evan's drink.

'Excuse me,' asked Green, 'but I promised I would call my father. Do you know, is there a public phone here?'

'In the other bar, towards the back,' said Evan. Then 'You'll need coins' at Green's back as she walked away.

'Oh, thank you, I have plenty!' Green called to him as she headed through to the public bar.

The landlord put Evan's ale down as he drained the last of the first pint. I fished out a shilling and placed it down on the bar. He took it away, along with Evan's empty glasses and went back to his work.

'Cheers!' said Evan. We both took a sip of our beer. 'You're a very lucky man if you don't mind me saying so, Albert.'

'And no, I don't mind, you're right, we're both very happy.' I knew what he was saying though, Green was a good ten years younger than me and, though not in Milady's league when it came to salon elegance, had a pretty perkiness about her. The guide was probably wondering how on earth I managed to land her.

'I could see it as we went around today. Lucky lad, I thought. Quite a looker and bright too. Some odd views of course, and an American as well but you can't have everything, eh?' He raised his glass and drank again, then frowned as if a thought had suddenly occurred to him. 'Hey now,' he asked, 'she's not a journalist, is she?'

'A journalist? Good God no! Just a hobby.'

'Oh, right. By the look of the sparkler on her hand you'll be getting married soon, would I be right?'

'We are, the month after next,' I said.

He looked thoughtful for a moment. 'Expensive business, marriage. And you have the look of an old soldier about you, would I be right thinking that?'

I nodded. Took a sip of beer. 'Infantry.'

'I thought so. An officer by the sound of it?' I nodded again. 'And let me guess, for I know a bit about this sort of thing,' he went on, 'you spent almost all your discharge money on the ring and,' gesturing with his glass, 'the rest on that suit by the look of it.' He looked at me thoughtfully, sizing me up. 'London's an expensive place for an old soldier and there's not many who'll take us on is there?'

I made a noise that could have been taken as an affirmative.

'Well,' he continued, 'If you ever need a bit of work, cash in hand, you know, ask for me here and I'll have you set up.'

'What sort of work?' I asked.

'Ohh,' he replied, with a slow wink, 'this and that.'

'Thanks, I'll think about it.'

'You do that, lad. Even officers need an extra bob every now and again, don't they?'

'You're right there,' I replied, giving what I hoped was a wry smile.

'Oh, dearest one.'

I looked up at Green, who was standing in the entrance to the lounge. 'Yes, Rose, my dear?'

'Daddy wants to speak to you.'

I sighed slightly and followed her back out to the telephone, held up the receiver.

'Sterling. Church.'

'Oh hello, sir, yes, your daughter and I are having a wonderful time,' I said loudly, for the benefit of any of Evan's friends who might be listening.

'Do you know St George's Hospital, on Hyde Park Corner?' I said I could find it. 'I'll see you there at four.'

'Yes sir, I'll make sure your daughter is safely home.'

'You do that.'

He ended the call. I walked back to the other bar to find Green and our new friend locked in jovial debate.

'Rose, dear, your father wants you home now and I'm to see you there.'

Green stood up. 'Well, Evan, thank you so much! It has been a wonderful afternoon.'

'Thank you, ma'am, you are most welcome. Bert, do let me know if there are any other questions that you find yourself with. Just leave a message here with Teddy.'

We shook hands and Evan gave me the firm grip, steady eye and cheery smile of one honest man to another. I nodded as we shook hands. 'I will'.

Outside as we looked for a cab, I thought about Evan's performance on the tour, his patience with the old ladies, his easy-going attitude with the rest of us and his charitable camaraderie with me while Green was on the call. And a phrase of the soldier whose name I'd borrowed came to mind as I thought about that handshake. 'I wouldn't trust him,' as I once heard the real Bert Norris say about someone, 'further than I could spit into the wind.'

9. *Call*

I arrived at Hyde Park Corner a shade before four. The day was already darkening, the evening chill setting in. My cab pulled up a few doors down from the main entrance to St George's, behind another that was already by the kerb.

'There you go, boss. St George's Hospital.'

I stepped outside, closed the door behind me. The cabbie rubbed his hands together, warming them, while he waited for me to pay.

'Here,' I said, passing him up a half crown, 'keep the change.'

'Thank you, sir, very kind.' He touched his forehead and threw the hansom into gear, the engine rattling into life as he pulled away from the kerb and back into the swirl of traffic coming down from Piccadilly.

As I watched him head towards Knightsbridge, I realised it was colder than I had first thought and cursed myself for not bringing a hat and scarf. I put my hands into my coat pockets, feeling my new papers there as I walked along. Patience had had them ready for me when I dropped off Green; for the purposes of this evening's visit I was Kenneth Wilkinson, a representative of Gadd, Shanks & Pincock; solicitors, based in Chatham. They were good enough for a meeting or two, she had explained when she gave them to me, and would check out if someone decided to call the number on the card or look up the company but she had warned me that they wouldn't fool anyone who 'knew their onions'.

It felt odd to be walking out in the open and while part of me felt committed to follow through on the deal I had made with Milady, there was another part of me that was thinking that the first chance I got I should start running without looking back. The years in Canada meant I was a long way changed from the carefree layabout I had been eight years ago so I might hope to avoid identification. Besides which, if she was to be believed, Patience had rendered me invisible to the Bureau's engines. All I had to do was steer clear of Fuller's search parties and every constable in London. And what I imagined to be the far higher hurdle of evading Milady.

'Sterling.' I jumped, startled to hear my name. The voice came from the parked cab and I glanced to see Church's impassive face at the window. He pushed the door open and gestured me inside. I ducked in, tugging the cab door closed behind me and sitting opposite him, the leather seat creaking as I did so.

'How was Whitechapel?' he asked. 'What did you make of the tour?' I glanced up at the roof and raised an eyebrow. Church shook his head briefly. 'One of Mac's lads,' he said. 'So. What are your thoughts?'

I felt myself warming to Church. He reminded me a bit of our RSM in Canada – solid, dependable, but canny and the kind of man I would want on my side in a fight. I shrugged at his question. 'Not much to say. I liked the tour more than I thought I would. I can see why it would be popular. There are two questions that come to mind though: where is the money coming from and why haven't they been robbed?'

'What do you mean?' asked Church.

'The tour bus and horses were better quality than I would

have expected, and the little details were all far better done than I would have thought. It all seemed,' I shrugged my shoulders, 'too good for a tour like that. The tickets are a few shillings each and they run a few times a day. They obviously have an arrangement with a theatre but even so, I can't see how they make their money. Who knows, perhaps they have an eccentric backer with a yen to shock well-heeled tourists? But even so: why wasn't the bus robbed? There was plenty of money on display amongst the passengers. We were going down some very poor and, I assume, highly criminal areas yet were completely unmolested. The driver was armed but, really, I couldn't see that as a major disincentive to a determined gang.'

'Paying someone off, most likely,' said Church. 'I don't know which mob is on top in Whitechapel these days, but I'll find out. Rich tourists you said they were?' I nodded. 'Could be they mark them and rob them later. I'll get Green to check on it. Was that it?'

'The guide spotted I was an old soldier; offered me a job when Green was calling her Papa.' Church smiled and I continued, 'I received a distinct impression it was not as a tour guide. And he wanted to know about Green's interest: was she a journalist?'

Church was silent for a moment, then said, 'So the tour was too good, and the guide was too chatty?'

'In a nutshell, yes, I suppose that's that. Insubstantial, I know.'

'Insubstantial is meat and veg for us, Sterling. You'll get the hang of it soon enough.' He fished out a pocket watch and flipped it open. 'Talking of which, time for us to pop inside and see the good Sir Anthony. Green brief you before you left?'

'Yes,' I replied. 'We're lawyers representing families of post-Ripper victims claiming police negligence. We want to know if Sir Anthony will agree to be a witness. We'll see how he reacts.'

'Strictly speaking you're a lawyer,' said Church, 'and I'm your firm's enquiry agent. Hardly matters, though, it's all just pointless goose-chasing to keep some high-ups happy so don't expect too much excitement.'

I pointed at the pair of overnight bags that sat on the floor of the cab. 'Are we going somewhere?'

'Yes, thanks to you and your fiancée.'

'What do you mean?' I asked.

'Didn't they tell you? We're off to Blackpool once we've finished here.' He picked up his hat from the seat next to him, a dark grey bowler, and settled it on his head.

'Blackpool?'

Church reached out for the door of the cab. 'It seems one wild goose is not enough for us so we're heading to the seaside to see the gent your new friend Evan the guide mentioned; Herbert Richardson, some lunatic conspiracist. He's in Blackpool apparently, so we're on the 6:10 from Euston. As I say, more goose-chasing. You know the score: if in doubt, look busy.' He opened the door of the cab. 'After you.'

He followed me out onto the pavement, and we walked up a set of steps to the front doors of the hospital, standing to one side for a pair of nurses on their way out, dark blue capes wrapped tight about them. Their conversation suddenly silenced as they saw us, then was re-joined with loud laughter as they reached the bottom of the steps. We headed into the warmth of the hospital reception.

The reception was a large oval room, brightly lit, with doors leading off it in either direction. Church dropped back to let me take the lead as we walked across a tiled floor to a long, low desk. Behind it sat a sombrely dressed middle-aged woman scribbling away on the outside of a large, beige envelope. Behind her, through an open doorway marked private, a telegraph machine clicked away. She closed the envelope and carefully wrapped the string round the envelope's button before putting it on the smaller of the two piles of similar ones to her right. She looked up at us with the weary cheer of a person determined to fulfil their role even in the face of the crowd of tasks more important than dealing with the two of us.

'Hello,' I said. 'We're here to see Sir Anthony Willard. We have an appointment but we're a little late.' I smiled apologetically and handed her one of the cards Patience had provided. 'Kenneth Wilkinson and associate.'

She reached under the desk for a metal clipboard and scanned down the sheet of engine print-out attached to it. 'Let's see. Ah yes, Mr Wilkinson, I have you here. And can I just have your colleague's name?'

'Dent,' Church said.

'Thank you very much,' she said and briskly turned the clipboard round. 'If I could have your signatures here and here, gentlemen.' She carried on as we signed. Patience had had me practising Kenneth Wilkinson at the Map Room until I had managed a fair facsimile of its neat, un-fussy flow. 'You'll need to go through those double doors and walk down to the teaching wing then take the lift there to the top floor. When you come out, turn left and walk along the corridor. Sir Anthony's office is at the very end. His secretary will be expecting you.'

Church lifted his hat with a friendly 'much obliged to you ma'am' and we headed through the doors and along the corridor. We walked along black-and-white patterned linoleum past a series of doors, the round windows in each affording us glimpses of white rooms with two or three beds apiece. Some had patients in them but most seemed empty. The corridor was brightly lit with large, very modern fluorescing lights set into the ceiling of the kind one might see in a smart office. A faint smell of disinfectant was in the air, though masked to a good extent by the perfume from fresh flowers that stood on plinths at regular intervals along the walls. The nurse working in her office at the end of the corridor didn't look up as we walked past her into a small foyer with a staircase and lift.

A group of young men in white coats who I took to be students chattered over each other as they hauled themselves tiredly up the stairs. Church and I walked over to the lift and pushed the call button. The doors opened immediately and we walked inside. There was no one there to work the lift; fully automatic cage doors slid apart of their own accord. We got inside and pressed the third-floor button. After a pause the doors closed again and, with a low whine, we were carried upwards.

The lift chimed and we stepped out of it into a very different world. The lights here were gas rather than electric and of an older style that gave off light with a yellowish tint. The walls were panelled with dark wood, the floor a richly coloured geometrical parquet. The doors here were windowless, closed and brass labelled: Head of Tropical Diseases, Dean of Research, Bursar, Vice Principal. Finally we came to a door towards the end of the corridor with 'Sir Anthony Willard, Principal' in a larger plaque than the others, then, underneath that, engraved on a black wooden sign 'Enquiries: Room 1a.' We walked a little further and found the next door open: a tall, smartly dressed secretary sat at a plain, uncluttered desk, her fingers deftly racing across the keys of a typewriter. When she looked up they danced for a few more seconds before they came to a halt and stayed there, hovering above the keys.

'Mr Wilkinson and Mr Dent?' I replied that we were. 'Please wait here for a moment, gentlemen.' She used a pencil to mark a point on the sheaf of notes she was evidently typing from and walked from around the desk, knocked lightly on the door connecting her room to the Principal's and went inside, closing it behind her. A brief snatch of telephone conversation escaped as she did so, dropping to a distant murmur as the door closed.

Church took off his bowler, holding it by his side, and glanced around the office. Filing cabinets filled the right-hand wall while on the left behind the desk was another, much smaller table on which sat an engine terminal.

The door opened and she came back out. 'Sir Anthony is ready for you, gentlemen. Please, let me take your coats.' She stood to one side, folding our coats over her arm as we handed them to her. Church gave her his hat and we walked through the doorway. It pulled shut behind us with the briefest and softest of clicks.

Sir Anthony's office was much larger and far more luxuriously furnished than that of his secretary. The wall opposite the windows was covered in bookcases, the wooden floor almost entirely hidden by a vast silk carpet that stretched the length of the room. Sir Anthony was at the far end behind a broad, leather-topped desk. On the wall behind him hung a few portraits of severe-looking men in dark suits and a smaller painting of what looked like a Venetian piazza. Sir Anthony was standing as we entered, smartly dressed in a dark, three-piece suit. He was younger than I had pictured him, perhaps in his early forties, shorter than both myself and Church, and with a complexion and midriff that suggested that the position of Principal was one that attracted regular invitations to formal dinners. His dark hair was beginning to thin and, as if to partially make up for this, he wore a neatly trimmed goatee beard. 'Please, gentlemen, do sit down,' he said in an amiable manner, indicating the two green leather swivel chairs on our side of the desk. We walked over and sat down and I handed him one of my cards.

He looked at it for a moment. 'You are a lawyer, Mr Wilkinson?'

'Yes, Sir Anthony.'

'And what can I do for you and your colleague, Mr…?'

'This is Mr Dent, he acts as an enquiry agent for our firm.'

'I see,' he said. 'And what brings you to St George's?'

'My firm represents a number of clients who have lost loved ones in the last eight years.'

He gave me a puzzled look. 'There is no connection with St George's, surely? Our survival rates for patients are the best in the country. We also have an impeccable record when it comes to surgical and diagnostic errors. Are you sure you're in the right place?'

'Oh we're sure,' growled Church, grim faced next to me, causing Sir Anthony to give him a slightly nervous glance.

'Perhaps if I explain a little more of the case,' I said.

'Oh please do. That would be useful.' Sir Anthony smiled again, this time a little less certainly.

'Thank you, Sir Anthony,' I replied. 'By the way, I must say how impressive the hospital wing was that we passed through. Was that a recent improvement?'

'Yes indeed,' he said, instantly more comfortable in the role of extolling the hospital's virtues, 'the result of a most generous bequest we received a few years ago which enabled us to modernise and extend the hospital, an improvement that was well overdue.'

'Well I must say it looks tremendous and must be of great benefit for the patients,' I said.

'And for the students, of course!' he replied with the tone of a real enthusiast. 'Which is such an important part of what we do here.'

'Of course. But to bring us back to the case we are hoping for your support with?'

'Of course, of course.' Sir Anthony seemed to have overcome Church's blunt interruption, and was cheerfully polite again. 'If there is anything I might be able to do.'

'Our clients,' I said, 'have all had female family members murdered in London since November 1888 and we are—' I got no further before Sir Anthony interrupted me with a note of exasperation in his voice.

'My good Lord, is this that blasted Ripper case again?' He shook his head. 'I honestly don't believe it. It's like a damned millstone.' He looked at us both in turn, calming himself. Shook his head again. 'Gentlemen, I apologise for that outburst. However, I am afraid I have no wish to be involved in your case, whatever it is.'

'Sir Anthony, if I could just explain a little about what we are asking of you and, either way, we will be on our way without delaying you any further.'

'You can,' he replied, 'but be warned I have very little patience for the subject.' He fished in his pocket and pulled out a gold watch which he consulted. 'And I'm afraid I have a phone call that I must make so the briefer you can make it the better.'

'Very well,' I said. 'And apologies, Sir Anthony. I hadn't imagined that the mention of the case would cause you such distress; after all, it was eight years ago.'

He smiled thinly. 'You would think so. But you are the second pair of gentlemen I have seen today who have seen fit to do so.'

'Really?' I said. 'Who were the others?'

He paused, obviously considering whether or not to answer my question. 'If you must know, they were police officers.'

Church looked at me. 'Not good news for us, Mr Wilkinson.'

'Not at all, Mr Dent,' I replied. 'It seems they may have got wind of our case even at this early stage, which is most tiresome. You see, Sir Anthony,' I continued 'our clients' case is simply this: that the Metropolitan and City police forces should have learnt a great deal from the way that the Ripper cases were tackled which, when put into practice, would have made Whitechapel and other parts of the City safer. In fact, this has markedly not happened; there has been no decrease in the level of assaults on women in the time since and in fact the number of murders has increased, particularly those of a vicious nature.

'We will be seeking to prove grievous negligence on the part of both forces, negligence which has resulted in the murder of a number of women who would otherwise be alive today. And from you, Sir Anthony, we were hoping to take a statement attesting to the poor nature of the police investigation and review of the case. Given your review of the original murders as part of the investigation at the time we thought you would be well placed to do that.' I smiled, hopefully.

'Well, Mr Watkins—'

'It's Wilkinson, Sir Anthony, Kenneth Wilkinson.'

'Whatever your name is, I am afraid I won't be able to help you. I have no wish to rehash what wasn't a particularly pleasant task for me and one, quite frankly, that I wish I had never been persuaded to be involved in. In my opinion the police did their best in somewhat challenging circumstances. Now, if you'll excuse me.' He stood: clearly our time was at an end. We both stood as he pushed a button on his desk.

'There was one other thing, though,' Church said and pulled a copy of the aerial photograph from Miller's Court. 'Are you familiar with this photo, Sir Anthony?'

Irritated, he looked down and I saw the shock of recognition flash briefly in his eyes before he managed to give the appearance of a much vaguer familiarity. 'Er. Yes, I think so. That was in the papers wasn't it, at the time of the murders, I mean? They thought it was the Ripper.'

'Almost,' said Church, 'This one is a larger version and look, you can see another man in the picture.'

'Another man?' Sir Anthony paused, brow creasing. 'You mean the figure in the street is just a passer-by then?'

'Oh no,' said Church. 'The fellow I got this from said he thought they were in it together. Two rippers, not one, do you see?'

'Not really, No. I really must ask you gentlemen to leave me to it, I'm afraid.' A fragile smile clung to Sir Anthony's face as he ushered us towards the door. He pulled the door open and looked around. His secretary was just coming back into the room as he did. 'Milly, where the devil have you been? I was buzzing you and there was no answer.'

'I am sorry Sir Anthony, I had to take your correspondence downstairs to make the last postal collection. I thought that these gentlemen would be with you for longer.' The girl looked quite taken aback.

'Well they aren't. So please see them out. Gentlemen.' He nodded curtly and went back into his room, not quite slamming the door behind him.

The secretary passed over our coats and Church's hat. 'I'm sorry, gentlemen, I apologise for the delay.'

'No apology necessary,' I said supportively and shrugged on my coat. 'I expect Sir Anthony was just worried about missing his call.'

'His call?' the girl looked blank for a moment then recovered herself. 'His call, of course, one of the governors has asked to speak to him. Well,' she said, trying for and almost managing a bright smile, 'thank you, gentlemen, I'm sure that Sir Anthony will be in touch if he wants to follow up with you.' I had had enough experience of NCOs suddenly fabricating pretexts for discrepancies during my time in Canada, sometimes on my behalf, to recognise it when I saw it. Catching Church's eye, I saw that he was thinking along similar lines.

I thanked her and asked her to pass our thanks onto Sir

Anthony. All smiles and casual conclusion, we headed back down the corridor and pushed the button for the lift.

'Interesting,' Church said softly, as he looked at the indicator above the door climb its way to three.

'Most,' I replied.

'All smiles until you mentioned the Ripper.'

'Wasn't he, though?'

'And he'd seen that version of the photo before.'

'Yes he had,' I agreed.

Church made a short, thoughtful noise. 'I think I'll ask Patience to run the good doctor's cards.'

We stood in silence as the lift arrived, chimed its bell and opened its doors. We both got in and I pushed the 'G' button. I turned to Church. 'How does that goose seem to you now?'

'Not so wild,' said Church.

The lift moved downwards smoothly, stopping gently and letting us out at the ground floor. We retraced our steps to the reception where the same woman was still working steadily at her labours. We thanked her with a smile, signed our names again and left.

After the warmth of the hospital the street felt even colder than it had done earlier and I hunched into my coat again as we walked back to the cab. The driver materialised from behind it and sprang up into his seat as we got there, bringing the engine back to life as we clambered inside.

'Euston,' Church shouted up through the hatch once we were in. 'And I'll give you a note for Green.'

'Aye, sir,' came the shout back from our driver.

Church pulled a small leather notebook and pencil from inside his jacket and wrote quickly on it. 'I'll tell Patience to get to work. Anything else?' He looked over at me.

I thought for a moment. 'Yes. Tell Green that the doctor's assistant, Milly, should become her new best friend. And ask both of them to find out why he has a painting of a Venetian square on his office wall.'

'Venetian?'

'Yes it didn't look like San Marco; one of the smaller ones, San Lorenzo perhaps?' I said.

Church finished writing the note, folding it and, opening the hatch, passed it up to the driver. 'Make sure Green gets this,' he said.

'Aye, sir.'

Church closed the hatch again and sat back in his seat. He breathed out, took his hat off, rubbed a thick-knuckled hand over his close-shaven head.

'Good work for a first-timer,' said Church.

'Thank you, Church,' I said. 'It seems that that not being shot at, imprisoned or dragged along a riverbed immeasurably improves my mental acuity.'

'It surely does,' he replied. He looked me over thoughtfully. 'You let me know if you're not okay. Understood?'

'Don't worry. I'm fine,' I said. And I realised that I half meant this. I had been so intent on observing the surgeon that, for those moments, everything else had faded from focus. Perhaps, I thought, the role with these Map Room people could be more than a legally expedient refuge. Perhaps, it could help me keep Edgar and the rest of it out of my mind, the way that the sharp end of army life had done.

We sat in silence for a few minutes before I decided to show some willing. 'What do we know about the chap in Blackpool?'

Church glanced over at me. 'Not much. Worked in a pharmacy not far from Whitechapel at the time of the murders. Bit of an obsessive. Wrote about a dozen letters to the papers with advice for the police. Suggested that specially chosen constables should dress up as women to act as bait for the Ripper. Arrested for obstruction twice. Ran an on-wire salon for Ripper theorists for a while then, six months or so after the last murder, sold up and left London. Almost nothing since. Patience dug up an address in Blackpool. A boarding house, she says. No wife or family. Seems to have a low but regular income. Nothing unremarkable. But because, apparently, we have nothing better to do, we're off to bloody Blackpool.'

'Now then,' I said, 'I'm sure it will be a delight. We can see the Tower, take in a show, go for a walk along the pier perhaps?'

He looked at me glumly. 'The pier? In November? It will be bloody freezing.'

'Bracing, Church, I think the word that you might be looking for is bracing.'

10. Illuminations

The rain hammered down relentlessly.

It danced on the dull, grey cobblestones and swept ragged shreds of urban flotsam along the gutters. It hissed and spat on the gas lights that burned at the end of the side street we stood in and it drummed down on the borrowed umbrellas of questionable efficacy beneath which Church and I stood, hunched and sodden.

The round, ruddy face of the doorman looked out at us impassively through the small square hatch in the door, a unique source of warmth and light in this narrow street of silent warehouses and boarded up shops. 'I'm sorry, lads,' he said, 'We're closed. Might be there's a club somewhere by the Tower.' He pointed up past us, out of the street to where the Tower was dominating the skyline, its restaurant lit up and its lower frame glowing in the lights from the promenade beneath.

Lightning flashed somewhere out to sea and a slow roll of thunder made its way across the sky. A drip of water made its steady, infuriating way down the back of my neck and past my shirt collar.

'Look, sunshine,' said Church, taking a step closer to the

door, 'we're not tourists that just fell off the train. We're not here for a polka. We're here for the club you're standing in. Now open up and let us in. It's pissing down out here.'

'Look lads, it's like I've already told you, we're not open tonight. That's just how it is, I'm afraid.' And with that, he closed the hatch.

Church swore, briefly, coarsely and loudly and turned to look at me.

A crisp, star-filled sky had covered our departure from London but the weather had worsened the further north we had travelled and by the time we got to Blackpool it had been doing, in Church's words, a pretty fair impression of a monsoon.

We had taken a cab to the hotel, dropped our bags, been loaned umbrellas by a concerned receptionist who did her best to persuade us to stay and sample the delights of the dining room, and headed out. Richardson's lodgings had been easy enough to find based on the address that Patience had provided and I think, though we didn't discuss it, that we were both hoping for a short conversation and an early supper. Richardson was out when we called, however, and at first his landlady was adamant she didn't know where. This changed after a careful explanation from Kenneth Wilkinson of Gadd, Shanks & Pincock of our search for Mr Richardson in connection with a large inheritance. At this the landlady was more than happy to tell us that he was at work, work being a club of some kind. She didn't know exactly what sort of work. She didn't know the name of the club. She wasn't sure where it was, she had told us, but probably in the same place as all the rest of them. She didn't know what time Mr Richardson was expected; he had his own key. She hoped we found him and cheerily waved us on our way.

So we had visited the few pubs, bars and clubs that were

open on a bleak November evening, starting by the Tower and working our way townwards from there. Still introducing myself as Wilkinson, I showed Richardson's photo to everyone we talked to, saying we were lawyers sent by his family but no more. As we did, I found that, despite the rain, I was enjoying being Agent Sterling and sleuthing around the grimier alleys of Blackpool's seafront. I was warming to Church and I think that the reverse was also true and it seemed that we were slowly building a working camaraderie, albeit one that wasn't turning into results.

We cajoled, smiled and, in Church's case, looked silently menacing, but were none the wiser and about to call an end to the evening when we had a small stroke of luck. In a less salubrious club, a few streets in from the seafront, we encountered a patron who thought he recognised the picture and whose confidence in this identification positively soared with half a crown in his hand. Richardson, he told us, could be found working in a club not far from the one we were in.

'What's it called?' Church had asked.

The man hesitated but on being prompted by Church proffered the name: The Filthy Lanes. It was French, he had added by way of an explanation. I hadn't had the heart to contradict him and I puzzled at what the original words might have been as we continued on our rain-soaked tour of Blackpool's nightlife. After a quarter of an hour or so we had found the place he'd directed us to, in a short street of dark and shuttered shops and storehouses. And so here we were, standing in the rain, in front of what looked like the stage door of an old music hall, attempting to argue our way past a particularly intransigent doorman.

'We should go back to the bloke that steered us here, get back our two and six. Have a word.' Church took out a handkerchief and wiped his face.

I knocked on the door. Then again, more loudly. The hatch opened to reveal the doorman once again, his face a picture of noncommittal vigilance.

'Look,' I said to the doorman. 'I'll be honest with you. We haven't come here from the other side of the country just to visit a club, wonderful though I am sure it is. I am from a firm of lawyers endeavouring to speak to one of your employees, a Mr Richardson, about a matter of inheritance.' The doorman said nothing. 'You see, a great uncle of his has died and left him a substantial estate which would settle on him a very healthy annuity for life, should we be able to find him before the deadline which is tomorrow at noon. After that time, the money reverts to the government which, I'm sure you'll agree, would be a shame. So we're quite keen to find him.'

The doorman's brow furrowed. 'What's his name, this man?'

'Richardson, he's called. Herbert Richardson.' I showed him the photo and saw a brief flash of recognition in his eyes. He shrugged his shoulders.

'No one here of that name,' he said.

'He might have changed his name. He is estranged from his family you see. This great uncle of his was the only person who had any sympathy for his beliefs. The rest of them turned their back on him.'

'That's as maybe,' came the reply 'but I still can't help you and like I told you both, we're closed.' He leaned back and reached to close the hatch.

'Wait!' I said. 'There are, of course, discretionary disbursements available for information or actions that enable our successful execution of duty.'

'You what now?' He paused, hatch half closed.

'He means we'll pay you,' said Church.

'Oh absolutely,' I followed on. 'We have full authority to offer payments for anyone who can help us progress our search.

What would you say, Mr Dent? Ten pounds might be suitable in this case?'

'I'd say so, Mr Wilkinson.' Church reached inside his coat and slipped out a crisp new banknote, folded in half, and held it up. The doorman looked at what was probably two months' wages and seemed quite quickly to reach a decision.

'Inheritance you say?' He asked.

'That's right,' I replied, 'so it's a very good cause, all things considered.'

'And you're lawyers?'

'That's right,' I reassured him and smiled in what I hoped was a matey sort of way.

'Not rozzers?'

I shook my head, amused at the thought. 'No, not at all.'

'He looks like one to me,' said the doorman, pointing at Church.

'Ah, well, he was once but now he works for my firm,' I replied. 'What they call an enquiry agent nowadays. But a police constable, certainly not.' I smiled again.

He paused for a moment. 'Alright then,' he said and nodded to Church, who gave him the note. It quickly disappeared inside the doorman's coat and we both stepped up to the door, keen to get out of the downpour.

'Wait a minute,' he said, and pulled out a sheet of paper that he held under his umbrella. 'You have to read this. Out loud.' I glanced at Church: he shrugged and I read what the doorman was holding up.

'I have been asked to confirm my identity and have done so. I am not a police constable nor in any way employed as an investigator, officer or agent of the law. I realise that if that is the case and I have not declared it, by concealing this identity I indemnify the premises against any investigation resulting from my visit.'

'Right then,' he said. 'Welcome to the Fees Willanes.' And he opened the door, ushering us into a short corridor lit with dimly glowing gas lamps. 'Entry is sixpence, coats on top of that.' And he stood aside for us to walk in. We collapsed our umbrellas and headed in through the doorway. I let Church walk in first and as I made to follow to him in the doorman grabbed my arm.

'Ask for Lily.'

'And she will introduce us to Mr Richardson?' I asked amiably.

'Just ask for Lily.'

He closed the door behind me. I joined Church, who was halfway down the corridor, shaking himself out of his coat while a sharp-faced young woman in a maroon theatre usher's uniform waited unsmilingly for him to finish. He did so and put his hat and overcoat down on the counter. I added my own and she took them up, managed a wan smile and busied herself finding empty hangers for them. Judging by the others there was no shortage of patrons already arrived.

'That's one and six,' said the usher, putting two brass discs and two numbered, cardboard tokens down on the counter. 'Entry and coats. First drink included.'

I gave her one of my dwindling supply of half-crowns and cheerily told her to keep the change. This brought a smile to her face which, if not exactly bright, seemed to be fuelled by something like genuine enthusiasm. 'Have a good evening, gentlemen, welcome to the Fever Lens. Straight through the double doors.'

The front door was soundproofed in some way, I realised as we walked along, for not only was the rain now inaudible but I could also make out the sound of music, then cheering and applause coming from within the building.

And it suddenly clicked.

'I know what this place called.'

'So do I, she just told us. It's the Fever something,' said Church.

'No it's not. It's pronounced "Les Filles Vilaines".'

'That's what she said,' he replied.

'No it isn't.'

'Alright, Jean-Pierre. What does it mean?'

'Naughty girls. Wicked girls. Something like that.'

'So, it's a brothel,' said Church. 'French dancing maybe?'

'Sounds like it.' I pushed open the doors and we found ourselves in the auditorium of a theatre, enveloped by an atmosphere of warm beer, loud laughter and cigarette smoke. A dozen or so large, round tables were arranged across the floor of the auditorium. The tables were mostly filled with older men except for the few brightly dressed, younger women dotted here and there among them and a raucous group of overdressed young couples sitting near to the stage.

The applause was fading as we emerged from the doorway. Sitting at the back of the stage a small ensemble bashed out something loud and cheery with varying degrees of success as a boatered and blazered Master of Ceremonies ran on from the wings, shouting through a megaphone for the crowd to raise their hands one last time for the wonderful Stella. The audience responded enthusiastically, clapping, cheering and, in not a few cases, hammering the tables to show their appreciation.

A woman walked up to us, raising her arms in welcome. 'Messieurs! Bienvenue aux Filles Vilaines!'

She was wearing a man's three-piece suit the same colour as the coat girl's uniform, though closely tailored in a way that accentuated rather than masked her form. A stiff, high collared white shirt and slim black cravat completed her outfit. Her short hair was slicked back from her face, her face powdered and rouged. She beamed a warm smile at us.

'Enchanté mademoiselle,' I replied, 'Nous sommes ravis d'être ici et nous attendons avec excitation un spectacle merveilleux.' I gave a slight bow.

Her smile faltered a little and when she replied it was with a broad Lancashire accent. 'Right, well, we've nothing down by the stage,' she said, 'but there's a table on the top if you like?' I nodded and she led the way across the rear of the auditorium, out through some doors at the back and up some stairs. The first floor was set up in a similar way, with the chairs removed, tables in their place and a small bar along the back. She led us across to the far side to a small table, just big enough for the two of us, and waited till we sat. 'Now then. What would you like?'

'A pair of coffees and a pair of large whiskies would be wonderful,' I said. 'Soda please, but no ice. And would you mind telling me where I might find Lily?'

She smiled. 'Oh she'll be along. I'll let her know you were asking. She likes an admirer does our Lily.' And she walked off to the bar.

I looked around the tables on this floor. Again, mostly men: well, though not richly, dressed. A few glanced across at us but otherwise our entry attracted little attention. The MC was back on stage, running through a comedy routine ahead of the next act, doing an impression of the Prime Minister and what I realised was General Gordon. He capered elegantly between the two imitations, as if they shared a house together. He ran through a pretended conversation over breakfast, with the two statesmen awkwardly exchanging pleasantries, discussing the weather, home life and so on and, in doing so, inadvertently letting slip excruciatingly embarrassing details about themselves. The crowd delighted at his antics, greeting each double entendre with peals of laughter. I had to admit that, even three or four drinks behind the majority of the clientele, I thought he captured the two of them, and the faux politeness of their election campaigning, perfectly. I found myself laughing out loud a few times, not a sound I had heard myself make very often in the last eight years.

Our drinks arrived: mugs of coffee, tumblers of whisky, a half-size syphon. I splashed some soda in my whisky, swirled it round and drank a sip. Church drank his neat, downing half of it and putting the glass back down on the table. He nodded to himself and looked around. 'Not a bad place is it?'

'Seems popular.'

'It does,' said Church. 'Mostly regulars if that rigmarole getting in is anything to go by.' He poured the rest of his whisky into his coffee, then spooned in some sugar from the bowl on the tray. 'I didn't see Richardson anywhere on the way in.' He tasted the coffee. Added another spoon of sugar.

'Neither did I. The staff are mostly women by the look of it.' I swallowed down the rest of my whisky, the warmth of it starting to permeate. 'Maybe you're right,' I said, 'and there is a brothel in here somewhere. View the goods on stage with a private visit later if you can afford it?'

'Maybe.' Church took a gulp of coffee. Looked at the mug with narrowed eyes. 'Now that,' he said, 'is horrible coffee.' He put the cup down. 'Let's get hold of this Lily, find out where Richardson is and get ourselves back to civilisation.'

Back on stage the MC had finished his sketches and was announcing the next act. Behind him the musicians were readying their instruments.

'My Lords, Ladies, gentlemen, other gentlemen and associated hangers-on. Les Filles Vilaines is profanely pleased, profligately proud and partially paroxysmal,' he waited for the brief burst of applause to die down, 'to introduce that most sylphlike of songstresses, the lovely, the luscious, the lyrical... Lily Lovelace.'

The tables around us burst into cheers, applause and whistles as the singer walked out onto the stage, dressed for a walk by the Serpentine in a canary yellow dress that was extravagantly sleeved and grandly adorned with a floral motif. A parasol of the same colour completed the outfit. As the whistles and shouts continued, Lily began to walk about the stage in a winsome manner to the tune of 'Strolling through the Park One Day'. The overall effect was, it has to be said, most becoming and only partially spoiled by her short, neatly trimmed, but still very visible, dark grey beard.

'Well,' said Church. 'that's two solved for the price of one. There's Richardson and this,' he caught the eye of a waitress and beckoned her over, 'is a molly house.' He raised his voice. 'Two of these.' I shook my head. 'Make that one more of these darling, but without the coffee this time.'

Down in the auditorium Lily had enticed one of the men from the audience up on stage with her as she began to sing of how she had been 'taken by surprise by a pair of roguish eyes', circling her new-found paramour to delighted whistles and shouts from the audience.

'And how does this compare to the others you have been in?' I asked once the waitress had gone.

Church smiled. 'Looks better than most. Of course,' he added, 'the view's a bit different when there's a van load of peelers charging through the place.'

The waitress arrived with our drinks and put them down on our table. I asked her to wait and passed over the tokens we had been given plus a few coins to cover our bill.

Below us the hapless volunteer was being helped down off the stage by the MC, to raucous applause from the audience and a blown kiss from Lily.

Church downed his whisky in short order. Looked at his

watch. 'Right. Let's find our welcoming host and see how much a ticket backstage costs.'

11. Arpeggio

The room was small, the decor fading, and badly lit by a pair of mismatched standard lamps. There was a faint smell of fresh perfume on the air that did a fair enough job of covering the background odour of longstanding artistic residence. A collection of male attire variously hung or lay on a small armchair at one end of the room. At the other end an old and battered bureau stood in as a dressing table. A few cards from well-wishers were tucked around the large mirror that hung on the wall above it. On the right of the dressing table was a three-tiered wooden box, the top halves pulled open, showing a jumble of partially tidied creams and cosmetics; brushes and pencils lay abandoned in haste next to it. Next to this box stood a bottle of champagne, part of our price of entry, the cubes in its ice bucket tinkling as they melted in the warmth of the small room.

Church leaned on the wall by the door while I made myself almost comfortable on a low wicker stool next to the dressing table. We waited in silence as the distant roar of music and applause began to die down. There was a moment or two of quiet, then more applause, slowly fading, and we heard the sound of heels hurrying in the corridor outside. The door opened and in walked the singer we had watched from the balcony, parasol in hand, dress swishing noisily. He strode into the room and sat in the chair in front of the dressing table, swivelling it round to face us both. There was a moment of artful arrangement, the yellow satin dress rustling, before we were given full attention.

Richardson was thinner than his photograph with slim, delicate features. Seen close up the make-up was careful and not too exaggerated; more demi-monde than panto dame. It struck me that, without the beard, he could easily pass for a woman. When he spoke, the voice was light and airy; feminine rather than falsetto.

'Champagne! Well how lovely! What darlings you are.'

'Good evening Mr Richardson, thank you for seeing us. My name is Wilkinson. I am a lawyer.' I reached across and gave him a card.

He looked at it. 'A lawyer?'

'I work for a firm in Kent,' I said. 'I'm here to talk to you about a case of police negligence that we are currently pursuing.'

Richardson glanced at the card I'd given him then looked up at me. 'Well I must say, Mr Wilkinson, you don't look much like the kind of lawyer that I usually come across and he,' indicating Church with the card, 'doesn't look like any kind of lawyer at all.'

'Mr Dent is our firm's enquiry agent,' I explained. 'He, well, enquires for us.'

'I haven't done anything wrong, though, have I? I mean there's nothing against singing in a theatre is there?' He was trying to make a joke of it but there were nerves now, just creeping in at the edges of his voice.

'No, Mr Richardson, nothing like that. Actually, we are in need of your help.'

'Well. I can't imagine what that might be, but do carry on and if this is to be a protracted conversation, might we please have some refreshment?' A gloved hand indicated the bottle of champagne.

'Of course. Most remiss of us. Mr Dent, would you be so kind?' I asked. Church nodded slightly and moved to open the bottle.

'The matter of it is, Mr Richardson—'

'Actually,' he said, 'would you mind doing me the kindest favour?'

'Of course.' I smiled, encouragingly.

'Would you mind calling me Lily?' Richardson said. 'It's just. Well, I have to go back on again in twenty minutes and I try to stay Lily when I have a break. It makes it so much easier when I'm back on stage.' He smiled. 'I am sure you understand?'

'Of course,' I said, as Church popped the bottle and began to pour a glass 'So… Lily, my firm is acting on behalf of a number of clients who have lost loved ones, murdered in and around Whitechapel over the last few years—'

'My God,' Richardson interrupted. 'Is it the Ripper? Is it happening again?'

'Our enquiry is connected to the Ripper murders, but I can assure you that they are most definitely not happening again. We have been engaged on the premise that both Metropolitan and City police forces should have learnt lessons from the Ripper case and become more expert at preventing the recurrence of similar violence.' Church handed Richardson a glass a champagne which he half emptied with a first, long sip as I carried on. 'Our contention is that this has not happened. The number of assaults and, even worse, murders of women has increased. In short, if the police had done their job our clients would not be grieving the loss of their wives and daughters. '

Richardson took another sip of his drink. 'Won't the two of you have some with me? It's very nice,' he said.

I nodded at Church who poured me a glass then came and leaned on the wall behind me. I took a sip. Much to my surprise it actually tasted like champagne. I reached over and lifted the bottle half out of the bucket. Bollinger. I raised an eyebrow in surprised salute.

'It is good isn't it?' Richardson said to me. 'Gwen is always so particular about making sure we have the best available, particularly for special visitors.' He smiled, his voice even, his confidence returning.

'It is,' I said, then put my glass down on the table. 'Do you think you can help us? We are interested in anything that looks like mistakes were made and covered up; where the self-image of the police was put ahead of the safety of our citizens.'

'I don't know that I can, Mr Wilkinson. It seems like such a long time ago and I wasn't really that involved, just wrote some advice to the papers. I'm not sure that there is much I can tell you.' He sipped his glass then realised that it was empty. 'Oh, would you mind?' he asked Church brightly.

'Please,' I said, 'allow me.' I stood and reached behind Richardson for the bottle and filled his glass up, a touch too quickly. 'Sorry about that,' I said to him as I put the bottle back in its bucket.

'Oh don't worry at all.' He waited till the bubbles receded before he took a sip.

'We appreciate that you may not be able to bring all the details immediately to mind,' I said to him, 'but Mr Dent and I were hoping that you might be able to give us some pointers. Any ideas about where to start looking would be most helpful. For example, were you aware of anything untoward in the investigation?'

'Only if you would describe mislaying paperwork as untoward,' said Richardson. 'I mean things were chaotic – the Met and the City teams were getting in each other's way, the press were having a field day. All kinds of citizens' groups were up in arms.' He shrugged his shoulders. 'I'm sorry, I don't think I'll be much help to you. I just can't really remember much at all.' He smiled and shrugged his shoulders.

'Lily,' said Church. Richardson looked up at him. 'We know you ran an on-wire salon called the Ripperography Club. Is that correct?'

'It is,' replied Richardson. 'Do you know Mr Dent, I am having the oddest compulsion to call you Inspector. Were you ever a policeman before you became a lawyer's agent?'

'I was... ma'am,' Church said.

'How funny! I suppose I must have met enough in my time to know!' Richardson's tone was one of breezy jocularity, but his hand was shaking as he took another sip. 'Ripperography. I haven't thought about that for years. I did take part in a few discussions there but that was so long ago. You might be better off seeing if there is an archive of the salon on an engine somewhere.'

'It's funny you should say that,' said Church. 'We've got a girl in our office. Genius with engines. She looked for an archive, called it exactly that, but couldn't find it anywhere. Said the only explanation was that it must have been completely erased after it was shut down. Which is unusual, apparently, for that kind of thing. It happened at about the time you moved up here to Blackpool.'

'Well I don't know what to tell you, Mr Dent. I don't think I can help you,' said Richardson.

'Perhaps,' I said, 'you could just give us a sense of the kind of discussions that were happening in the salon. What sort of topics were popular?'

'Oh. Well. A lot of it was quite far fetched,' said Richardson.

'Speculation. Thought experiments I suppose you could call them.'

'You mean conspiracies,' said Church.

'Yes, or you could call them that.' Richardson smiled uneasily.

'What sorts of things were people saying?' I asked.

'Just the sort of things that were in some of the papers,' Richardson replied. 'You know, guessing who the Ripper was and why he did it. He was a religious fanatic, or perhaps a foreigner from one of the embassies, or maybe a Mason carrying out some esoteric mission. But in the salon we did more than just pass around ideas, we tried to test them as much as possible to see what was and wasn't feasible. Sometimes it meant research. Sometimes it meant going out in the field.'

'Out in the field?' I asked. 'You mean Whitechapel?'

'Oh yes,' replied Richardson. 'For example, a few of us walked different ways between the September double murders, to try and gauge which route the Ripper took.'

'Did they ever mention more than one person working together?' I asked.

Even in the warmth of that small room and beneath his make-up, Richardson visibly paled. 'What? Why do you ask?' he managed to stammer out.

'Well. We came across this photograph, you see.' I reached into my inside pocket and took out the Miller's Court photograph, turned it so it faced Richardson and passed it across to him. He took it and held it in both hands, staring at it. His head dropped slowly towards the photograph as if mesmerised by what he saw.

He looked up at me, eyes wide in a mixture of wonder and alarm. 'Where did you get this?' His voice was low, disbelieving.

'We have police contacts who are sympathetic to what we

are trying to achieve. One of them provided us with this picture.'

He looked up at me in a daze. I saw the beginnings of tears in his eyes.

'You don't understand. This shouldn't exist.' All the artifice was gone from Richardson's voice and fear was in its place.

'Why? Tell us, Lily, what does it mean?'

'One to cut them and one to mask his work.' Richardson gripped the photograph tightly. He was talking almost to himself now and whatever he was seeing as he spoke wasn't in this room.

I reached over and gently took his wrist. 'The people in your salon. This was something they talked about?' He nodded. 'Explain it to us.'

Richardson pulled his hand away from mine and looked around his dressing table. I took a handkerchief from my pocket and passed it to him. He thanked me quietly, took it and dabbed gently at his eyes, then held it tightly in his lap. Took a deep breath. 'You're not lawyers,' he said to us. 'Who are you?'

Church stopped leaning on the wall and stood up straight, arms held loosely by his side, suddenly looming large in the room. 'It doesn't matter,' he said. 'You want us out of here and we want to be on our way. So. Tell us what you think this means and you can go back on stage and pretend you never saw us.'

'Or what? You'll arrest me?' Richardson moved the chair away from Church

'For what? Singing in a dress?' Church replied. 'No one gets arrested for that these days, especially not in Blackpool. And we're not police. But let's say we are something similar. Maybe we'd have a word with the Branch, get them to come in and close this place down for good. Because I bet there's enough going on in here for someone to get arrested. If that's what you want.' Richardson stayed silent and Church waited for a few seconds before continuing. 'But we don't want to do that. We just want to know about the men in the photograph. So have a good think. What did your salon have to say about them?'

Richardson closed his eyes and took a few deep breaths. When he spoke it wasn't as Lily any more but in his own voice, quiet and level.

'Most of what we argued about was who he was. What his occupation was. Where he was from. Early on people were saying he was a slaughterman or a butcher. Then, when some of the details from the post mortem reports came out people were saying he was a doctor or surgeon, perhaps a medical student. And on the salon we debated it back on forth until someone suggested that maybe it wasn't a choice, maybe it was both. But we found it hard to describe a realistic man who could be a surgeon skilled enough to remove organs so cleanly and at the same time a clumsy slasher to make such a mess of the bodies. Especially Miller's Court.' Richardson shuddered and I filled his glass up again and handed it to him. 'Thank you.' Poise regained, he took the merest of sips and carried on. 'So. One of us hit upon the idea that it didn't have to be a solitary man of two halves, that it could have been two people working together.' He pointed to the picture. 'A brute to kill and mutilate and a surgeon to remove the organs.'

'But why remove the organs?' I asked. 'As keepsakes of some kind? And wouldn't two men be more difficult to hide than one?'

Richardson handed me back the picture. 'Two men would be easy enough to hide if they were careful. Even more so if you involve others: people who can spirit your killers away and obfuscate the evidence. We knew that the picture the newspapers published was altered. We had someone in the salon who developed pictures for a living and he could tell it had been substantially cropped. But no one could find the original. Even one person who I'm almost certain was a policeman. They were perpetuating the idea that it was a lone killer you see.'

'Who was?' I asked.

'The same conspiracy that doctored reports and misdated evidence and statements to keep the killers' alibis intact.'

'And what was the surgery for?' Church asked.

Richardson looked at us both. 'What are you going to do if you find out? If you catch the men? Will you put them on trial?'

'I told you,' said Church. 'We're not police.'

'Then why do you care? Why bother now?'

'Because what happened wasn't just,' I said. 'And finally someone has taken notice.'

Richardson leaned back, started to sip his drink, then thought better of it and put it down on the dressing table. Church and I waited in silence for him to speak. 'Of course,' he said, 'I'm sure the sudden urgency wouldn't have anything to do with the election, would it? Don't tell me this is going anywhere near a court room. What are you going to do if you find these men, and whoever protected them? Just take them away nicely and quietly and lock them up where no one will ever see them again?'

'I wouldn't say nicely,' said Church, 'but they'll disappear, you have my word.'

Silence again from Richardson. Then he seemed to reach a decision. 'The surgery was to remove organs for transplant into a human recipient. The mutilation was to mask the fact. It's true,' he said, responding to the look that Church and I exchanged. 'You don't believe me but I can explain. I have papers in my room that prove it. It's been tried in South America and there have been trials on animals here in England.' He waited for a moment again. 'I know it sounds preposterous, the idea that a surgeon in this country would dream of carrying out such a procedure but that's why it had to be done in secret. In the limited examples I have read about, the donor in the operation never survives. That's why they used the kind of girls they thought wouldn't be missed.'

'Preposterous is the right word. Who would go to all that trouble for something that might not even work?' asked Church.

'Someone very rich and very powerful and very desperate,' I said. And somewhere, out on the furthest reaches of my long out-of-service imagination, warmed by the whisky and helped along by the Bollinger, the tiniest of bells rang for the briefest of moments, and the merest suggestion of an idea flared and faded before I could fully grasp it.

'You're right, Mr Wilkinson. I can show you a dossier of papers and other materials that demonstrate what I'm saying is feasible.' Richardson smiled eagerly. 'And there's something else.'

'Go on,' I said.

'The member of our salon who worked with photography, he said he had proof that it was two men. He had photographs taken at a crime scene with a hidden camera that showed how they escaped. Before I left he gave them to me. They're in my dresser. If you come and see me tomorrow morning in my lodgings I can show them to you. Can we say ten o'clock?' I nodded. Richardson let out a sigh and breathed in deeply, relaxing in his chair as if something heavy had slipped from his shoulders. When he spoke again it was once again with Lily's voice.

'Now, if you gentlemen will excuse me, I have to be on stage in five minutes and my eyes are simply a travesty.' He span his chair around and viewed himself in the mirror.

I stood. 'Thank you for trusting us,' I said.

Richardson's reflection gave a thin smile at me. 'Do I really have an alternative?'

'Not one that ends well,' said Church.

'Tell me something, Mr Dent,' said Richardson as he squinted at the mirror and picked up a brush.

'What's that ma'am?' Church stopped on his way to the door.

'Would you have arrested me back when you were an inspector? For doing this I mean? Being in club like this?' Richardson put down the brush and picked up a small jar of something from the box.

Church thought for a moment. 'No. No, I wouldn't have.' He opened the door then turned back. 'But some of your friends out there, the ones that are along tonight looking for a young lad in trouble, impressionable, maybe short of cash, I'd have locked them up without a second thought.' He paused. 'And I'd have made sure they fell down the stairs a few times on the way.' He stood silently for a short moment then gave a brief nod. 'Good night to you.' And he stepped out through the door.

'Goodnight.' Richardson said. 'And thank you for the champagne!' he called.

'Goodnight to you, Lily. We'll see you tomorrow,' I said and closed the door behind me.

Church and I were a few paces down the corridor when we heard Richardson start singing. It was nothing special, just arpeggios, but he sang it very well, all the same.

12. Dresser

My first CO in Canada, Major Harrington, was a lifelong soldier who, unlike most of the troops under his command, was in Canada through choice rather than as an alternative to some worse punishment. An amiable man, he was more a conversationalist than a reader and, when called back to headquarters for a briefing every now again, would usually take myself or one of the other officers along with him. This was ostensibly to give us 'a feel for the responsibilities of higher command' but I rather got the impression that we were mainly there to help him pass the time on the journey. It was no great chore: he had served in almost every corner of the Empire, amassing a wealth of anecdotes that he was happy to relate with very little prompting.

The briefings I attended mainly concerned any new general orders, upcoming troop relocations, progress reports on railway construction and updates from the other Canadian provinces. These were always followed by a long and often boisterous lunch where the more senior officers, many of them Crimea veterans, would argue about Balaclava, swap tales of society's moral decline and heatedly agree on the idiocy of politicians, particularly those situated in the War Office. The rest of us tended to stay as long as was politely necessary before slipping out of the dining room for a game of billiards and the opportunity to make the most of the Brigadier's excellent cellar.

It was on one of these visits to HQ that I met my first spy. His name was Talbot, introduced to us at the end of the briefing as an 'exploring officer'. I had heard of them but never met one before. His role, we were told, was to scout out along the border in order to gather intelligence on enemy activity. He didn't look much; a smallish man, in his forties, perhaps five-and-a-half feet tall, dressed in cheap-looking civilian clothes and with a short, straggly beard. At lunch he didn't make of much an effort to speak to anyone beyond the Brigadier and the Major, who acted as his head of intelligence.

In short this Talbot fellow didn't make much of an impression on me or the CO at the time to the extent that, when he arrived out of the blue at our outpost a month or so later, I had to rack my brains to think where I'd seen him before. He had papers with him, signed by the Brigadier, instructing us 'to extend every aid and courtesy' to him. They gave his rank as major, though, as at the briefing, he was wearing civilian clothes and could easily be mistaken for a local. Much to the CO's visible vexation, Talbot let us know that he intended to be with us for a few weeks. We had little choice but to find a bunk for him and put up with him as best we could.

As it turned out, though, Talbot was very little bother to us. He spent most of his time away from the camp, often staying out overnight and when he was around he kept to himself. He didn't go out of his way to make friends with any of the rest of us and even the normally genial Major Harrington didn't take to him. One evening over supper he confided in me that he considered Talbot, and exploring officers in general, to be indulging in the kind of questionable activities that were entirely unworthy of Her Majesty's Army and, all things considered 'best left to the French'. Talbot was nothing more than a spy, Harrington had declared, and the sooner gone the better. He had come across a few of them during his time in India apparently and, according to him, they were forever intriguing and stirring things up for no good reason. 'More trouble than they're worth, Maddox, you mark my word, more trouble than they're worth,' were his final words on the subject.

Three weeks or so into Talbot's stay, the CO and I were going through some of the seemingly endless paperwork demanded by HQ when Talbot interrupted us to request our help on the next of his trips. He went on to tell us that he might be meeting, and potentially bringing back, a vital source of intelligence. As a result, he said, he was requesting a section-strength patrol to escort him and the source back to camp.

'And just where is this vital source?' the CO asked him.

'I'm sorry, sir, I'm not at liberty to say, and,' Talbot replied. 'you don't really need to know. I just need a patrol to meet me tomorrow evening. I'll give the time and place to the patrol lead and he can choose his men. They'll need to be sharp; good scouts and good fighters if it comes to it. Though I doubt it will.' He smiled casually, as if what he was asking for was of no consequence.

Major Harrington pondered this, stern faced for a moment. 'Very well, Talbot. Captain Maddox here will lead the patrol and pick the men himself. Be assured that every man chosen will be more than up to the task. Now,' he picked up his spectacles and looked back down at the papers in front of him, 'if that is all for now, the Captain and I must get this finished. I'll send him along to see you as soon as we do, if that will suit?'

It didn't sound much like he was expecting any answer that wasn't an affirmative and Talbot took the hint, gave a surprisingly smart salute and left us to it.

'Odd sort of chap, don't you think?' said Harrington, once he heard the outside door close. 'Keep an eye on him, won't you Maddox.'

'I will, sir.'

'Good fellow. Right then, let's finish off this pen-pushing.'

So it was that the next night I and a dozen of my men were edging carefully along a series of barely discernible forest trails on our way to rendezvous with Talbot. In addition to the troops, the Major had lent us his guide, a Mohawk tribesman called Tayo, attached to the camp as an irregular and who knew the area like the back of his hand. His trail-finding abilities were somewhat legendary amongst the men, as was his skill with knife and pistol and I was very glad to have him along, scouting ahead of us as we threaded our way through the dense forests that lay between us and the rendezvous. Even without him, though, I knew enough of the territory to realise that our trip was taking us a few miles the wrong side of the border.

We made slow progress and arrived at the rendezvous, a log cabin at the edge of the forest, a few minutes after the allotted time. It was halfway through the short Canadian autumn and, though no snow had fallen yet, it was the kind of night that told one winter wasn't far off. Walking at the head of the small column with Tayo, I walked a little quicker, looking forward to even a moment's rest out of the cold when a sharp tug on my arm pulled me to a halt.

'Wait.' It was Tayo, his pressure still on my arm, and I was about to give him an earful when he released it then motioned for us to move back into the cover of the trees. Behind us, Sergeant Jones had seen him signal and, without waiting for me to tell him, instructed the men to take cover. I crouched down with Tayo at the edge of the trees. The log cabin was a few hundred yards from the treeline, a simple single-storey structure typical of the region. No lights showed and it looked deserted. If Talbot was there, he was understandably playing a very cautious game.

'What is it?' I whispered in his ear.

Tayo shook his head. 'Wait here.' He moved off slowly and quietly round the treeline. There wasn't much of a moon and he moved without making a sound so I lost him a few times as he made his way towards the cabin, suddenly catching sight of his silhouette as he reached the rear wall.

Jones moved alongside me. 'What is it, sir?' he whispered.

'I don't know. Something's spooked Tayo,' I said.

'That doesn't sound good. Shall I disperse the men, sir? Set a picket down the trail?' asked Jones in that not-really-a-question way that he tended to employ when he thought I was about to do something inadvisable.

I nodded. 'Carry on, Sergeant. But keep it quiet.' He moved back slowly to the men and I heard gentle rustlings as they moved into position. I had fallen into the habit of carrying a rifle myself as well as my pistol and I slipped mine off my shoulder and pushed it out in front of me, sighting across the clearing.

Jones came back and dropped down next to me. 'All set, sir,' he said, voice low. 'Any sign of Tayo?'

'Not yet,' I replied.

Neither of us spoke for the next few minutes as we both stared across the clearing, trying to catch sight of Tayo.

'You think an ambush, maybe?' Jones said. 'The Confederates setting us up?'

'Seems like a lot of trouble,' I said. 'Why wait till we get to a clearing when they could have had their pick of good spots in the trees?' Jones nodded agreement but didn't look particularly reassured.

Just then I caught a glimpse of Tayo as he came back round

the treeline towards us. Jones and I rose to a crouch as he arrived, eager for news.

'We must go,' Tayo said, gesturing back down the way we had come.

'What do you mean?' I asked 'Is there no sign of Talbot?'

He was silent.

I turned to Jones. 'Sergeant. Half the men to come with us, the rest to cover our approach. Tayo, you show us the way.'

'Please, Captain, it is better we go,' Tayo replied.

'If Talbot isn't here or if something has happened to him, we need to know. We can't go back to the Major empty handed. Come on, Sergeant.'

Somewhat reluctantly Jones called out names in a hoarse whisper and half a dozen of the men spread out behind us in loose skirmish order as we walked towards the cabin. Tayo waited for a moment then suddenly he was there beside me, a vicious-looking throwing axe in his hand. He quickly moved ahead of us, glancing around us as he led the way.

'Stay out here, Sergeant,' I said as we arrived at the rear of the cabin. 'Keep watch and stay out of sight.'

Jones gave me one of his special 'sir's, neither 'yes' nor 'no' appended, a sure sign that he wasn't wholly convinced by the order he had just been given.

'I'll just be a minute, Jones,' I said. 'then we'll go.' He nodded and gestured to the men with us who moved out to positions around and beyond the cabin while Tayo and I walked round to the front. Firewood was neatly stacked along the outside but the windows were shuttered and there was no sign of life from within. As we reached the door I saw that it was slightly ajar. Tayo looked at me and I nodded, holding my rifle ready as he opened the unlocked door. I followed him inside and waited for my eyes to get used to what little light the door let in.

Most of the furniture had been moved to the walls, leaving

a clear space in the centre of the room. In the middle of that space was a single chair, facing the door. Talbot was tied to it. His naked body bore the marks of the torture they had carried out before they killed him. The blood looked black in the half-light but some of it was still fresh, its metallic tang in the air. Talbot's clothes were in a pile next to the chair.

'Captain.' Tayo's voice, suddenly quite loud, and I realised that he must have said it a few times without getting my attention.

I looked at him, not nauseous or shocked but dazed.

'Captain.' He put a hand on my shoulder. 'We must go. They are watching. Perhaps many. We must go.'

I wanted to say that we should untie him, take him with us or bury him there but I just nodded again, unable to find the words quickly enough. I took a deep breath and walked to Talbot's clothes carefully keeping my eyes away from the ruin of his corpse. On top of the pile was a notebook I remembered him using. I opened it and saw that it was just the covers and blank pages; any notes had been removed. The message was loud and clear. I pocketed the notebook.

'Captain.' Tayo again. 'There is nothing else here. We must leave him.'

'Just a moment, Tayo,' I said. He stood silently by the door as I moved to the fireplace and held my hand over it. Still warm. I used my knife to rattle the embers back to life then pulled them out onto the floor, stacking kindling and a few logs around them before throwing Talbot's clothes on top. Looking around I saw an oil lamp in the corner of the room, opened it and poured its contents onto the pile. I waited for several seconds till the kindling caught then left the hut. Tayo followed me out, closing the door behind him.

Jones was waiting for me outside.

'Is it Talbot, sir?' he asked. I nodded. Jones looked around.

'We should go. They'll be out there somewhere, waiting to see who turns up.'

I took another deep breath and I could still taste the room at the back of my throat. I breathed in and out a few more times then looked at Jones. 'Let's go, Sergeant.' Jones gave two short, low whistles and several dark shapes unfolded from points around the landscape and began their slow retreat, working in pairs, taking up firing positions, covering us and each other as we went back to join the rest of the patrol in the treeline.

We made it back to the camp without incident, arriving just before dawn. The Major was awake, waiting for us nervously. I let him know what had happened and gave him Talbot's note-book then caught a few hours' sleep, shaved and wrote my report for headquarters. I realised afterwards, when I thought about it, that I should have known what I would find before I had even opened the door. There was something about the stillness, the silence of the place, that should have told me.

I had tried to put it out of my mind, tried to rid my thoughts of the scene in that cabin and I had been mostly successful. Eight years later, though, as I pushed at the half open door of Richardson's lodgings in Blackpool the memory of that far-off cabin flashed suddenly into my mind and I knew, without a doubt, that Richardson was dead.

Church came in after me, and closed the door without a sound, and the two of us stood still on the tiled surface of the hallway for a moment, listening. We were earlier than arranged but even so the house was quieter than it should be, no sound coming from the landlady's room on the ground floor. A tall, square table was near the door. On it was a hand-written card that said 'All post to be collected within 24 hrs'. On the floor next to the table was a painted wooden box that I recognised as Richardson's make-up box from his dressing room.

I walked to the landlady's door, rapped sharply. Nothing. I tried the handle and found the door unlocked so opened it. Church followed me through into the landlady's rooms. Her living room was warm and tidy, a low fire burning in the grate. Her bed was made, the breakfast crockery washed and drying in the rack. An automated clothes washer was quietly rattling its load in the kitchen. Of the landlady herself, however, there was no sign.

We walked upstairs, me in front with Church following. I didn't know what floor Richardson was on but, as the only lodger, I assumed he would be in the closest room. The landlady hadn't looked like someone who found much enjoyment in stairs. The door on the first floor was ajar so I pushed it further open and walked in with Church close behind. The room we walked into was a sitting room with a tiny kitchen area in one corner and a small bureau in the other. The curtains were undrawn and the light was muted. A small and overladen bookcase stood next to the window. The door to the bedroom was off to the right.

Richardson's landlady was slumped in the only armchair, arms hanging down, one leg stretched out in front of her. She was wearing a lilac day dress and a much-laundered pinafore which had been pulled up to cover her head. Church walked over, gently tugged it down from her face and briefly felt for a pulse. He looked back at me and shook his head. He stood up and I saw the mass of raw bruises around her neck.

I felt a slight judder of nausea, and did my best to swallow it down, to detach myself from the scene. Church seemed completely unaffected by the scene and it struck me that Agent Sterling should probably be the kind of spy who didn't lose his breakfast over the trivial matter of a dead body.

I went to the bedroom door and opened it.

Richardson was hanging from the clothes rail of his

wardrobe. He was slumped forward away from the wall, legs half bent. Richardson's face was purple and horribly swollen, his tongue protruding. The navy-blue cord that was round his neck matched the dressing gown that he was wearing over pale blue pyjamas. The room was a mess, a pile of clothes on the bed, an odd shoe lying on the floor. A shaving mug and brush stood ready on the small sink next to the wardrobe. The grate was full of ash and burnt paper, the smell of which just managed to eclipse the odour of human soil that hung in the room. Another judder sprang up my oesophagus from my stomach and this time Church heard it.

'You can step out if you like. Get some air.' I shook my head, swallowing hard. 'It's fine, I can handle this on my own.'

Mastering the nausea, I shook my head again. 'It's fine.'

'Okay. Do it in the sink if you have to.' Church pointed at the small sink over by the window where a pair of grey socks hung drying next to a pair of white silk stockings.

He stepped carefully around the room, looking over the scene from a few different angles before moving closer. He crouched down next to Richardson's body. 'You poor bastard,' I heard him say softly as he began to feel around Richardson's neck.

I couldn't help but agree. I thought about Richardson, tucking himself away up here and shuffling along a carefully drawn line between dreary day and starry night. Putting a past behind him that we'd brought with us and pulled him sharply back into.

I scanned the small bedroom; a single, iron bed, a shabby wooden dresser whose top drawer was open and a cheap bedside table were the only furniture in the room besides the wardrobe. The carpet was worn and the curtains had seen better days. On the bedside table was a single piece of notepaper, a few lines of handwriting on it. Picking it up I saw there was no date or signature. A rough edge down one side showed it had been torn from a notebook.

'What does it say?' Church asked over his shoulder from where he was carefully examining Richardson's hands.

'Not much. He was unhappy, ashamed of living a lie. Ashamed of even bigger lies than that one. Nothing about wanting to end it all. No mention of the landlady. It looks like it has been torn out of a notebook,' I added.

'So,' Church said. 'Richardson strangles his landlady then hangs himself in a fit of remorse. Because he likes to sing in a dress every now and again, and maybe, maybe he's a molly. Fair enough, I've seen men top themselves when someone finds out they are a homosexual, but that tends to be men with a reputation to lose,' he gestured at the room, 'and they tend not to murder other people while they're doing it.'

Church stood up and reached into the wardrobe and gave the rail a sharp pull. It held. He turned back to me. 'What's the first thing you would do if you were going to hang yourself from this wardrobe?' he asked.

'I would imagine,' I said, doing my best not to look at Richardson's face, 'I would make sure it was strong enough.'

'Exactly,' said Church. 'And the paint on the rail is flaking so if you did that, you would expect to come away with some on your hands. Church held up his hands and, sure enough, his palms were covered in flecks of paint. 'Richardson's hands are clean,' he continued. 'Now maybe he saw the paint and thought to himself "oh I couldn't possibly top myself with dirty hands" and gave them a wash, so he was nice and neat before he strung himself up. Or maybe he's been planning this for a while and tested the rail some other time. Maybe. But it doesn't look like that to me.' He bent down again to study the body.

The methodical manner with which Church worked his way through the scene seemed well practised and it reminded me that he'd told Richardson he had been an inspector. 'What kind of inspector were you?' I asked him.

'No kind really.' He replied tugging the knot away from Richardson's neck. 'Military Police for a while. Worked with the Branch on a couple of things. Went private for a while, overseas mostly.' He bent closer, looking carefully at the marks on Richardson's neck. 'But, you know, you pick up a few things along the way.'

'Right,' he continued after a short pause for thought, 'here's what I think happened. There were two of them. They got here this morning, strangled Richardson and did their best to make it look like suicide. You can get away with it if you know what you are doing but they had to rush it and they didn't quite get it right. They searched the place and burned whatever papers they could find. As they were doing it, they found a journal, had a read and thought to themselves "aye aye, let's grab a page of this while we're at it, make it look nice and proper". At some stage the noise brought the landlady up and so they killed her too. Because I bet you a ten bob note that if you measure your man's fingers here and compare them with the marks on her throat, they'll be apart by a mile. But please, don't take my word for it.'

'I believe you.' It was my turn to work it through. 'It was our conversation last night. They knew that Richardson had spoken to us.'

'And knew that we were coming here this morning,' said Church.

'They had someone in the club?' I suggested.

'Maybe. Or that guide Evan let them know you were asking questions down in Whitechapel and they came up here as quick as we did. Or a microphone in the dressing room. Which would mean they were looking for the photos that he told us about. Poor bastard. What time do you make it?'

I looked at my wristwatch. 'Quarter to ten.'

'We need to be going,' said Church.

'Why?'

'If it was a microphone, they heard us arrange to meet and, if I was them, I'd be calling the Old Bill right about now and encouraging him to send a van round here. I'll give the other room the once-over, you see if any of those papers are worth rescuing and let's get out of here.'

I poked around in the remains of the fire. What paperwork remained was badly charred, but I picked out a few pieces of paper showing parts of medical diagrams and what looked like the edges of a couple of cardboard folders, their labels still just about readable. I carried the pieces next door to the bureau, found an envelope and dropped them in, then sealed it and slid it into my jacket pocket. 'Anything else here?' I asked Church, who was looking over the bookcase.

'Nothing. Time to go.'

I followed Church downstairs then stopped as he opened the door. 'Hold on,' I said.

'What?'

'He said the photos were in his dresser.'

'So?'

'I think dresser means something different in the theatre. Something to do with costumes. Maybe it's the same for make-up?' I pointed at the make-up box.

'And?' asked Church

'And maybe that's his "dresser"?'

Church closed the door and put the box on the table, then unfastened and unfolded it and the two of us rifled through the contents. Nothing looked promising until we got to the bottom layer where I spotted a large, round powder dish. I took it out, carefully prized the lid off. Inside there was a glass disc, about five inches in diameter, with a crack running across its middle. Around the outside of the circle were six small, circular images.

'It's from a Stirn,' said Church.

'A Stirn?'

'A hidden camera. You wear it under your waistcoat,' Church replied.

I tilted the plate, trying to see what was in the images. 'They're too small to make anything out. That could be a boat.' I pointed to one of the images. 'Which doesn't make sense if these are from Whitechapel.'

'We'll get them back to Patience, see what she can do with them,' said Church. 'Let's go.'

I put the glass plate back into the dish then put the dish into my overcoat pocket and we left. The street was relatively empty, and we joined a few mid-morning strollers as we walked back towards our hotel. We were both, I think, glad to leave Richardson's sad little rooms behind us. We were a few streets away from the B&B when the first dark blue van shot past, its bells brash and loud in the morning air.

13. Fox

We changed at Preston. Church left me to look after the bags while he, suffering from a moderately grave deficiency of tea, went in search of a Lyons amongst the shops and stalls dotted along the length of the central platforms. The people on the platform were a mix of daytime travellers: elderly couples, businessmen, gaggles of small children being corralled with varying degrees of expertise by mothers and nannies. News sellers threaded their way through the crowds in raucous rivalry, seeking readers of staid headlines and shocking sensation alike. In addition, at the end of the platform, a small, watchful group of railway enthusiasts waited. Most carried well-worn notebooks, a few had cameras hanging from their necks, while one of them was carefully adjusting a tripod-mounted kinematographic camera. There was little conversation between them, I noticed. In the main they were silent, waiting with patient attention as they stared down the track, checking their watches, pencils at the ready.

'My dear sir, could you possibly spare a sixpence for a worthy cause?'

Tugged away from my idle observations, I found myself confronted with an elderly clergyman, beaming away at me across a tray full of miniature flags hanging from a canvas strap around his neck. His black suit had seen better days and dots of breakfast clung here and there to the front of his waistcoat. 'Disabled soldiers and sailors, sir. Heroes uncared for in the country they gave their all for. The smallest contribution could make a difference,' he added, lifting a collection box from the tray in my direction and giving me an encouraging smile.

'Of course,' I said, fishing from my pocket what felt like a sixpence but turned out to be a shilling and dropping it into the box.

'What a kind gentleman you are, but of course I should have known an old soldier wouldn't ignore the plight of his comrades.' He saw my slightly puzzled look. 'Standing at ease,' he continued, shaking his head with a smile, 'is one of the hardest habits to leave behind. Please allow me,' he continued, lifting one of the flags from the tray and leaned in to pin it to the lapel of my coat.

'By the by,' he said in a low, confidential voice, 'were you aware that you are being followed?' Then, more loudly, the shakiness of old age returned: 'Soon have this fixed for you, sir, such a generous donation.' He fiddled with the flag a bit more and lowered his voice again. 'A young woman in a dove-grey overcoat, an older, red-headed man with side-whiskers and a brutish-looking companion. They seem to be caught between keeping an eye on you and watching out for someone else.'

'What?' was all I could manage in the moment. 'How do you know?'

'How do you not?' he replied. 'But perhaps a young lady's attention is nothing of note for a young man such as yourself?' He raised his voice again as I glanced behind him at the crowds around the platform trying to see anyone resembling the pair that he was talking about. 'Thank you so much, what a kind man you are. The veterans of our great nation thank you!' A quick scan of the crowds around me revealed nothing and I was about to tell him what I thought of his powers of observation when I got that sense of eyes glancing away an instant before my own reached them. And saw her, a young woman in a dove-grey overcoat, assiduously reading the available choices at a chocolate dispensing machine.

I turned to the clergyman, intent on quizzing him some more only to find him silently vanished. I looked around the crowds nearest me but saw nothing then, suddenly, caught a glimpse of his white hair bobbing against the tide of passengers coming down the steps to the platform.

'You alright?' Church asked, as he arrived holding a waxed cardboard mug. 'You look like you've lost something.'

'I think we're being followed,' I replied quietly.

'How do you know?' Church asked.

I thought about it for a moment. 'Just a feeling. There's a girl over there who seems to be taking an inordinate amount of time to choose a chocolate bar. At the machine by the stairs. She's wearing a grey overcoat. Well, dove-grey really.'

'Hold on,' said Church, taking a gulp of his tea and handing me the mug. 'I'll be back.' And he was gone, not hurriedly but smoothly, easing his way through the people on the platform like a breeze through long grass. I stood watching the crowds and did my best to appear unconcerned. A slight change in the tempo of activity amongst the waiting enthusiasts at the end of the platform suggested the train's arrival was imminent. This was confirmed a moment later by an announcement over the loudspeaker readying us for the arrival of the Caledonian and reminding us that it would be pausing at Preston for ten minutes, and that the service ran fast from Rugby to Euston.

The Caledonian pulled in moments later with a cacophonous hiss of steam, a modern-looking locomotive, dark red and streamlined. The express line was imperial gauge, much wider than the branch line we had taken from Blackpool and the train itself was similarly scaled, the Caledonian's scarlet-and-gold-liveried carriages dwarfing those of the trains on the station's outer tracks.

The train slowly drew to a halt. Mothers gathered charges, salesmen clasped their sample cases and elderly wives waited patiently while elderly husbands conducted final and thorough checks of tickets and itineraries. At the far end of the platform, the train enthusiasts had leapt into activity, a gleeful but precise flurry of notebooks and cameras. Doors began opening up and down the train and a sort of shuffling negotiation began between those ardently seeking their seats, those hurrying for a connection and those merely keen to stretch their legs.

Church emerged from the throng and took his tea back from me. 'Cheers.' He took a long draught from his mug. 'You were right,' he said. 'There's three of them. Your girl in the coat, a ginger bloke and a nasty-looking cully with a beard like a bush. Well done. You've obviously got a good instinct for it.'

'What do you think we should do about them?' I asked, hoping to move the conversation along and avoid any more detailed questioning of my brilliant instinct.

He swallowed a mouthful of tea. 'Nothing at the moment. We know they're there, they might not know we've spotted them. So let's just pretend we haven't and see what turns up. If they're still with us at Euston we'll have a little fun. If not, we'll get their descriptions to Patience, see what she digs up.' He finished off the rest of his tea. 'I needed that.' Looking around for a rubbish basket, he saw one several yards down the platform and threw the empty cardboard mug in its direction. It bounced noisily in, much to the disapproval of a plump nanny clutching a pair of young boys, both of whom looked round at Church with undisguised awe on their faces.

'Come on,' he said, picking up his bag, 'we're in First.'

'Special treatment for the new recruit?' I asked as we walked off to the rear of the train.

'More likely Patience trying to wind up Collier. He's a bugger for expenses. Used to be a civil servant, watches every penny. Whenever he thinks we're out of control he gets everyone in the briefing room and gives us a talking to. To be honest I think Patience wants to see what Collier looks like when he's angry.'

'Why? What does he look like?' I asked.

'Nobody knows,' replied Church. 'Right, this is us.'

Church opened the door and stepped into a plush compartment, where four seats upholstered in blue velvet faced each other in pairs, a low, veneered table set between them. The day's *Times* lay neatly on the table next to me, copies of *The Strand* and *Sporting Life* on the other side. We set our bags up on shelves, hung up our coats and sat down next to the window, opposite one another. The inner door leading to the corridor stood open and I was thinking of closing it when a uniformed inspector popped his head in.

'Tickets please,' he said. Church passed our tickets across to him. 'All good thank you, gentlemen. Would you like drinks?' he asked.

'That would be most pleasant,' I said.

'I'll send the steward down then. Is there anything else I can do for you gentlemen?'

'Actually yes,' said Church, reaching into his pocket. 'Can I rely on your discretion?'

'Of course, sir,' replied the inspector, sounding slightly shocked at the idea that we might think otherwise.

'Very well, my name is Detective Sergeant Church.' He showed an ID to the inspector, who immediately stood a little taller and straighter. 'This is Detective Superintendent Sterling. We are in the midst of a delicate investigation and it may be that we are being followed. I'm interested in three of your passengers. The first is a young woman in her early thirties, five-and-half feet tall, pale complexion, brown eyes, navy outfit under a grey coat. The second a man in his forties, medium height, short ginger hair and side-whiskers, dressed in a dark brown suit. Might be wearing a flat cap. The third is well over six feet, coarse faced with a large black beard and wearing a black overcoat and a bowler the same colour. They might be travelling together or apart.' He paused. 'I'd be obliged if you could confirm for us whether they are on the train or not and, if so, whether they are with any other people. Can you do that for me?'

'I can, Detective Sergeant, you can count on me,' replied the inspector.

'I'm sure I can,' said Church. 'I shouldn't be saying anything about this at all but you seem like the kind of man I can trust.'

'That is most kind of you, sir,' said the inspector, pride in every word.

'Good. And, of course, you can't tell anyone about this, not ever. National security is at stake here.'

'Of course, I completely understand.' The Inspector paused. 'What is it? Anarchists?'

'I can't say any more than I have already, sir, but rest assured there is no immediate danger to the train or its passengers,' Church said.

The inspector seemed as though he wanted to salute but made do with a curt nod. 'I'll be back once we're under way.' He retreated more respectfully than he had arrived, taking care to close the door in silence.

'Good man,' said Church. 'Here you go,' he said to me, once the ticket inspector had left, passing me over a leather ID-holder. I opened the holder and saw a relatively recent head and shoulders photograph of me sealed into a plasticised Special Branch warrant card.

'It's a good fake,' I said to Church.

'Because it isn't,' he replied. 'The Branch let us have a few of them, on the condition that they are issued in each agent's codename. That way they can come back to us if we get up to anything too out of order. You know, murdering a Member of Parliament, that kind of thing. It isn't a magic wand but officials like officials so it can sometimes smooth things along.' He pointed to the door. 'Case in point. Plus of course the Branch's reputation for being right bastards adds a helpful dose of fear. Don't lose it or it will be more than a telling off in the briefing room.'

'Understood,' I said, putting the ID into the inside pocket of my jacket.

There was a knock at the door and we saw a white-jacketed steward outside. I beckoned him in and he slid the compartment door open and stepped inside.

'Drinks, gentlemen?'

'Tea,' said Church.

'We have our own breakfast blend, sir. Or you might prefer Assam or Darjeeling? Orange Pekoe? We also have a Chinese blend as well if that's to your taste?'

Church stared at the steward for a moment. 'Just tea. And some of those round biscuits. The ones with jam in.'

'Breakfast blend it is. And I'll see what we have in the way of biscuits, sir,' the steward replied. 'And for you, sir?' he asked me.

'The same,' I said. 'But without the biscuits.'

'Very well gentlemen, coming right up.' He stepped back outside, closing the door behind him.

The last few doors slammed into place, shouts rang along the platform and whistles were blown before the train jerked into motion. I picked up *The Times* and scanned the front pages. General Gordon speaking at a Neo-Chartist rally in Trafalgar Square. A hotel in Manchester evacuated because of a bomb threat, presumed to be Fenian radicals. I skimmed through the rest of the pages: nothing about an explosion at Millbank, no headlines about a fugitive army captain. Nothing on the possible resurgence of the Ripper.

'Anything I should know about?' asked Church.

'Nothing much. Nothing about Millbank.' I folded the paper and offered it to him. He shook his head and I put it back on the table.

'Well the Bureau are hardly going to admit someone broke out of their most secure gaol,' said Church, 'and they don't want some local copper running you in and hearing whatever stories they think you might have to tell. Right, here's the tea.' He stood up and pulled the door open for the steward, who had returned with a tray of drinks and, to Church's obvious delight, biscuits that did indeed appear to have jam in.

'Gentlemen. Your tea.' The steward put the tray down on the table next to Church. 'Will there be anything else?' I shook my head and he left us to our devices.

Church poured the tea, passed mine over to me. I thanked him and settled back to look out of the window, watching the scenery pass by while Church made a start on the biscuits.

The train soon picked up speed and we left Preston's soot-grey industrial landscape behind, the brick and grime of factories and warehouses replaced by the smudged browns and greys of outlying villages. I sipped my tea carefully, enjoying the sight of a landscape where people took the peace for granted and went about their days unbothered by patrolling soldiers or the worry of what trouble might visit from across the border.

'It all looks so peaceful,' I found myself saying out loud.

'How long were you away?' asked Church.

I looked at him, startled away from my thoughts. 'You don't know?'

He shook his head. 'Milady doesn't tell us much when she brings someone new in. And people tend not to ask. I know you served but that's about it.'

'Eight years,' I said. 'Canadian border. Rifles.'

Church raised his eyebrows. 'Really? I had you figured for Guards, cavalry maybe.'

'Nothing so glamorous,' I said. And less likely for me to run into someone who might be aware of the whiff of scandal that clung to my sudden departure for Canada.

'First time I came back from a long stint,' said Church, leaning back against his seat. 'South Africa it was, about fifteen years ago. Eighteen months running security on supply columns.' He looked at me. 'I got back here, flush with pay, went out for the night on the town I'd been promising myself every day of my last month there. Of course, it wasn't like I thought it would be. London, I mean. I couldn't get over the way everyone was just walking around without a care in the world, oblivious. No checkpoints. No mines to look out for. No shots coming out of nowhere. Just people, laughing. I wanted to run up to every single one of them, shake them, tell them there was a war on.' He shook his head. Gave a short, unsmiling laugh. 'I was meant to be here for two weeks. I was there two nights when a bloke I knew called me about a job in India, so I checked out the next day.' Church dunked a biscuit in his tea and bit a piece off thoughtfully.

'Did you meet Milady there?' I asked.

'What's that?' Church's brow furrowed slightly.

'I wondered if you'd known Milady. In India.'

'Here's the thing then, Sterling. Part of being here with us is knowing when to ask questions and knowing when to look out the window.' He polished off the rest of the biscuit, emptied his teacup after it.

A knock at the door heralded the return of the ticket inspector.

'Any news?' asked Church.

'Well, Sergeant,' the inspector answered. 'No sign of the young woman you mentioned but I did see your ginger-whiskered fellow and his large friend. They are sitting in second class with a group of men who would have drawn my attention even if you hadn't already told me, if you catch my meaning.'

'Rough sorts?' Church asked.

'I'd say so. Not their clothes, you understand, which are smart enough but more their manner. Hard faced.'

'How many are there?'

'Six in total, Sergeant, including the men you described to me.' said the inspector.

'Thank you inspector,' I said. 'That's incredibly helpful. You can leave things to us now, though. Don't pay too much attention to these men beyond your normal duties. We don't anticipate that there will be any trouble on the train.'

'Right you are, Superintendent. But if I notice anything else I'll come and find you.' said the inspector.

'Ideal,' I replied.

'Is there a bar at this end of the train?' asked Church.

'There's a dining carriage between here and Second Class if it's lunch you're after,' said the inspector, 'or there's a bar at the rear of the train with a billiard room where you could get—'

'Did you say billiard room?' Church interrupted.

'Yes, sir,' replied the inspector, smiling, 'a three-quarter size table but very playable. First Class passengers only.'

'Excellent, well thank you for your help, inspector, and please remember, not a word about us or this conversation.

And if all goes as we expect,' I said, reaching out to shake his hand, 'I'll make sure to write a letter of commendation to your company.'

'Thank you, sir, that's very kind,' he replied.

'Not at all,' I replied with a smile.

Church waited till the ticket inspector had left before speaking. 'What are you thinking?'

'That somewhere between Crewe and Rugby we should expect a visit from Ginger and his friends,' I said.

Church glanced around the compartment. 'Bit pokey in here.'

'Billiards?' I asked.

'Billiards it is,' said Church.

We left our bags in the compartment but took our coats with us, mine with the waistcoat camera plate still tucked safely into a pocket. We followed the signs for the bar towards the end of the train, past two more carriages, one of which, I noticed, was the home of the train enthusiasts I had seen on the platform. They seemed perfectly delighted with themselves and were chattering away noisily as they compared notes and tucked into their packed lunches.

The bar took up an entire carriage, the half-glazed doors and the glass panels on either side all covered by blinds. We opened the doors and walked in to find a small bar immediately to the left of the door, a few armchairs and small tables opposite it while further, fixed to the floor at the rear of the carriage, was the billiard table. Pairs of short, red velvet curtains were drawn and corded back either side of each of the large windows that were spaced along both walls. Between the windows were three-branched electric lights, fashioned to look like candles. Two chandeliers of a similar design hung overhead. I nodded to the barman as we walked in. 'Thought we'd play a little billiards.'

'Can I bring some drinks over to you, sir?' the barman asked.

'Not just yet, thank you. In a while perhaps,' I replied. He nodded and bent briefly under the bar in front of him, evidently to switch on a cylinder player as piano music suddenly boomed from speakers around the room, the volume swiftly reduced to a background level as the barman frantically darted back down. Above the bar a hunting horn and riding switch hung either side of an inexpertly stuffed and rather startled-looking fox.

Church and I walked past the billiard table to where a selection of cues was clipped to a rack on the rear wall. On either side was a chair where we dropped our coats. A small set of drawers under the cues proved to contain different sets of ivory balls.

'Look here,' I said, opening the bottom drawer, 'they have a set of pool balls. We used to play with these in Canada. What do you say to a game?'

'Why not? Let's have a go at it,' replied Church.

'It's easy enough to pick up.' I pulled out the box, reached for the triangle on top and set up the pack. 'You break,' I said, walking over to the chalk board. 'When you pot a ball, you score the number on it. First to sixty-one wins.' Church bent to the table and set the cue ball on its spot, then hit it down the table to smash open the pack with a loud crack, immediately potting two balls.

'Hmm,' he said, looking down the table. 'What was that? Eleven for me? I think I might have the hang of this.' He bent down for another shot and over the next thirty minutes proved himself right, winning our first game and the next in quick succession. I pulled back the next while Wigan came and went and we still had the carriage to ourselves. We had paused for a glass of ale at the barman's thoughtful suggestion and I was setting up the balls for another game when the doors at the end of the bar opened and several men walked in, our red-headed friend at their head, the bearded bowler hat wearer next to him.

They walked down the carriage towards us, the four behind spreading across it in a ragged arc behind their leaders. Their suits were smart enough, but no one would have mistaken them for anything but the thugs that they surely were. The Inspector had been right in his assessment of them. They were large framed and hard faced, bruisers all, and filled the carriage with the promise of imminent violence.

'Could I see your tickets, please gentlemen?' asked the barman in an understandably nervous voice.

The leader, who in my head I had christened Ginger, stopped in his tracks, his men doing the same. He his eyes on both of us, moving his head only slightly to shout over his shoulder. 'Pipe down and fuck off.' His voice was harsh and loud, the London accent sharp. The barman didn't need telling twice, edging his way speedily out through the door. 'Ralph. Watch the door.' Again, he didn't stop looking at us to speak and started moving again without waiting for an answer. Behind him one of his men pulled a cosh out and, holding it at his side, walked back to the door. The rest of the group stopped a few yards from us, confident in their aptitude for the task at hand.

Church and I matched most of them for height except for one: the monster of a man next to Ginger whose thick, black beard looked in severe need of horticultural attention. He caught my eye and smiled. Next to me Church shifted as he put his glass of beer down on the side of the billiard table, leaning his hand on the edge of the table.

'Right,' said Ginger, 'I am here to give you a message. I don't care who you are, I don't care where you're from. I only care what happens when you get off this train and that is nothing, fuck all, do you understand?' Neither of us said a thing. 'You went poking your stupid faces around in Blackpool and some-one died.' He paused, waiting for a reaction but, finding none, continued. 'Stop asking questions. The past is the past so don't go raking it up. If you do it again, you will get properly hurt. And when I say properly, I mean properly. You understand?'

I waited for a few moments before replying. Behind him, a gloomy palette blurred past the window: the dark dirt of ploughed fields, damp green of low hills, sullen grey sky.

When I did speak, it was with the apologetic but cheery tone of a minor baronet who may have shot someone's dog by mis-take. 'I must confess,' I said, 'I'm dreadfully sorry to tell you this but I don't speak English, so I'm afraid that I don't have the faintest idea what you're talking about.' I heard Church give a low chuckle from the other side of the table. I shrugged apolo-getically. 'I am so sorry.'

I saw a few furrowed brows in the back row as they tried to work out what I was playing at. Ginger didn't miss a beat. 'You don't speak English?'

'Not a word. Sorry, it really is the most awful bother, I know.' I smiled at him and shrugged my shoulders again.

One of the men behind Ginger stepped forward but he reached out an arm to stop them. 'Hold on,' he said and stepped forward until he was only a few feet away from me, close enough for me to see the small patch of stubble on his chin that he had missed during his morning shave.

'And what about your friend?' he asked. Does he speak Eng-lish?' I turned slightly to look at Church, stepping slightly in his direction as I did.

'Do you know, I'm not sure?' I said. 'But then, even if he did I wouldn't be able to tell you because, you know, I can't speak a word of it myself.'

'Actually, old son, It's even worse for me,' Church said.

'Is that right?' asked Ginger.

'Oh yes. You see I'm a deaf mute,' said Church.

'What?' Ginger asked. Behind him his men had caught up and by the looks on their faces were about ready for a game of 'beat the lights out of the jokers'.

'Yes, it's tragic really, my old mother always hoped I'd be on the stage.' Church smiled a broad smile.

'Well that's a real shame for you,' said Ginger, his face colouring in anger, 'because now we're going to have to find another way to get the message across. Right lads?' He turned his head to the right as he added this, nodding to the men behind him as he did, a signal to ready themselves.

I was never much of a sportsman growing up, consistently disappointing throughout my schooldays as far as rugby and cricket went. Even association football was beyond me. But there were two areas in which I always excelled. In the first case I have always been a more than fair shot with pretty much any sort of gun. In the second case I am, as I was delighted to discover during a turbulent time in my first year at school, a natural boxer. And so, as the tension wound up in the carriage, I found myself shifting my feet slowly, unnoticed by my ginger friend, into the required position.

Thus, it was a good punch that I struck against the side of his jaw. As good, I think, as any I ever landed, a fluid rotation that ran from foot to shoulder into a right cross that put our red-whiskered friend down and I knew, as I felt it connect, that he wouldn't be getting up again.

I was moving past Ginger before he even hit the floor, back on balance, feet moving and guard up as surprise turned to fury and the nearest of the other men came for me, stocky and grim faced with an evil-looking scar that ran up the right side of his face. A fighter he was; a boxer he was not. I slipped past the punch he threw at my head and sent a left hook into his body that must have hurt but not enough to put him off; though staggering, he still managed to send a wild swing of a punch in my direction. I bobbed under it, then rose smoothly to plant a sharp combination to stomach, face and chin that sent him crashing back into a window and grabbing onto the curtains for support. Abandoning Queensbury for a moment, I kicked his legs from under him and he crashed to the floor, the curtain coming away in his hand and pulling the curtain pole with it.

He stayed down and with Ginger out for the count I turned my attention to the others, revelling in the joy of the moment as, for the first time since I had landed, I was in a situation where I understood the objective, the rules and the opposition. I smiled as I watched Church twirl one of the billiard cues like a quarterstaff, one ruffian lying senseless on the floor at his feet, a second being subjected to a series of rapid strokes to head and body that had him crashing backwards into the bar and thence to the floor at the feet of the only two of Ginger's merry band left standing. As if emphasising the point, Church swung the cue around his body in an impossibly quick series of arcs ending with it pointing downwards from under his arm, like a swagger stick. I smiled and caught Church's eye. Nodded in recognition. This was almost too easy, I thought to myself.

And suddenly I was flying.

I crashed into the corner of the carriage, all the wind gone from me. Trying to pull myself to my feet, I heard someone shout 'Do for him, Ralph'. I desperately threw myself to one side and heard something narrowly miss my forehead, instead catching my left arm just above the elbow and all but paralysing it with a blow that cause me to exhale sharply in pain.

I got to my feet to see Ralph the door-watcher step cautiously towards me, waiting to see if I would get back up. He was smaller than the others, a rodentine specimen of a man dressed incongruously in a pin-striped suit that gave one the impression of being assailed by a renegade bookkeeper. Clutching his cosh, he stood still for a moment, sizing me up, then suddenly threw a wild, overhand swing at me. I moved outside it, sent a hard right into his face and aimed a ragged punch at his chin as he followed through. He swung at my head again, and I threw myself backwards, narrowly avoiding the blow. Encouraged, he threw a third blow at me and this time I moved in close, barging him into the wall and, still unable to feel my left arm, used it to pin him there while I sank punch after punch into his body with my right. The air exploded out of him and he staggered. I waited for a moment, fists ready, but he dropped the cosh and sank to the ground, grey faced and whining in pain.

I turned back to the room, trying to massage some feeling back into my arm. Church was moving around, keeping his distance from Blackbeard, cue smoothly spinning from one hand to the other as he rained blows onto the larger man's arms and body, though with little discernible effect. The giant laughed at him and, when the next blow came, he grabbed the cue out of the air and pulled Church towards a vicious head-butt that, had it landed fully, would have ended the fight there and then. Church twisted and the blow glanced off the side of his head, a lesser hit but still throwing him off balance. Seeing his opportunity, Blackbeard wrenched the cue out of Church's hand, before grabbing his lapels and throwing him bodily in the direction of the bar. Church somehow turned the fall into a shoulder roll that brought him back to his feet as Blackbeard, looking disappointed, stepped forward to finish the job.

My swing with the cosh caught him on the back of the head and I was expecting that to be the end of it but Blackbeard's skull must have been made of teak for all the good it did. Far from taking the fight out of him it only seemed to further enrage him and, forgetting Church for the moment, he turned and slammed me into windows of the carriage, unperturbed by the few, feeble blows I managed to throw into his body. A single, flat-handed blow from him set my head ringing and a moment later his hands were around my neck and slowly but surely tightening their grip. I struggled, flailing at anything I could reach with my right hand and my slowly un-numbing left but he laughed off the blows and pressed harder.

Suddenly Church was behind him and grabbed him, locking his forearm to create a tight stranglehold on the larger man. It seemed to have little effect. My head felt like it would burst, my limbs strange and distant lumps over which I had no control. Light and colour leached from my vision till all I could see was darkness.

A bright explosion roared close to my head and I felt the fingers slacken ever so slightly. Another came and a third and the grip on my neck fell away so that I slumped against the window and slid down it to the floor, drawing in short, painful gulps of breath, vision slowly clearing, hearing deafened. I realised that my face was wet and, putting my hands up to my head, saw them come away smeared with blood and fragments of flesh and bone. Glancing next to me, I saw the big man lying on his back, arms by his side, sightless eyes staring straight up, while a red stain spread around his head and into the carpet. Church stood the other side of him, leaning on the snooker table, a small revolver smoking in his right hand.

He stood up straight, stretching his back, and stepped across to where I lay on the floor, offering me his left hand. The muscles in my arm protested and I let out a gasp of pain as he pulled me to my feet and helped me across to a bar stool.

'Okay?' he asked me, concern briefly overlaying the look of murderous determination on his face.

'No,' I said, in a hoarse and painful whisper.

Church slipped his pistol back into a holster in the small of his back and picked up a bar towel which he used to wipe my face and shoulders. He patted me on the shoulder, saying, 'There you go, good as new.' He left me where I was and went around the room, searching the pockets of the men and throwing the contents onto the billiard table as he did: coins, a few banknotes, a knife, a wallet. There were no protests from the men lying on the floor.

'It's alright, inspector,' he said, 'you can come in.'

The inspector opened the door fully and walked into the room, the barman hovering outside the doors. Both stopped in shock.

I tried to speak but couldn't manage little more than a croak.

'Hello, inspector. Rowdy bunch,' said Church. 'Got a bit overexcited but they're having a little lie down now. Don't worry, though, we'll keep an eye on them till we get to Rugby. Is there a transport constabulary detachment there?'

'Er, yes, there is,' the inspector replied, eyes fixed on Blackbeard's body.

'And do you have a wireless telegraph on board?'

'Yes, we do.'

'Well, tell them that they'll need to pick up four men to charge with disorderly conduct. And there'll be one to box up.'

The inspector paled. 'He's dead?'

'Resisted arrest,' replied Church. 'We'll be taking Ginger here into custody and escorting him back to London by the way. Probably best if we stay here for the rest of the trip don't you think?' The Inspector nodded quickly. 'Which reminds me,' continued Church, 'do you have any kind of restraints on board?'

'We have some sets of police handcuffs but they're for emergencies really.' The Inspector paused for a moment and Church gave him a meaningful look. 'Which, of course, this plainly is. I shall be back as quickly as I can. Come on, Laurie.' This last to the barman who followed him out and back down the corridor.

'You idiots. Do you have any fucking idea who I am?'

I looked over to where Ginger was pulling himself up by holding onto the billiard table. The side of his face was already swelling up nastily. A few of the others were stirring themselves into motion too, struggling to lift themselves to their feet.

'Well it says here "Detective Sergeant Harris, Birmingham Special Branch",' said Church, reading from one of the wallets that were lying on the table. 'So that would be my first guess.'

'That's right.' He tried to smile but it obviously hurt too much so stopped. 'And as soon as we get to Rugby the two of you are going to be in a vast heap of shit.'

'Oh, I wouldn't worry yourself about that,' said Church, holding out his own ID open, 'they'll give these to anyone nowadays.' With his other hand, he reached inside his jacket and pulled out another pistol, a boxy automatic that was much bigger than the one he had used to kill Blackbeard, and pointed it at the other man. 'Now, Detective Sergeant Harris, you come over here to one of these chairs and make yourself comfortable unless you want a taste of what did for your friend over there. And the rest of you useless shower: stay where you are and lie down facing the floor. And behave yourselves like good little boys because, rest assured, if you don't your day will most definitely take a turn for the worse.'

14. Frame

I stood at the French windows staring through the panes at the small garden outside the briefing room. It looked lifeless in what little of the day's light remained, trees and bushes drearily bare, the last of their leaves long since swept away. A lone sparrow darted down for a hopeful inspection of the lawn, hopping lightly around for a few seconds before taking flight for better prospects. I edged past the screen and projector, still set up across the window, and walked back to the mantelpiece to pour myself a cup of tea. It was cold but I was thankful for its soothing coolness on the still-painful rasp of my throat.

The room was less starkly furnished than it had been yesterday. Someone had found a large dining table for us to sit around and against the wall opposite the door stood a pair of noticeboards, supported on large easels, displaying a collation of papers and photographs.

I walked over to the dining table and sat down, gingerly relaxing into the chair and trying to find a position to sit in that didn't hurt.

To give my mind something else to do, I looked over the display while I waited for the others: Sir Anthony was in a photograph of what looked like the opening of his new hospital extension while Richardson stared out nervously from an identification card headshot. An old police personnel file photo showed DS Harris as a younger but no happier police constable. Beneath the photos were typed cards describing background, connection to the Ripper murders and current whereabouts, while some presented only a question. 'Venice?' asked a card beneath Sir Anthony's proud smile. There were also some blank pieces of cards where photos should have been, respectively labelled Patron, Director, Agent. Red string ran between the three; another piece of it ran from the last of these to Harris. On a small, felt-covered card table next to the boards was a neat stack of blank cards, a handful of pencils, a box of drawing pins, and a ball of red string. Out in the hallway the clock struck four.

Collier had brought me in here as soon as Church and I had arrived, ordering in some tea and sitting me down for a conversation while Church had wandered off upstairs with the blindfolded Harris to an interrogation room. Collier had started by congratulating me on a successful trip.

'Successful?' I asked.

'Indeed yes,' had come Collier's reply. 'As I understand it you flushed out the opposition and, in doing so, I would say, gave a strong indication of the existence of some sort of conspiracy. You retrieved some vital information and captured a potentially useful source of intelligence, so yes, I would call that a success.'

'People died,' I said. Seeing Richardson then, purple face bloated, hanging mute in his cheap pyjamas.

'True,' Collier replied, 'and, of course, most regrettable but whether such a cost was worth paying we won't know until you bring the directive to a successful conclusion. What we can be sure of is that they were not killed by you,' continued Collier, 'and not killed because of you. The conspirators could have silenced or made Richardson unavailable some other way, but they decided not to. It was their choice, not yours, that killed him. It might be difficult, but as a field executive you have to put such mishaps behind you.' He took a sip of tea. 'Which I hope you will be able to do?' There was a note of minor concern in his voice, as if we were discussing the availability of a particular condiment at lunch.

'I've seen worse,' I said, 'But I can't help wondering whether, if we had had more information before we headed to Blackpool, we might have been able to proceed differently, with less serious consequences.'

'Certainty is an often-absent luxury when it comes to the kind of work we do, Sterling. Proceeding without it is something to which you will have to become acclimatised,' he said. 'But I trust you would let me know if you have any personal qualms again about the course of action we are taking.'

'Of course,' I said, not really meaning it and suspecting that any disagreements would, in reality, be less than welcome.

'Excellent,' said Collier. 'Well, let's put that to one side for now. To continue, would you mind talking me through the main points of your trip.'

I did so briefly, covering our meeting with Richardson, our discovery of his and his landlady's bodies the next morning followed by our encounter on the train. It wasn't until I started on the last part of our journey that Collier interrupted.

'You weren't aware of being followed till you were at Preston?'

'No.'

'And what alerted you to that fact?'

Describing a whispered warning from an alms-seeking vicar seemed a little fantastical and I thought better of mentioning it. 'Just a feeling, really. It's difficult to explain. Something about the way the girl was acting just caught my eye.'

'I see.' Collier seemed happy enough with that. 'When it came to your confrontation on the train would you say you had any other recourse than the one you took?'

'I would say not,' I replied. 'Harris and his men were clearly intent on delivering much more than a warning. Given their treatment of Richardson I guessed that their aim was to render us incapable. If we hadn't acted first, they would have done so and your directive would have been dead in the water.'

'Very well,' replied Collier. 'Well, let's see what information Church can procure as a result.'

Collier had excused himself and left me to my own devices at that stage, saying as he left that we would reconvene at four o'clock. I had taken the opportunity for a welcome soak in a bath and a change of clothes before coming back down here to wait for the others.

A set of photographs had been dropped in the middle of the table and left to lie there like a deck of poorly shuffled cards. Some of them were spotted and streaked; evidence of their rushed development. A fair number were blank, unused frames from the Eastman that I'd borrowed from one of the enthusiasts on the train, his initial reluctance overcome by a rental offer of twice the camera's worth. The rest were of the train's arrival and a few of the owner's fellow enthusiasts. The shots I had taken of Harris and his gang were with Patience, she having assured me that she was somehow able to derive their Bertie numbers from the images and use those for a quick search of police records. As well as this task, waved away as barely worth her attention, Patience was also tackling the challenge of deriving enlarged prints from Richardson's waistcoat camera plate. I had popped down to her room earlier to check but it had been locked, with a sign saying 'NO. GO AWAY' taped to the door. Knocking had received a shouted and less polite version of the sign.

I leaned back carefully and looked again at the display laid out on the board; something about the titles niggled me, but I couldn't put my finger on it.

'I didn't know you were here!'

I turned around in my chair, grimacing slightly at a twinging rib, and, after the merest instant of hesitation, recognised the blonde stranger in the doorway as Green. The sober and professional Gibson Girl had been replaced by a winsome, blonde-ringleted gadabout, her clothes a little too colourful and a little too frothy in the way that might lead an observer to quickly deduce, in approximately this order: tourist, rich, American.

'Why, sir!' she exclaimed loudly in an accent I recognised as being from the Southern States. 'If I didn't know any better, I'd say you didn't recognise me!' She stopped suddenly and looked around the room. 'Did you know that it was almost dark in here?' Without waiting for an answer, she flicked a switch by the door, setting the electric lamps around the walls into life with a steadily brightening glow.

'Miss Green,' I said, standing.

'Mr Sterling,' she replied, this time in her own voice.

'Unless I should be using a different name?' I asked.

She laughed and gave a deep curtsey. 'Virginia Cobb, at your service, sir. Just a tourist on her first trip to London and,' she slipped back into the southern accent and raised her voice, 'it is just the most exciting place!'

'You're right. I barely recognised you,' I said. 'For whose benefit?'

'Sir Anthony Willard's assistant,' said Green. 'I managed an accidental meeting this lunchtime.'

'And?'

'Just a brief chat,' she replied, 'but I know that she is originally from Surrey, has never been to the America, prefers hot chocolate to coffee and on a sunny day she has her lunch in Hyde Park. I'm crossing my fingers that the weather will be kind for us tomorrow.' Green reached for the teapot.

'All gone, I'm afraid,' I said.

'Oh well,' said Green, 'no doubt fresh supplies are on their way.' She walked across to the table and sat down on the other side from me. 'How was Blackpool?'

'Wet,' I said. Then, after a pause: 'Eventful.'

'That's what I heard,' Green replied. 'It sounds like you stirred up a hornets' nest and then some.' The last added in her new-found Southern twang.

'Ah, Miss Green, Mr Sterling. Good to see you both here on time.' said Collier, entering the room with the same casual pace as the day before, one hand in his pocket, the other holding a thick-edged Manila folder. 'Mr Church will be joining us shortly as, I am assured, will be Patience. So, my main concern at this present moment,' he said, casting an appraising eye over the mantelpiece, 'is refreshment.' He stepped back into the doorway and leaned his head into the corridor outside. 'March!' he called, then turned back to us. 'You are well enough rested, Sterling?' he asked.

I nodded. 'Well enough.'

'And Miss Green, your initial foray this morning was a success?'

'Yes Mr Collier,' said Green, with enthusiastic formality, 'Contact has been made and I am convinced that I can secure an information source for the Directive.'

'Excellent news. Ah, March,' said Collier as the butler appeared in the doorway. 'Could you sort out a pot or two of tea for us?'

'Of course, Mr Collier. And something to eat? I had some sandwiches prepared in case you required them.'

'An excellent idea, March. See to it, would you? And do

let Mr Church and Miss Patience know that we are ready for them.'

'Indeed, sir.' March swept away in that discreetly grandiose manner that experienced butlers pride themselves on. As he did so a young man in shirt sleeves showed himself briefly at the doorway to let us know that Church was on his way down.

'Excellent. Thank you, Mr Wallis,' Collier called to the young man then came over to sit at the head of the table, facing the windows. He placed the folder on the table in front of him and reached into his pocket for a fountain pen, which he placed on top of the folder.

'God, I'm parched.' Church walked in, folding his jacket and coat over the back of a chair and sitting down at the table next to Green. His collar was undone, as was his waistcoat. He nodded at me with a curt 'Sterling', then dropped a few sheets of handwritten notes in front of him and looked Green over. 'Nice outfit, Green. I like the Barnet.' Green's brow furrowed in confusion till Church took pity on her and pointed at his head. 'The hair.'

'Why thank you, sir,' Green responded, a Southern Belle again for a moment.

Collier gave a gentle cough. 'Did you see any sign of Patience as you came in, Mr Church?' he asked.

'Standing to attention in the corridor? Waiting keenly for the meeting to start? Not a glimpse. I can go down and drag her out of her cave if you like,' said Church, dropping his tie on the table next to him.

I shifted to a slightly more comfortable position in my chair, happy for the moment to let the conversation wash over me.

'No need, thank you Church, I am sure she will be here in a moment,' replied Collier.

'I doubt it.'

'Actually Church, you know some of us take our responsibilities seriously.' Patience walked in, shirt and trousers still slightly too big for her, her hair piled up under what looked like a train engineer's cap. A collection of translucent envelopes was held under one arm; she closed the door behind her and walked around to sit next to me, putting the envelopes on the table. 'Hello Mr Collier, sorry if I was a little late. All ready now and very much looking forward to hearing what everyone has to say,' she said and sat up straight, smiling at Collier with a mix of attentiveness and contrition on her face. Church shook his head.

'Thank you, Patience.' Collier took a sheet of paper from his jacket pocket, unfolded it and smoothed it out carefully on the table in front of him. 'Miss Green, would you mind making any relevant notes and updating the boards after the meeting?'

'Of course, Mr Collier.' Green produced a small, cardboard-backed notebook and a pencil and readied herself.

The door opened and March walked in carrying a tray arranged with the paraphernalia of tea. Behind him the young man that Collier had called Wallis carried a platter of sandwiches. Conversation paused as plates were deposited, cups arranged, sandwiches distributed and tea poured, March and his helper working quickly and deftly before departing with the tray from the mantelpiece and closing the door behind them.

'So,' said Collier, 'the Blackpool trip has borne fruit, perhaps more than we had expected, including a demonstration of serious and harmful intent from the conspirators. I assume, Mr Church, that your experiences have convinced you that this is more than, how did you put it, "a jolly for the new lad"?'

Church nodded slowly, swallowing down the second half of a ham sandwich.

'Good,' continued Collier. 'And how did you fare with the good Sergeant Harris?'

'We got on very well. I'll spare you the details but suffice it to say that after a little chat he started singing like the proverbial.'

'Did he take much convincing?' asked Green.

Before Church could respond, Patience interrupted from the end of the table. 'Did you give him the third degree? A right going over? I bet you did.'

Church glanced at her. 'Now look, Patience,' he said, 'when you are locked away working your supposed magic—'

'Literal, actual magic,' interjected Patience.

'Whatever you call it,' said Church, 'I don't ask you how you go about your business and I expect you to do the same for me.'

'Oh my God, Church, did you break a chair over his head?' asked Patience, before continuing in one of the worst fauxcockney accents I had ever heard. 'Did you give him a bunch of fives in his Alberts?'

'Thank you, Patience,' said Collier, voice stiffening slightly.

Patience sat up straight again and smiled. 'Of course, Mr Collier. I am so sorry, Mr Collier.'

'Here's the thing,' said Church, treating Patience to a stern look. 'Our man Harris has had one of the worst days of his life today.' Church drank a quick mouthful of tea, put the cup back down on its saucer with a slight clink. 'For the last seven years he has had a nice little life in the Special Branch back office in Birmingham. As of this morning, he has become an accessory to a capital crime, he's been on the losing end of a short and painful round of fisticuffs with Sterling here,' Church pointed at me across the table, 'and he's been arrested. He may look like a bit of a hard man – we saw that on the train. But once you poke him: paper thin.'

'So how much has he told you?' asked Collier.

'Plenty.' Church took another swig of tea and looked down at the notes in front of him. 'It starts in the spring of '88. Harris is enjoying life as a CID sergeant until his inspector finally catches onto the fact that, while he seemed to be effective enough at catching thieves and the odd violent husband, none of the better-off criminals in the district were getting put away, and one in particular had developed an oddly accurate ability to guess when police raids were on their way. Not enough proof to turf Harris out, though, so they did the next best thing and transferred him to a job in Central Records, hoping that he would get fed up and quit.

'So there he is, angry at being half found out and narked off at being stuck behind a desk when one day he gets a telegram, anonymous, no sender. It asks him to print out some information from the files and drop it off the next day at particular post office to be collected by someone called Smith. The information wasn't too serious – staffing lists, that sort of thing – but still confidential, so mindful of his recent near miss, he ignored it.' Church paused and referred to his notes again. 'The next evening when Harris gets back to his rooms there is a copy of the telegram waiting for him. Along with it was an additional page listing a series of events; failed raids, missing evidence and changes in witness statements that Harris recognised as being his dirty work. Being smart enough to join the dots, as soon as he got to work the next day he printed the files out, dropped them off in a package as instructed and was delighted to find the sum of thirty pounds appear in his bank account the day after.'

'And Harris never tried to find out who was behind the messages?' asked Green.

'He called the post office to try and track the sender of the telegram but they couldn't find any reference in their system,' said Church. 'After that he says that he didn't bother.'

'Are untraceable telegrams a possibility, Patience?' asked Collier.

Patience looked up from her plate where she had been opening sandwiches, removing the filling and replacing it with
carefully sprinkled spoonfuls of sugar, and stared thoughtfully
at the ceiling. 'I suppose so. You would need to know the
GPO system really well, and have full access.' She paused. 'It
would be easier to create a false account for each telegram that
you wanted to send then delete it afterwards. Either way it
means breaking into the GPO engines which is very tricky and
very illegal and ridiculously hard these days since the Bureau
upgraded the GPO security procedures.'

'Not something that your average tapper could pull off
then?' asked Green.

'God, no,' Patience replied. 'Thinking about it, it would
probably be far easier to just bribe someone on the inside to do
it for you or just create a paper forgery and deliver it by hand.'

I had a thought. 'What if you're on the inside already?'
Patience and Collier looked at my sudden interjection. 'What
I mean is, what if sending using the system itself is your easiest
option because you have full access as part of your job?'

'Someone from the Post Office?' asked Collier.

'Either that or the Bureau themselves,' I said. 'You said at
the first briefing that if there was a conspiracy it might involve
police or someone to do with security. Why not the Bureau?
Someone there would have exactly the kind of access you
would need to do this, isn't that correct, Patience?'

'Totally and absolutely so, Sterling. They'd have all the back
door codes, administrator shortcuts,' she paused for a moment,
her eyes sparkling with excitement at the thought of it. 'Tapper's paradise.'

'Thank you, Patience,' said Collier, 'Miss Green perhaps you
could make a note of Mr Sterling's suggestion and we can continue. According to Harris, did this arrangement continue, Mr
Church?'

'It did. Every few weeks in the summer of '88; Harris would get a telegram specifying some confidential but unimportant data, he would drop it off wherever the telegram said and the next day he was paid. Then, just after the first Ripper murder in August he was asked to send post mortem details, reports and investigation notes and he baulked at it. He says he ignored the request, but the telegram turned up at his home address again, this time matching the same list of events he had been sent already against payments into his bank account. So, not really having a choice as he saw it, he did what they asked, all the way through the Ripper investigation, and for several months afterwards. I couldn't get him to admit to it, but I also think he moved information the other way, altering or replacing files. Let me have another crack later and I'll make sure of it.'

'So how did he end up in Special Branch?' I asked.

'Came out of the blue according to Harris,' Church said, 'about six months after the last Ripper murder. It meant moving to Birmingham, but he took it anyway and, by his account, made a good fist of it, broke a few big cases. The telegrams stopped and he thought it was over. Knuckled down, bought a house, got married, had a child.' A pause while Church filled his cup again, added milk, spooned in some sugar. 'Harris thought that was the end of it until last night when he got a phone call telling him that unless he did exactly what he was told, details of his leaking of documents, along with photographic evidence, would go to his superiors. He tried to put them off, said that was all behind him, but they threatened his family. So, he said yes. They gave him Richardson's address and description, told him to pay him a visit at eight o'clock the next morning and threaten him into silence. Then they gave him a number and told him to call them after it was done.'

'What time did he get the call?' I asked.

'Late evening, he thinks around 10pm,' said Church.

'About the time we saw Richardson at the club,' I said.

'Yes, someone tipped them off. I bet it was that bloody doorman,' Church said. 'So Harris went to Richardson's place but before he did he looked up our dead thug, a mister,' Church looked at his notes again, 'Baller or Baz or Barry Johnston who he had used before for similar work. Harris used his Branch ID to get in and the landlady took him upstairs. He said Richardson was nervy and when they started in at him, Richardson apparently told Harris where to go; he had kept quiet for long enough and he was going to say anything he wanted to anyone he wanted. Harris got shirty, grabbed Richardson, tried to threaten him and he said Richardson just laughed at him. So, Johnston stepped in to give him a scare and grabbed his dressing gown cord, aiming to strangle him unconscious a few times. Didn't quite get it right.'

'What about the landlady?'

'Pretty much what we thought. She heard the noise, came in with her own key to see Richardson being strangled so Johnston killed her as well. Harris panicked, did a quick search of Richardson's place and burned what papers he could find and rigged Richardson up as a suicide,' Church said. 'A bloke like Johnston, killing that easily; he's done it before. And he would have done it again, starting with Sterling. So at least we know we did one thing right.'

I suddenly realised that I had been gently rubbing at my still-sore throat and I stopped, moved my hand down to rest on the table again.

Church went on. 'Then Harris did what he had been told to do and called a number to confirm what had happened. They didn't seem unhappy, just told him he had one more job to do, to meet a woman at Blackpool station and she would tell him what would happen next.' Church looked down at his notes again. 'So, he gets to Blackpool station and a woman in a grey coat comes up to him. She knew his name, knew he was expecting her and said that he was to follow and warn off a couple of lawyers who were asking some awkward questions. She asked him if he knew any likely lads who could meet them at Preston and give these two men a bit of a roughing up. He did, as it happened, and she waited while he got in touch with the thugs for hire that we met on the train. She came with him as far as Preston, made sure he had identified us then left him to it.'

'Did he describe her?' asked Green.

Church referred to his notes. 'Twenty-five to thirty-five, slim, quite tall, maybe five feet eight or nine, pale skin, brown hair, green eyes, dressed well but not flash. Quiet voice. Northern accent but not too strong. "Didn't seem like the kind of girl you'd expect to be mixed up in something like this," he told me. All sounds far fetched, I know but I believe him. Like I said, he has had a really bad day.'

'We are assuming the woman he talked about is the same one that Sterling noticed?' Collier again. He looked at me for confirmation and I nodded.

'I would put her in the middle of that range, maybe early thirties.'

'So following Mr Sterling's idea, we're looking for someone of that description with a role in the Bureau or a related agency. Patience?' asked Collier.

Patience nodded. 'Two hours.'

'Good. Where is Sergeant Harris now?' asked Collier.

'Upstairs, chained and fretting,' replied Church. 'He's meant to call the same number again, tell them what happened.'

'I see,' said Collier. 'Let him make the call with your supervision. Patience, can you disguise our location while finding out theirs?'

'Sans doute. I'm hooked into a public phone box in Picadilly. We'll use that.'

'And Miss Green,' Collier continued, 'if you could check Harris's account against his official career record?' A short nod from Green. 'Excellent. Now what about the fragments of papers that Sterling and Church found in Richardson's rooms in Blackpool?'

'I managed to identify one of the papers, something that was published in an Argentinian medical journal in the early '80s,' said Green. 'It was exploring the theoretical possibility of human organ transplantation. It caused quite some scandal at the time and the author, a fairly respected Argentinian surgeon called Rodolfo Pereira-Garcia, was forced to resign as a result. Nothing much was heard from him after that except from some informal, on-wire monographs and interviews on a similar theme. He died in 1890. The other fragments seem to be facsimiles of private, unpublished papers. It's almost impossible to say much beyond the fact that they were medical in nature.'

'Organ transplantation?' Collier seemed genuinely unhappy at the idea.

'That ties with what Richardson told us,' I said. 'He said that the prevailing theory in his on-wire salon was that the Ripper was two people. One of them was a surgeon whose job was to remove the organs and the other, the real 'Ripper' if you like, mutilated the victims afterwards to cover up the surgery.'

'With our man Harris doctoring any evidence to make sure that no one realised later on,' said Church. 'Even so, it would be tricky work.'

'Such an undertaking would entail a substantial risk,' said Collier.

'And a substantial reward to match it,' said Green.

'Something like an unexpected promotion to Special Branch,

perhaps?' I said. 'I imagine there would be similar rewards for the others involved.'

'Did you have something in mind?' Church asked.

'Well,' I said, 'I was thinking that a knighthood and a brand-new hospital wing might be suitable inducements for a medical man.'

'Sir Anthony Willard,' said Church.

I nodded. 'Indeed. I'd be interested to know when his meteoric rise began. Keep your ears open, won't you Miss Green?'

'Of course,' she replied, though I got the impression she was less happy taking direction from me than she had been so far from Collier.

'And would you do some more research into this idea of organ transplantation? Has it been done successfully? How long does it last? And how quickly does the organ have to be transferred from body to patient?' I said, thinking of the picture from our initial briefing of the two men by Miller's Court, one in the doorway while the other hurried on his way with a black bag. For the first time I wondered at the man staying behind, alone with the body in Miller's Court and the charnel mayhem of the scene that he left there.

'I'll see what I can find,' said Green.

'Excellent,' said Collier. 'If there is nothing else to add, let's move on to the photographs. Patience, if you would?'

Her earlier enthusiasm had slumped slightly during the first part of the meeting, but Patience perked up at this, moved her plate out of her way and gathered up her envelopes in front of her.

'Just a moment,' I said. Patience paused half out of her chair then slumped dramatically back down, rewarding me with an eye roll that seemed to take in her whole head. Ignoring her, I pulled myself up out of my chair with the merest of winces and walked over to the boards. I took a card and wrote 'Tapper' on it and pinned it to the board next to the card with Harris's name on it. I took two more cards, wrote 'Surgeon' on one and 'Driver?' on the other and put them next to the one that said 'Ripper'. Then I took another, wrote 'Patient?' on it and pinned it high up at the top of the board. And as I did, that bell that I'd heard in Richardson's dressing room gave another low chime in the back of my mind.

'Are you finished, Mr Agent, sir?' Patience from her chair, mockingly respectful.

'A few more things,' I said, as I walked back to my side of the table. 'We'll need to make sure that the gang from the train stay out of circulation for a while. And make sure that Richardson's death is treated as open and shut by the locals. We want Harris's anonymous bosses thinking that everything went smoothly for as long as we can.' I eased myself back into the chair. The moment I did Patience pushed back out of hers and went to the projector.

'Special Branch will be holding onto the gang for the next 72 hours before they pass them to the locals for charging,' said Collier, 'and as far as Richardson goes, once his stay in a sanatorium becomes public knowledge, people will be more inclined to believe that he was responsible.'

'Excuse me, Mr Collier, but I don't remember seeing anything about a sanatorium,' interjected Green. 'It wasn't in his file.'

'Really? I'm sure it will be there somewhere if one were to look again,' replied Collier. 'Would you mind adding it to your list, Patience?'

'Right you are, guvnor!' came a chirpy reply from Patience, tweaking buttons on the projector. Church shook his head in mild exasperation.

'Oh, and we should call Harris's wife, say that he has to stay away on Branch business,' I said.

'Church?' Collier said.

'Done. I'll get the cockney sparrow here to let me have the line after Harris has made his call.'

'Wonderful,' said Collier. 'So, unless there is anything more, that leaves us with whatever you have found for us, Patience.'

Patience made some final adjustments then stood facing the rest of us. 'Just so you know, I've done my best but the disc you found was quite deteriorated, and on top of that Stirns have a fixed aperture and these were taken at night. So, don't expect miracles. I've enlarged them as much as I could without losing too much clarity and pulled up the contrast but even so there's not much to see. I'll show you them in order. Could someone switch off the lights?'

Collier walked to the switch and turned the lights off as Patience brought the first image on the screen. It was almost white.

'They were all pretty dark,' said Patience. 'So I've tried to bring them up as much as possible. To try and get some detail.'

The view was of a street. From the angle it looked like the photographer was lying on the ground. The cobbles in the foreground were clear enough in places, and here and there it was possible to pick out details: a lamp post, kerb stones, a window ledge. Two blurred figures stood in the background.

'Difficult to tell from this where it was taken,' Patience's commentary continued, 'but I think we can assume London.'

The second image was clearer, the two figures still there, their hats visible now. It seemed obvious now that one of them had a case. They were turned, their backs to the camera.

'And the next one.'

In the third the scene had changed dramatically: the camera was angled up away from the pavement showing a blank sky between the edges of buildings. And in the middle a fattened teardrop, a shade lighter than the sky around it. What I had thought was a boat when I had first seen the disc in Richardson's lodgings.

'It's clearer in this,' said Patience as the next slide clicked into place.

Closer now, the shape resolved itself into an airship, filling the sky between the buildings as it descended. The details were hard to make out, but it looked small, perhaps smaller than the one that had taken me to Millbank.

'And in this.'

The airship was barely above the rooftops in this shot, blocking the sky, its shape clearer to see, its hull obviously lacking identification numbers. A light-coloured line that might have been a rope ladder hung down from the 'ship, one of the figures making his way up, the other standing at the bottom holding the ladder steady.

'And finally.'

The airship was rising again in this photograph, the remaining figure alone now and walking along the pavement towards the photographer but on the other side of the road. He was indistinct but one could just make out his top hat, his shoes and, in the hand closest to the camera, a walking stick, the shank thin while the top was heavy and round, almost the size of a fist.

'That's all there is.' Patience ended her presentation but left the last image up which faded to be almost invisible as Green brought the lights back up. 'And now,' she said, walking over to the boards, giving me a smug look as she did, 'we just need to make one small alteration.' Without waiting for a response, she took the card that said 'Driver?' off the board, reversed it, wrote 'PILOT' in large block capitals, and pinned it back up on the board.

'And a bloody good one, to get that low in a street,' Church said.

'Where do you find one of those?' asked Green. 'The army?'

'Maybe,' replied Church. 'Maybe ex-army.'

'Excellent work, Patience,' said Collier.

'Should be easy to find wherever he's from. There aren't many pilots that good.' Church again.

But I wasn't really paying attention to the voices in the room; the conversation suddenly seemed like it was happening a thousand miles away. Because I was suddenly certain that I knew that walking stick. Had watched it ordered in a shop on Jermyn Street, the large head of the stick weighted to make it suitable for self-defence. Had been there when it was picked up, felt the weight of it and seen it tested on a chipboard dummy set up in the back room of the shop. It wasn't clear from the photo, but I knew that the top was carved like a wolf's head. And when, just over eight years ago, I had woken, bleary-eyed on the floor of a bedroom in Cooper's, the head of that stick was the first thing I had seen, lying on the floor next to me, its end matted with blood, hair and bone.

15. Rag

'Where to, squire?' The cabbie's mouth was obscured, his scarf wrapped high up around his face. His cab was steam powered, of a much older design than the electric or diesel versions I had seen since I had been back in London. It was larger than the newer types, with an extended rear supported on its own set of smaller wheels and where a tall, thin chimney puffed. These days, I imagined, the driver would be relying on tourists to enjoy its vintage appeal but as far as Church and I were concerned, it was a busy Friday evening and every other cab we had passed so far was already taken.

'A bar in Canning Town called Boston's,' said Church. 'It's off Victoria Dock Road. I'll give you directions when we get there.'

'Right you are,' the cabbie said as Church pulled the door open. 'Canning Town you say?'

'Too far for you?' asked Church, half in and half out of the door.

'Nowhere's too far for a pair of gents like yourselves. If it's company you're after, though, there's plenty of good clubs around here, guvnor, much quicker to get to and the ladies are much friendlier, if you catch my drift?' He smiled, gave

Church a conspiratorial wink. 'I could have you there in two shakes.'

'Not tonight,' Church said.

'Right you are, guvnor, Canning Town it is. You and your friend hop in and we'll be on our way.'

Church ducked in through the door and I followed him into the cab's threadbare interior. Church waited till I was settled, then rapped on the roof and we set off with a whistle along the thick bustle of the Strand as Friday evening began in earnest.

Omnibuses crawled along while cabs jostled for space, depositing bands of excited nightlife-seekers, swapping them for weary-legged shoppers, briefcase-clasping office workers, and at least one group of lengthily lunched tycoons, swaying cheerily together at the kerb. The evening was clear, the fog at bay for now, and the lights on the theatre awnings sparkled brightly, blazing out the titles of the shows at us as we slipped by. One or two of them seemed familiar to me. Perhaps, I thought, it was from one of the magazines that had occasionally found their way into the officers' mess in Canada, thoughtfully dispatched by a far-off loved one and, once read by the lucky recipient, the tales of angling or golfing or London life shared with the rest of us.

There were screens on a few of the buildings, larger versions of the one that I had briefly watched in Marie's room in Cooper's. Adverts rippled into place, replacing one another in a parade of perky proclamations and, on one screen, the evening's headlines: 'Ripper expert dead in murder suicide!'.

Then we were heading past Drury Lane, the cabbie weaving smoothly to avoid the theatregoers as they wandered towards their shows, excitement at the experience to come rendering them less sensible to the more mundane activities of the here and now. I watched them closely, focusing on their clothes and faces, anything and everything, in an attempt to hold at bay the loop of memory that I could feel pressing in on me, a sliver of numbing horror that I had thought I had damped down and forgotten, raked to a blaze again by the picture from Richardson's camera.

'Penny for them,' said Church

'Just thinking how cheery it all looks out there.'

Church nodded. 'And dangerous. Once your Preston filly and whoever she works for find out Harris and his friends didn't put us off, which they will, they'll try and find us again and this time they won't be as gentle. Luckily, we're hard people to find, but better safe than sorry.' He patted his left side under his arm where I knew he was wearing a large, Belgian-made semi-automatic in his shoulder holster. My own pistol was a Webley, a newer version of the army regulation one I was used to, lighter and better balanced, less of a kick according to Church. It felt odd to wear a pistol again. In Canada I had switched to a rifle after a brief exchange of fire on one of my first patrols gave me a decided preference for range over regulation. It felt doubly odd to wear a pistol under my arm instead of in a side-holster and Church had made me practise before we left, drawing it again and again until I had the knack of it.

There had been more discussion about the airship in the photograph in the briefing room before we left. Collier had thought that army and naval pilots should be our first port of call whereas Church's view was that pilots with the skill, and the nerve, to fly that close to buildings were rare and, given the use it was being put to in this instance, were more likely to be found employed in criminal, rather than military, enterprises. With that in mind we were on our way to see an old contact of his, a club owner and more besides who, Church had assured Collier, would be able to point us in the right direction.

We lapsed into silence as the cab took us along the Embankment, through the City and skirted the south of Whitechapel. Church finished his first cigarette but didn't light another. We passed the Tower of London, being spruced up for next year's Jubilee, the newly gleaming walls and open spaces of its grounds in stark contrast to the tightly packed tenements that stretched away northwards. Then we were in the docklands, smoke thicker in the air here than in the West End, drifting up from factories and warehouses but also the ships at anchor all along the docks. The ships themselves were as varied as their cargoes: tall-masted clippers, short, chunky steam ships and larger, more modern vessels. The majority of the flags they flew were British, or from one of the colonies, though the other major powers were well represented and I saw more than one ship with the 'Stars and Bars' of the Confederate States fluttering at the rear. Cranes and mechanical lifters were thick in attendance beside most of the ships, working quickly to lift a wide assortment of bales, barrels and crates onto the dockside for onward transportation.

The traffic changed as we drove, with commercial vehicles coming to dominate the further east we went; I saw trucks, lorries and even the occasional horse-drawn cart drive past while above us a short and ragged arc of airships waited sullenly, propellers gently turning, for their turn to load or unload. The people changed too; more men than women, rougher clothing and rougher faces, the spread of nationalities reflecting the breadth of the trade that poured into London. Finally, we came to Canning Town and Church rapped on the roof of the cab and a small hatch opened up. The directions that Church called up took us away from the dock and into the blocks of warehouses, factories and workshops that led away from the river, finally bringing us to a halt in a wide street, warehouses lining each side. Several had their doors open, goods being loaded or unloaded, bright electric lamps above the entrances lighting up patches of the road like day. We stopped alongside an alley between two of the unlit warehouses.

'We'll walk from here,' Church shouted up to the driver.

'Right you are, sir,' replied the driver.

I opened the door and went out first, waiting while Church paid for the cab. The driver took Church's money, making change from a large leather pouch that he drew out from the seat beside him. 'Are you sure this is the right place, sir?' He looked nervously around him.

Church handed him back a few coins as a tip. 'What do you mean?'

'I wouldn't want to be walking around here at night.' The cabbie replied, looking pointedly at a pair of dock hands trudging tiredly along the road next to us, both dark faced. 'I mean, you don't know what they get up to.'

I was in London when the Americans started arriving in large numbers. It was the summer of '83. The Confederates had just bombed Washington and it was pretty clear to most people that the Union was going to lose. The majority of refugees came to Britain, and, as is often the case, they settled first where they landed, building new lives alongside their fellows before venturing further. Those who were black soon found that, despite the entreaties of a Queen determined to show the world what Christian charity looked like, they were far less welcomed than their white counterparts. Shouted abuse, printed vitriol and attacks in the street were not uncommon as some people rejected the notion that we should welcome these newcomers with open arms. Even amongst my own friends, whom I had considered well travelled and open minded, the sentiment was largely hostile, the language casually spiteful. This cab driver's tone was tame by comparison which, taking the London cabbie as a barometer of social sentiment, made me think things had shifted slightly since I was last home.

I saw Church stand straighter, though, and stare at the driver. 'You know,' he said, 'I served alongside men like them when I was in Africa. They fought well, and died well when they had to. And got along well enough. Because what it came down to is this: soldiers are soldiers. And people are people.'

'Well I meant no disrespect, of course, sir. Didn't know you were a soldier. Of course, I would have served myself except for this leg.' The driver lightly slapped his right knee a few times.

Church gave him a sceptical look. 'Well, no need to put yourself in danger now. We'll make our own way back.'

'Aye aye, sir,' said the cabbie, throwing Church his best approximation of a salute and turning his cab around in the street to drive back the way we had come, blowing the whistle as he did.

Church shook his head and set off down an alleyway between two of the buildings. The light faded as we walked away from the main street.

The alleyway was too narrow for us to walk abreast so I followed just behind, thinking about my own troops in Canada, the majority there in preference to a gaol or the gallows, our nationalities a distillation of the Empire. And Church was right. After a while, soldiers are soldiers and bonds do form, though, in my experience, not quite to the extent of the caring brotherhood Church had implied to the cabbie.

'Did your soldiers really get along together?' I asked.

'Eventually,' said Church. 'More or less.' He paused. 'Once I'd cracked a few heads together anyway.'

The alley was long and narrow, the light almost disappearing as we reached a point where two more warehouses backed onto the two that we were walking between. Rubbish was scattered sparsely along it and something small started in the gloom ahead of us and disappeared through a broken grill in the wall before I could see what it was. Another light from up ahead became slowly stronger as we continued along the alleyway until we emerged from the end and, to my surprise, I realised that its source was a set of particularly ornate gas lamps, arranged at intervals around a cobbled square formed by the backs of several buildings. The next thing I saw was a cab pulling away from the pavement on the far side, looping around the square and out along a wide, lamplit street that led away north. Where it had been parked a small group of people were walking to join a queue of fifty or so others where they stood waiting outside a dark building with a brightly lit doorway, above which was a large red, illuminated sign that read 'Boston's'. And below it, in smaller letters: 'Bar. Music. Dancing.' As I watched, one of the doormen unclipped a velvet rope and let a handful of people from the queue into the club.

Church stood taking in the scene in silence, his brow furrowing as he did.

'I assume this has changed a little since the last time you were here?' I asked.

'Yes, it bloody has,' he replied then set off across the square. I followed, walking alongside him. The queue was a mix of white and black faces, all of them were young, none older than mid-twenties and every one of them was dressed up for a night out, the women wearing frothy ensembles similar to the outfit that Green had been wearing that afternoon. The young men were likewise sharply dressed in three-piece suits, including some rather outré shades of tweed; a number of them sporting thick, ornamented gold watch chains.

We arrived at doorway, eyed suspiciously by those at the front of the queue. One of the four doormen standing behind the rope came over to us, walking slowly but purposefully to determine who had decided to disrupt his carefully arranged line of customers. He was smaller than us but broadly square in dimensions, not so much clothed as upholstered in a broadlapelled dark blue suit, his shirt and tie only a shade or two lighter. A bowler hat completed his outfit.

'What can I do for you gentlemen?' His voice was deep, his accent American, twanging.

'We're here to see Boston,' said Church.

'You're here for the club?' asked the doorman.

'For the owner,' replied Church. 'Boston Jack. I'm an old friend.'

'Well he didn't mention he was having any old friends over tonight.' The doorman folded his arms. Behind him, one of the others walked from around behind the rope to join him. Further along the queue was getting ragged as some people leaned out to see what was going on.

'Just tell him that Mr Church is here to see him.'

The doorman raised his voice. 'You want to come into the club, you queue like everyone else and maybe, if you look like genial folks, maybe we'll let you in.' Next to him the other doorman lifted the right side of his jacket up, showing an ivory handled revolver. 'What do you say?'

Church shook his head and started off for the back of the queue. I followed. As we did the door opened again, letting out a burst of loud, frenetic music and another group of people were let in. 'You see,' shouted the doorman after us. 'You two'll be at the front in no time.' I looked back at him. He smiled a broad smile, all affability and bonhomie now, and walked back to take up his position by the door.

Church was silent as we walked to the back of the queue. The club-goers nearest to us gave us a quick glance then carried on with their conversation, laughing as they did.

'How do you know Boston Jack again?'

'I met him just after he first arrived, must be over ten years ago. I was with the Branch then, met him when we raided a club in Limehouse looking for anarchists. Saw this black bloke, must have been about my age, not running, not fighting, just smoking a cigar by the bar. I walked over to give him what's what and he offered me a cigar. The two of us ended up having a smoke while everyone else got stuck in. Just hit it off you know, the way you just sometimes do. So I let him go, kept an eye on him and I watched him work his way up from whatever he was then to bossing his own show. And he helped me out every now and again. And sometimes, as long as he behaved himself and made sure his men did likewise, I did the same. By the time I left he was running, or had an eye on, anything outside the law down here.' Church looked down the line and shook his head. 'Last time I came here they were still patching up the bullet holes in the door,' he said, sounding almost sentimental.

'What's he like then, this fellow?'

Church smiled. 'Well. We always said: there are only two things you need to know about Boston Jack. One: he's not from Boston and two—'

'His name ain't Jack.' The voice came loudly from behind us, and I turned around to see a man with the same bulk as Church and similarly pugilistic features though, as much as I could judge at first glance, a much cheerier demeanour. He wore his hair and beard short, the latter tinged with grey. He was dressed casually; dark trousers and a white shirt with what looked like an army uniform jacket, sleeves bare of insignia but with the gold crossed swords of an American cavalry regiment sewn onto the collar.

Church moved forward, stretched out his hand. Boston Jack followed suit and they clasped in a handshake, stock still for a moment before firmly, slowly, shaking hands.

Church pointed to me: 'My associate, Mr Sterling.'

Boston Jack nodded a greeting at me as he stopped shaking hands and slapped Church on the shoulder. 'Let's get you inside. There's a fine old rye I came across that I've been waiting for an excuse to try.' He walked off down the side of the club, down an alleyway even narrower than the one we had emerged from. As he did I noticed for the first time the kinetoscope, painted black and almost invisible up near the roof of the building next to the club. Another further down focused on the door that Boston Jack led us too. He knocked on the door, which opened immediately and was held out of our way by a man dressed like the doormen outside. Crooked under the arm not holding the door was a large-calibre pump-action shotgun, its barrel severely shortened. It would be a deadly weapon in the confines of the hallway.

'Expecting trouble, Boston?' asked Church as we walked up a narrow and dusty set of bare wooden stairs. The rhythm and beat of the music from the club was just audible as we walked, faintly but insistently travelling through the fabric of the building.

'Just a little local disagreement,' came the reply from in front. 'I could ask you the same question, though. That's a lot of iron you're carrying around with you, Church.'

'You know what it's like, Boston, Canning Town's a dangerous place, especially for us white folks,' said Church.

Boston laughed, a sudden boom of sound in the tight space of the stairs. 'You tell that to the boys and girls downstairs.'

We arrived at the top of the stairs where a long, narrow corridor led past a single doorway to another set of stairs leading back down on the far side. Another of Boston's men leaned against the wall further down the corridor, no gun in sight this time but eyes on Church and me as we waited while Boston opened what I assumed was his office door. The music grew louder as he did and, following him inside, I realised that what was now Boston Jack's office had once been the warehouse overseer's, square panes of glass creating a rear wall that gave a perfect view of the floor below.

Boston walked over behind the desk that stood in front of the window. 'Please,' he said, 'take a seat, gentlemen.' His accent was definitely from the Northern States, what they had called the Union before the Second Civil War, but much beyond that I couldn't tell. He was confident, clearly used to giving orders. I had seen that kind of confidence before, in Canada, the kind that was a combination of inborn attitude, experience of command and surviving enemy fire. Now that I could see the jacket he was wearing in the light of the office, I could see the badge on the collar of the jacket more clearly: a number ten above a pair of crossed swords.

'Something on your mind, Mr Sterling?' Boston asked. I looked into a face that was unreadable, relaxed but not at rest. His eyes were hard, sharp and steady as he looked at me.

'I was thinking the 10th Cavalry was one of the few regiments that held together after Philadelphia fell,' I said. 'Didn't panic, apparently, held off Confederate forces so that refugees fleeing the city could escape.'

Boston made a quiet sound that might have been surprise. 'The man knows his badges,' he said. 'But this.' He pulled at one of the sleeves of his uniform. 'Nothing to do with me. It's just something I found in second-hand store.' He smiled. 'I guess I just like wearing it.' He gave a half-friendly smile that said the subject was closed. 'Now what say I get you fellows a drink?' Without waiting for an answer, he reached into a drawer under his desk and took out a brown bottle which he placed on the desk in front of him. The label was black and white, hand printed, the main part of the label taken up with a roughly etched portrait of what looked like George Washington. Boston Jack took out three glasses, apparently from the same place the bottle had been, and lined them up on the desk. With something approaching reverence, he held the bottle steady in front of him, uncorked it carefully and poured out three generous measures then put a glass in front of each of us. 'Cheers,' he said and looked at the glass for a moment before taking a sip. Church and I did the same. It was a vast improvement on some of the whiskies I had tried over in Canada, smooth and warming with a touch of sweetness.

Church put his empty glass on the table. 'Good stuff. Business must be good, Boston.'

Boston took out a cigarette case, opened it and offered us one of the Turkish ovals inside. Church took one and lit both with a lighter. Boston pointed over his shoulder with the cigarette. 'A year ago or so I took pity on a fellow countryman, recently arrived in London. Some sort of piano player.' He smoked. 'Next thing I know we've got people queuing out the door to come in and throw themselves around to something they tell me is music. Rag they call it.' Another draw on the cigarette. 'And not just locals either, we get plenty of fancier folks queuing every night and spending plenty when they're here.' He raised his eyebrows and nodded at the bottle. 'Another?'

'Don't mind if I do, thanks Boston,' replied Church.

'Enjoy it while you can,' said Boston as he poured, 'they don't make this one any more.'

'Why not?' I asked. 'It's very good.'

'Because the Confederates burned down the factory, summer of '85. Teaching us a lesson, you see.' He sipped his whiskey. 'So. What brings you here, Church? Must be something serious.'

'Looking for someone to help with a job,' said Church.

'What kind of help?'

'I need a pilot, someone who can fly an airship through a

city, land in between buildings, get out again without any problems and without anyone the wiser.'

Boston Jack raised his eyebrows again. 'Would have to be a small airship and a good pilot.'

Church nodded. 'It would. We have access to a 'ship that can run silent for long enough, just need the pilot.'

'And who is this we?' asked Boston. 'Not police?'

'Not police,' I said. 'And not army either. We're what you might call an independent endeavour.'

Boston laughed. 'Seems like there's a lot more of those around nowadays.'

'Do you know someone who fits the bill?' asked Church.

'I know two pilots you could use. One by the name of Sidney Buckman, specialises in quiet landings, mostly by the sea if you take my meaning. He's good, not too bright but dependable. Your better choice would be an ex-army guy, name of Lem Waller. But you might be out of luck there, I haven't seen him around for a good five years or so.'

'Do you have any idea where we might find them?' I asked.

'Well now, I thought your kind of independent endeavours would have the advantage over ordinary folk like me when it came to finding people.'

'Ordinary folk is it now, Boston?'

Boston Jack spread his arms wide, a gesture of hurt on his face. 'Just a businessman, Mr Church, strictly legitimate.'

'Whose doorman carry guns,' replied Church.

'I am sure we could find them,' I said, 'but any steer you could give us might save some time, and time is very much of the essence.'

'Well, then,' said Boston Jack, putting his cigarette on the end of a cheap metal ashtray on his desk and picking up a pen. 'Sid you can find here.' He took a small sheet of paper from a stack in front of him and wrote a few lines on it. 'In person or phone. But Lem I haven't seen for a while. Just sort of dropped out of sight a few years ago. Must have made his money I guess.' He smiled.

I took the piece of paper, folded it and put it into my pocket. 'Thank you.'

'Oh you are welcome. Always happy to help a friend of Church's,' replied Boston. 'Now, gentlemen, can I tempt you to sample the delights of Boston's while you are here? On the house?'

Church stood and finished off his second glass. 'We should get back.'

'At least let me show you the club on the way out,' said Boston.

Church nodded and we both followed Boston out of the office along the corridor and down the stairs at the other side of the landing. The man who had been outside on the landing fell in behind us as we passed him and Boston led us down the stairs. The music got louder as we descended and even louder as we turned the corner at the bottom and continued down a short corridor to a door at the end of it. Boston turned back to us, gave us a wink. 'Welcome to the future!' he said as he opened the door and we followed him through.

The noise was deafening, the loud and bright tones of a piano and the bleat and blast of brass underlain with the chunky strum of a double bass and the rattle and thump of drums. If the music was like nothing I had ever heard the dancing was even more surprising, as far from the sedate waltzes of my own youth as it would be possible to get. Clearly having the time of their lives, couples jumped raggedly at and around each other, feet together and arms flailing high.

'What are they doing?' Church shouted at Boston, pointing at a couple near us, his face a mixture of puzzlement and shock.

'I believe it's called the grizzly bear,' Boston shouted back. 'Can I get you that drink now?'

Behind us the music came to a thunderous crescendo and the couples on the dance floor gave up a cheer in the few seconds of silence that followed before the band started up again with a rippling solo on the piano.

Church nodded. 'Go on then. Just the one.'

16. Cowboy

I had been in Bermuda for an extended stint of Maddox corporate junketing when I heard that the Confederates had bombed Washington. The news that came through at first was sketchy but eventually it became clear that the Confederates had somehow acquired a fleet of airships and used them to carpet-bomb the Northerners' capital until barely a building was standing. Suddenly, the war that in the previous months seemed to have been heading for a barren stalemate had flared up again. Though Bermuda was by no means close to the field of battle, my family decided it would be best for me to return to London and a position was found for me at the Maddox Global Maritime offices there.

Along with the position I was given the keys of a brand new and perfectly nice, but certainly not extravagant, flat in South Kensington. My role at Maddox Global was by no means onerous, the tradition of family leadership having already been taken up by my elder brother Julius, and so I was required to do little more than ensure that any person of importance to the company who happened to be in town enjoyed their stay. My only other duties were going to meetings or functions whenever it was deemed necessary for a Maddox to be present and

Julius either could not or would not be there. Aside from that, I was free to throw myself into the sights, sounds and pleasures of London with as much gusto as I could muster.

And muster it I certainly did, enjoying the sheer variety of entertainments that I had so badly missed during my time in Bermuda, drinking swizzles and trying to muster up the enthusiasm for yet another private recital at Admiralty House. Parched of theatre, opera, comedy and music hall, I drank it all in whenever my evenings were free of corporate jollity. I went to every exhibition that I could find, from the Royal Academy to the smallest, most cramped artist's studio. It was at a commercial gallery approximately in the middle of this range, at some sort of opening (of something that never really stayed with me), that I ran delightedly by chance into an old friend from my Oxford days, the Honourable Edgar Theodore Huntingdon.

Having lost touch over the years, we quickly re-established the rapport than had made us fast friends in our youth. We were both well travelled. Both an intermittent bother for our respective families. Both in less than arduous employment and generously enough supplied with family funds. Each of us was young enough to appreciate the joy of profligacy yet old enough to possess the experience and imagination to ensure that our pastimes reached beyond the blunter and more obvious pleasures the capital had to offer.

Though of course we found time for those as well.

It was Edgar who introduced me to Cooper's, a place he had come across via an old school friend. I would never have found it otherwise, Mrs Cooper relying on word of mouth and personal recommendation to ensure that her clientele was of a particular quality, temperament and liquidity. I found it much to my liking, as most definitely did Edgar and it was where we seemed to end up on the evenings we weren't at Boodle's.

The last meal I ate with Edgar was a veritable feast at Wilton's. We kicked off with oysters before we moved onto lobster and an exceedingly fine bream. The group of us had spent the first part of the evening gambling in a rather vile den out in Seven Dials. We wagered first on cards then, later on, in a tucked-away basement, on bare fists. Venturing into that part of London was always a risk, even for a large group, and we had thought ourselves especially venturesome, so soon after the latest murder by the Ripper. This had been a particularly violent affair according to the men we had spoken to that evening, who gleefully regaled us with tales of mutilation and disembowelment.

It had been Edgar's idea to move on to Cooper's after supper. I thought at the time we would be lucky to get in, as drunk as we were, but, with Edgar to the fore and in typically persuasive form, we were welcomed in. It was the first time for some of the others and Edgar left me to show them the ropes while he went straight to the girl who had taken his eye that autumn, the 'young orphan Alice'. I had shown the rest of the fellows what was what as quickly as I could and, after a few minutes, left them with Mrs Cooper, answering their various questions about the girls as they stared at the paintings above the staircase, and went on my way to see Marie.

It was a few hours later when Edgar, unusually, knocked at the door and, a bottle of champagne in hand, suggested that we swap for a while, he having tired of his girl. His hair was wet I remembered, though not untidy. It wasn't unusual for him to do this, often tiring of a girl who he had proclaimed immeasurably fascinating only hours before. I was perfectly happy where I was, but, battered by his mockery of my keeping Marie to myself, I acquiesced and, after taking the proffered bottle of champagne, I walked a little unsteadily down the hallway and up the stairs to Alice's room on the next floor, drinking as I went. As is so often the case, it was only in leaving Marie's room and walking along the corridor that I realised how close to very drunk I was and I had to stop a few times along the way, take a deep breath or two and a gulp of champagne to try and snap myself out of it. The door to Alice's room was closed when I got there and, feeling worse if anything than when I had set off from the floor below, I struggled for a moment or two before I managed to turn the handle. The room was completely dark, I remembered afterwards, with the curtains drawn so that I could barely make out her shape under the covers on the bed. Then: nothing. And, no matter how many times I try and force myself to remember, there still is nothing.

I woke, lying stiff limbed on the hard, wooden floor. The room was bright with daylight, my head thick and empty. It took me a second or two to remember where I was in the unfamiliar surroundings. There was something in my hand I realised, as I pushed myself to my feet. Focusing on it I saw it was Edgar's wolf-head walking stick, tacky with something dark, larger blobs and specks of matter caught within the dark, sticky coating. I stood, staring at the stick, befuddled at the liquid's identity until a quick wave of comprehension shook me and, suddenly revolted, I threw it to the floor. As I did I saw that my hands and arms were likewise encrusted with blood. I turned to the bed, squinting against the light in the window and the hammering pain in my head, and I saw that the sheets which clung to the girl's form were soaked with blood and I stood still for a moment.

Then, and I still don't know what macabre instinct made me do this, I reached across the bed and pulled the girl towards me so that she lay over on her back. She was frail and slim and naked, her torso bruised and beaten and her face so badly attacked that it was barely recognisable as human. And I vomited, into my hands first as I tried to save her from that final indignity, and then onto the floor as I leaned against the wall, heaving my stomach dry. When I staggered out into the corridor the first person I saw was Mrs Cooper walking, then running towards me. When she saw into the room behind me she let out an involuntary gasp, closed the door and then took me downstairs and had one of her people make me some coffee while she called the police.

It was 11 November 1888 and my last day in England as a free man.

The evidence was damning, the witnesses, Mrs Cooper and my friend Edgar were both shocked but adamant that I was responsible. My protestations counted for little and I was held under house arrest in one of Cooper's rooms and questioned by Fuller until they eventually allowed me to call Julius. He arrived, silent, unsmiling and flanked by lawyers. It transpired that prior to his arrival Julius had been making a calculated disbursement of a portion of our family's hoarded influence and persuaded certain authorities at a suitably high level that it would be in everyone's better interest to see me enlisted rather than hanged. And so, three days later, I found myself on board a ship bound for Canada. Back in London, meanwhile, the kind of silence that significant wealth can buy washed gently across the press and life continued, untroubled and serene. My sudden departure was explained away to any who discreetly enquired as related to a liaison with a married woman and, readily believing it, society's hunger for disgrace was sated.

There were times in Canada, in those first few months after I arrived that I would lie awake and imagine the myriad of courses that my life could have run, pondering the choices that had resulted in exile to a remote, hellish and forgotten corner of the Empire. I picked decisions apart, reversed them and played 'what if'. I imagined myself still in Bermuda or back in a different London where I wasn't a murderer, had never met Edgar, never found Cooper's, never woken up in that room.

My plan when I arrived at the Canadian border was to sit out my exile quietly and, after a year or so, to ask Julius to petition for my return here, I told myself, I would be able to secure an acquittal. However, when I judged the time right and wrote my first letter it brought only a terse reminder from Julius of the strict terms of my sentence and a warning that any truncation thereof was utterly impossible. My letter to my father was returned to me unopened.

So, with little other option, I tried my hand at soldiering and, to my surprise and, I think that of my sergeant, I discovered that I was actually quite good at it. The months became years; with them my knowledge and ability grew while my yearning for London faded. In time, thanks in part to the sponsorship of Major Harrington, I progressed from being a farcically old ensign to a sadly over-aged lieutenant and, ultimately, a sage and battle-worn captain. I developed a reputation amongst my men for being even handed, no shirker in a firefight and even for standing up for them against the sort of nonsensical standing orders that floated down from headquarters on occasion. I met a woman, the daughter of a German pastor, on a mission to enlighten the heathen in the ways of Calvinism. And, despite the reason for being there, I began to be happy, to put to one side thoughts of returning to England and to make a new life for myself in Canada. Then came the news of my father's rapidly failing health and I came back to London, almost eight years to the day after I had gone.

Throughout my time in Canada the steadily accumulating stress and bleakness of life on the border had begun to supersede the horror of that one night in London, like the strokes of a painter overlaying an earlier, unwanted sketch. And, as the months turned into years and I left the earlier, dilettante incarnation of myself behind, so I began to believe that nothing remained of that night, that I could put it behind me and start again. Even on the flight across from Canada, as I ate and slept, admired the view and made small talk with fellow passengers, I managed to deceive myself that all was forgotten and without significance. But from the moment I stepped off the last stair down from the airship and set foot on the tarmac, images started coming back, until, jerked into place by the sight of Edgar's stick, I saw her again in horrible clarity, faceless and unmoving, and I realised that, far from erased, memory of that night was indelible.

'Come on, Sterling. There's only six of them. How hard can it be?' said Patience from her seat further along the desk, hunched in concentration over a set of old engine punch cards, working by the light of some differently sized and styled table lamps arranged around the desk.

Even more so than during my first visit to Patience's workspace in the basement of the Map Room, it resembled a haphazard blend of repair shop, museum and boot room, with several esoteric, mechanical projects in varying stages of completion dotted around the place. It smelt of oil and machinery and stale clothing. Patience's engine was running in the background, generating a low, soporific whirr as it did.

'It has to be one of them.' Patience said, out of the corner of her mouth. She was holding a thin metal cylinder the same width as the holes in the cards and as I watched she picked up a large metal hammer from the overlapping layers of engine-related disorder in front of her and started gently tapping away.

I realised that I was staring at the wall, jaw clenched. I took a deep breath, let it out slowly and looked again at the spread of grey folders in front of me. Six women with nothing to link them but age and height and hair. Sisters in data, they stared gravely at me from their engine-derived photographs, a random scatter of tiny printer smudges adding the illusion of a smirk here, a frown there. I looked closely at each in turn and tried to match their features to the memory of the grey-coated woman in Preston station. I didn't recognise any of them.

'Are you sure that these are the only ones that match the description?' I asked.

Patience stopped what she was doing and sat up straight in her chair. Even from the side I could see the height reached by her eyebrows.

'Fine,' I said before she could expel whatever barbed comment was being readied. 'I'll take another glance at them. You carry on.'

I went through the photos again, turning the chair away from the desk and looking at each of them in isolation. Still failing to kindle a glimmer of recognition, I turned to the folders themselves and read through the pages of detailed information in each one. The careers were similar, university followed by employment in army, police or government, and, for three of the women, a move to an agency of some sort: the Bureau of Engine Security, MO5 and the Field Intelligence Division. I went back to the photo of the woman who had ended up in the Bureau, covered her face with my hands so that just her eyes were showing. It was her. Lenora Mills.

I reunited the other photos with their folders and put them to one side, then read through her career history more carefully. Lovelace Scholarship at Manchester Municipal School of Technology where she studied Engine Programming. Graduated in 1885 and joined the Bureau a year later where a short string of letters and numbers took over: A9, C2, K17.

'Patience,' I asked, 'what are these numbers?'

'What numbers?' she replied as she held a punch card up to the light on the shelf above her desk and blew carefully on it.

'On this file, something to do with the Bureau.' I read the numbers out to her.

'Team designations. Typical Bureau: logical to the point of stupidity,' said Patience as she carefully slipped the card in her hands into a thick pack of similar cards and loaded them into a machine in front of her. 'Probably makes sense if you're an engine but it's not that exciting is it?' Patience put on a deep voice as she continued. '"I say, old boy, are you A9?" "Me, old chap? No fear, I'm K17 through and through."' Patience followed up this interchange with a peal of laughter. 'What a collection of idiots.'

'Can you find out what the letters mean?' I asked.

She gave me a look. 'Obviously.'

I passed the file across to Patience who looked it over quickly. 'So she went to the Tech did she? Very impressive.'

'Is it?' I asked, having been brought up to believe that there were only two English universities: Oxford and the Other Place.

'Oh yes,' replied Patience as she flicked switches across the desk and set her engine into motion. 'Tapper's paradise.'

I matched the rest of the women's photographs back with their folders and found room for them on top of a pile of textbooks.

That left a small pile of papers still for me to look at, the few details that Patience had managed to find on the two pilots suggested by Boston Jack.

Sidney Buckman's notes comprised his employment records (he had worked as a bargeman before progressing to be an airship loader and finally a pilot), summary arrest sheets (evading duty, smuggling prohibited goods, falsifying official documents) and the title deed for a public house on the Isle of

Wight, where he now lived. Lem Waller on the face of it was a simpler prospect having joined the Royal Aerial Navy at the age of eighteen before transferring to a newly formed Army Air Corps in '82. Both his naval and army records detailed unexciting, run-of-the-mill careers, his last position in the army that of an instructor before retiring on health grounds about five years ago. I was about to go back to Sidney Buckman as the most likely of the two when something jumped out from Waller's army notes, an eighteen-month period described as a 'temporary posting' and next to it a short word that I assumed was a location but then, looking at it again, read BES-K-17.

'Patience?'

'Yes?' she looked up from her screen.

'What does that word look like to you?' I leaned over, holding Wallers notes for her to look at them and pointing at the temporary posting.

Patience took the notes from me and held it under one of her many desk lamps.

Patience read aloud. 'BES.' She looked at me. 'Bureau of Engine Security.'

'K17. Like our friend from Preston,' I replied.

'So,' she said, throwing down the notes on the desk and attacking her keyboard, 'the question is, did Lem and Lenora hit it off?'

'Can you find out?' I asked.

'Not a problem. Just give me a minute or two to get up-line and into the Bureau engines.'

I stood, stretching my back and shoulders. 'Would you like some coffee?'

'You'll be lucky,' she laughed, 'March went home hours ago and Wallis couldn't make a cup to save his life.'

'I'll do it myself,' I said.

'You?'

'Yes, me.' Seeing a small panel of bulbs on her desk light up, I pointed it out to her. 'What's that?'

'Nothing to worry about, just the Bureau's engine checking our credentials, which of course are impeccable,' said Patience.

'And who are we today?' I asked.

'Night shift at the War Office, clearing up old pensions records,' she replied.

'Doesn't anyone ever suspect you?' I asked.

'Of course not,' said Patience, 'because I am very, very good and very, very careful.'

'Have you ever been caught doing this kind of thing?' I said.

'Me?' she said 'Caught? As if.' She made a derisive sound and went back to her keyboard as letters and numbers started flickering in across the screen. 'Right. Here we are. I'll run a search on K17, find out who's who and what's what in less than the time it takes you to find the kitchen.'

Taking the hint, I half-consciously checked my gun was still holstered and walked out of the room and down the corridor towards the kitchen.

'Oh and cream, no sugar for me!' Patience shouted after me.

I was about halfway down to the kitchen when I heard an explosion of mechanical clamour from Patience's room. I ran back as quickly as I could, gun suddenly in my hand. The noise died as I arrived, then started up again, thumping and clanging like a broken engine.

Patience was typing away at her keyboard, seemingly oblivious. She suddenly realised I was there in the doorway and looked up. She reached over to a cylinder player next to her and pressed a button. The noise stopped. 'What?'

'What the blazes was that?' I asked her.

Patience looked puzzled. Gave an exaggerated sigh. 'It's Electric Rag. You won't have heard of it.' Then she looked at me, saw the gun in my hand. 'Oh my God, did you think I had exploded or something?' Laughter bubbled up inside her. 'Or did you think we were under attack? That the bad men had come out of the wires to get us? Sterling, you are priceless!' When I didn't say anything, she shrieked with laughter and turned the music back on so that it blared out from two large speakers set against the end of the room. I mustered what dignity I could, re-holstered my Webley and walked back down the corridor to the kitchen, the noise of Patience's cacophonous music following me as I went.

The kitchen was pitch black when I opened the door, shutters closed, and everything cleared away for the night. After a few fumbling moments I managed to find a switch and turned it on, bathing the room in bright light from a rank of bulbs in the ceiling. A quick search turned up a bag of coffee beans and a grinder but nothing that I recognised as a coffee-maker. I thought for a moment. We had had a number of northerners in the regiment who had made their way up into Canada instead of either staying within the new Confederate States of America or braving the crossing to Europe. One of them, originally a Kansas cattleman, proved popular among the men partly for his skill as a storyteller but also for the pan-brewed coffee he could make. I felt confident that I had watched him do it enough times to be able to give it a good bash.

A further survey of the kitchen yielded some tin mugs which I used to measure the water into a saucepan and, a few patiently industrious minutes later, I had enough ground coffee to go with it. I heated the water to boiling, let it cool, then added the grounds. I stirred them and stood watching them settle for a few minutes. Clay his name was, the cowboy who made the coffee. Shot in the chest, I remembered, in an ambush on the wrong side of the border, and one of few who made it back to the camp. He died a few days later. I stirred the coffee again then put the saucepan on the tray along with the mugs, turned off the lights and made my way out of the kitchen along the corridor.

I was walking along, wondering whether I had remembered all the steps in the coffee-making process, when I had a sudden feeling that something wasn't quite right. I stood still for a moment in the gloom of the corridor, holding the tray and listening carefully. The music had stopped. Instead I could hear men's voices from the end of the corridor near the stairs, which seemed odd. Church had stayed on at the club with Boston Jack after I left and had no intention of coming back to the Map Room tonight. Wallis was the only other person here. This sounded like more than one voice. I set off again, covering the yards towards Patience's room with carefully quiet steps.

As the door came in sight, I saw a man dressed in dark workman's clothes. His back was to me and he was shouting up the stairs. He could have been a builder or a decorator except for two things: his head was completely covered in a red balaclava and from his left hand hung a short-barrelled automatic rifle, a large, black silencer fitted over the end of the barrel.

'Taff?' A pause. Balaclava called up again. 'Hey Taffy!'

I stood and, ever so slowly, without taking my eyes off the man, set the tray silently down on the floor, stepped over it and drew my gun.

An answer that I couldn't hear was called down from the top of the stairs.

'Fred says there's a little snowdrop down here if you fancy a poke.'

I started walking towards him with soft, wary steps to cover the ten yards or so that separated us, arm outstretched, pistol aimed at his head.

Another muffled response from above. Balaclava shrugged

his shoulders and called to someone in Patience's room. 'Taff wants to know is she American?' The man inside the room, presumably Fred, replied, though I couldn't quite make out what he said.

I covered a few more yards, tracking steadily on balaclava's head as I did.

He leaned into the stairwell and shouted up: 'Taff? She isn't American.' Another pause. 'I don't know, just some girl. We'll be about fifteen minutes. Alright? You go and keep an eye on the front of the house.' Another muffled shout. Then I heard a short cry of pain from Patience's room and the noise of breaking furniture.

Red balaclava turned back from the stairs and walked across the corridor, attention on the bright lights of Patience's room.

I hissed, a low whispered sound.

He turned, puzzling at the noise, eyes struggling to adjust to the darker corridor, then, suddenly seeing me, he started to pull his gun up to a firing position. But mine was already there and my first shot took him through the left eyehole of the balaclava. The second went an inch or two higher as he staggered backwards and his head snapped back, spraying blood and matter onto the wall behind him. I waited, following him down with my gun as he collapsed, but he hit the floor in a heap without firing a shot and lay there unmoving.

I heard an exclamation from inside the room and the sound of rapid movement. The man inside appeared in the doorway. He swore when he saw the bloody mess of his accomplice on the ground. This one was dressed similarly, with the same red balaclava. Glancing my way, he ducked back, and my shots missed. Then it was my turn to throw myself to the floor as a blast of automatic fire sprayed out through the doorway, bullets ricocheting off the corridor walls. I worked my way backwards along the wall.

'Sounds like you're all out, cully!' came the shout from the room. He came to the door of the room and leaned out just far enough to look down the corridor. 'Leave the gun there and up you get.' I did what he said. 'Now come back down here,' he said, then shouted in the direction of the stairs: 'Taff!'

I got to my feet and walked towards him, holding my arms out to show that I was unarmed.

'Who the fuck are you meant to be, then?' he said, as I stepped slowly towards him. 'Her dad?'

I shook my head slightly. 'Just a security guard.'

'You aren't much use, are you? Best I put you out of your misery I reckon.' He raised his gun and aimed it at me.

And didn't shoot.

Instead, he stumbled forward a small step from where he stood in the doorway, a puzzled look in his eyes. He blinked a few times then slowly let the gun slip from his fingers and reached up for the back of his head.

I heard a sickening crack and he fell forward onto his knees in the doorway. I darted forward to grab his gun as Patience stepped out of the room, stood over him and hit him again with the hammer. And then once more till he lay face down onto the floor, the back of his head a pulpy mess of hair and bone. His limbs shuddered and twitched for a few moments then he was still.

'George? Fred?' a voice called as the third of them, apparently only just hearing the noise, made his way down the stairs.

I picked up the automatic rifle, and waved Patience back into her room, then knelt and aimed at the topmost visible stair. He was half-wary as he came down, moving slowly but still exposing his legs as he did, and I put half the clip into them and walked a few rounds upwards. He screamed in pain and clattered down the stairs to slump in a heap at the bottom. He tried to raise his gun, but I was too quick and stamped down on his wrist, grinding at the bone until he let go, kicking the gun away from him.

He wasn't wearing a balaclava, instead relying on the tall, upturned collars of his coat to cover his face, an arrangement which had flattened in the fall, unmasking him.

'You're a long way from Whitechapel, Evan,' I said, recognising our guide from the Ripper tour. It had only been yesterday morning, but it felt like several lifetimes ago. I picked up the gun that he had dropped and slung the one I had fired on its strap across my shoulder.

He squinted at me. 'What?' he shifted himself to try and look at me and grimaced in pain, letting out a curse as he did. He stared at me for a moment. 'Fuck me, it's the soldier.'

'It is, and as you can see, I won't be needing that job after all.' I detached the magazine, making sure it was full, then replaced it and cocked the gun.

'It's not what it looks like,' he said. 'I was just the lookout.'

'Is that a fact?' I asked.

He nodded weakly. 'Couldn't find anyone else.'

'Who sent you?' I asked.

He shook his head. 'Don't know. Just a telegram.' He seemed to be drifting away so I stood on one of his legs and his eyes came open with a shout of pain. 'I swear it was a telegram. Told us to come here and clean house.' He slumped back down with the effort.

'Clean house?' I asked. 'Meaning kill everyone.'

He nodded. He closed his eyes and gritted his jaw as a spasm of pain swept through him.

'But you weren't part of that?'

Shake of the head.

'The other two were the killers?' I asked him.

Nod.

'Does the name Leonora Mills mean anything to you?

A slight shake.

'Special Branch detective called Harris?'

Shake.

'Right, well, that seems clear enough. Just one last thing, Taff?' I paused. 'Look at me, Evan.'

He opened his eyes to look at me.

'Why did you ask if she was American?' My voice was hard now and I saw the fear suddenly flash into his face at the question. 'Were you hoping that my friend from the tour was down here? Would you have come downstairs then?' I asked. 'Had a poke?'

He shook his head but the look in his eyes gave the lie to that denial and, anger suddenly flaring in me, I raised the gun and shot him in the head.

I turned back to Patience where she was watching from her doorway. He hair was dishevelled, her clothes tugged out of shape. She looked like she had taken a few knocks to the face but otherwise appeared unharmed. Blood was splashed across her shirt. It covered the hammer and the hand that held it. Her jaw was tight, her eyes bright with delight or fury or some combination of the two. She stepped across the body and, suddenly, the last thing I expected, pulled me into a hug. Taken off guard for a moment, I stood there as she clung on to me, face buried in my chest. I reached around her back, gun still in my hand, and placed my arm gently around her. For several seconds we stood like that, hammer in her hand, gun in mine while she cried a few brief and silent sobs. And, as she did, something that had been with me since Cooper's lightened and left me.

Patience pulled away from me, eyes red, took a deep breath, and gave me a brief pat on the chest. Then she walked back into her room, dropping the hammer on top of the man she had killed as she did.

The corridor stank of cordite and blood. I stopped at each body in turn, checking for signs of life. Finding none, I walked back down the corridor to the tray, picked it up and brought it to Patience's room, putting it carefully on the desk. She looked up at me, gave me a half smile, then carried on pressing buttons and switches on the engine.

'I pressed the alarm button,' said Patience. 'Jays should be here in,' she looked at her watch, 'six minutes.'

'Right,' I said, pouring the coffees out, adding cream to hers and putting it down next to her. We drank in silence, Patience's fingers tapping on the keyboard the only accompaniment.

The coffee tasted rather good.

17. Bustle

Regent Street on a crisp autumn morning. Pavements swept clean, coloured awnings catching the sunlight, windows polished to a shine and the final, deft adjustments being made to goods on display. Most shops were barely open but already the street was thinly populated with the earliest and most purposeful shoppers. Traffic was light; a few cabs and half-empty buses chugged and hummed along while boys neatly darted their bicycles between them, pedalling away the first packages of the day. Here and there along the street, hawkers were readying their stalls while paper sellers called out the morning's headlines.

Church and I walked in silence, each with our own thoughts as we went to our meeting with Milady. I had managed to grab a few hours of sleep and had showered, shaved and found a change of clothes waiting for me in my room, but the events of the night before clung vividly to me. Though physically draining me, the gunfight at the Map Room had seemed to fire up my mind, which whirled with thoughts of airships and surgery and the card labelled 'Patient' on the board in the briefing room. And a bell was beginning to ring more clearly. The brisk and business-like cheer of Regent Street that was unfolding around me felt like something that was happening at a distance. The activity seemed orchestrated and remote, a collection of players well versed in their roles and entrances, warming up for a performance of which I was no part.

We drew level with a news stand where the headline display read 'Blackpool Murder Suicide! Ripper found?'.

'Wait a moment, would you?' I said to Church, who did so while I bought a copy of *The Times*.

'What does it say?' he asked as we continued on our way. I scanned the front page.

'They've identified Richardson, dug up some of his background, some quotes from a police investigator who knew him from Whitechapel. He was always a suspect apparently,' I said.

'Of course he was,' replied Church. 'Since about yesterday afternoon, I'll be bound. Poor sod.'

'There's nothing about his personal life.'

'Yet. They'll find out though. And then they'll have a field day.'

I nodded, feeling a stab of remorse for what was being done to the memory of the sad, fearful man we had met, making the best of his life in a Blackpool dressing room. I folded the paper and put it under my arm. 'We're here.'

The shop was about halfway up Regent Street, a large emporium for women's clothes that advertised its wares in a series of extravagant window displays. The outfits on show were in different colours and styles but with one thing in common; they all looked as though they would be inordinately expensive. The shop's interior was decorated in a traditional style I recognised from reluctant shopping trips as a boy. Cabinets and shelves of polished walnut were arranged around the ground floor, showing off artful arrangements of ribbon, silk and woven fabrics as well as examples of the finished articles. A pair of counters, each attended by a smart and smiling young assistant, stretched away either side of dark wooden stairs leading upwards to the next floor. As we stepped through the door, I caught sight of Collier by one wall, holding up a pair of long, black opera gloves for inspection.

'Can I help you, gentlemen?' an assistant asked brightly from behind the counter to our right, standing in front of a collection of cheerfully coloured hats.

'We're with our friend,' replied Church, gesturing to Collier.

Collier put the opera gloves back on a counter and walked over to where we were standing. 'Gentlemen,' he said. Then, to the assistant: 'The fitting room is on the third floor I believe you said?'

'That's right, sir,' she said cheerily, Collier having evidently put her mind at rest as to why three men might be popping in to see one of her customers in mid-fitting. 'You will need to go to the third floor and someone will show you the way from there.' She pointed over to the stairs as she spoke.

Collier thanked her and led the way towards the stairs with a quiet 'I trust you are both well? Sterling, no lasting effects from the night's exertions?' From his casual tone he might have been talking about a session in the gymnasium or a heavy bout of gardening rather than a gunfight.

'All perfectly well, thank you,' I replied in kind.

'Good, good,' Collier replied. 'Terrible news in this morning's paper,' he continued, 'about that fellow in Blackpool. Did you read it?'

'Just seen it,' I replied.

'Quite shocking. Apparently, the police are convinced that he might have been the Ripper,' said Collier.

'I wonder why?' asked Church.

'Due to their admirable diligence and investigative skills I shouldn't wonder,' said Collier as we passed the first floor and carried up on our way. 'What a lovely day it is this morning, wouldn't you agree?

Church giving the appearance of a marked aversion to small talk, I answered Collier in the affirmative and joined in with him in a stilted sequence of inconsequential conversation until we reached the third floor. Directed by another young woman we found ourselves outside a door labelled 'Fitting Room' and, in larger letters below, 'Private'. Collier knocked.

The door opened to reveal Milady's driver, wearing the same dark grey uniform and unimpressed manner that I recognised from our first meeting. She held the door open and watched us as we filed into a large, light room with a high ceiling and tall windows running down the length of one wall. A few chairs and divans were arrayed nearby, low tables set near them. Large, blue silk dress covers were hanging from hooks next to the door, while on a nearby dressing table were piled a selection of material swatches and opened boxes of beads and thread. Against the opposite wall from the door a series of tall mirrored panels hinged out from the wall to form a pair of elongated semicircles. In the centre of this arrangement was Milady, standing on a small wooden block while a small, stocky man moved slowly about her, examining the dress she was wearing. His shirt sleeves were rolled up to reveal heavy forearms, thick with hair, their coarseness in contradiction to the nimble movements of his fingers as he carefully smoothed and adjusted the dress here and there. It was a long, sweeping ball gown in a sumptuous jade silk and embroidered exquisitely in coloured thread. On even a moderately attractive woman it would have been stunning; on Milady the effect was conversation-halting.

'Morning all,' called Milady from where she was standing. 'With you in the merest jiffy. Would you mind, Paul, giving us a few minutes?'

The tailor stood up from his task, smoothing down his waist-coat. 'Of course, my lady.' He held out his hand to her. She took hold of it as she jumped lightly down off the block. He followed her as she walked out from the mirrored screens and sat in an armchair by the windows and then, once she had set-tled, moved around her arranging the dress. Once it was satis-factorily positioned to whichever set of aesthetic principles he was working to, he straightened and gave Milady a half-bow. 'My lady. I will be waiting just along the corridor.' He turned to us and gave us a small nod. 'Gentlemen.'

'Oh, thank you, Paul, you are so kind,' Milady said as she opened the door, 'And Kitty, would you be a dear and slip out-side as well and make sure we aren't disturbed?'

A brief nod at Milady, a stern glance at Collier and Church with, unless I imagined it, a fractionally longer and sterner one for me, and Kitty strode outside, closing the door behind her.

Milady indicated the chairs near to her. 'Do sit down.' Col-lier sat in one of the two chairs, I took the other and Church dragged over a small, upholstered footstool that he found behind one of the mirrors. Close up, the embroidery on Milady's dress was delicately done; the branches of a stylised tree that swept up from the hem of the dress to curl up and around her waist, causing the tree's topmost tips to creep up to just below the neckline where, a few inches below, hung a piece of fruit picked out in what I now saw were rubies.

'Prussian ambassador's ball next month,' said Milady, notic-ing the direction of my gaze. 'The theme is "Paradise".' She gave a thin smile and raised her eyebrows at the tiresomeness of such a social duty. 'What do you think?' She indicated her dress with a sweep of artfully extended fingers. 'Not striking enough? Too much?'

I thought about the one or two Prussians I had met over the

years and imagined their reaction. 'It seems perfectly judged to me, ma'am,' I replied.

'Why thank you, Sterling, I'll pretend I can't hear what you are really thinking,' said Milady, 'and, in any case, I find that a moderate level of shock is a wonderfully invigorating way to start an evening. Now, though I am curious to probe your knowledge of ballroom fashion further, I fear we shall have to leave that for another occasion as I sense Mr Church's attention waning.' And in an instant the bonhomie vanished like sunlight suddenly covered by a cloud. 'So, tell me, what do we know about the attack?'

'It was organised by the group behind the Ripper murders,' Collier replied, 'which we believe to be either part of, or all of, a unit called K17 within the Bureau of Engine Security. I spoke to our man over there first thing this morning. He had never heard of K17 but made a few enquiries and called me back to say that it is listed as a small pool of secretarial staff.'

'They seem rather actively engaged for a roomful of typists,' I said.

'Well, quite,' said Collier. 'But so far the only named personnel we can identify are,' here he slipped his notebook from out of his jacket, 'Leonora Mills, the woman you and Sterling saw in Preston and who we think is their tapper. Then there is Waller, the airship pilot, and a senior Bureau official called Sebastian Fuller.'

'Fuller?' I spoke without thinking.

Collier stared at me for a moment. 'Do you know him?'

'No, I think I saw the name last night when we were looking at files,' I said. Fuller, the man who had come to Cooper's so quickly that night, who had been so convinced at Edgar's innocence and my guilt, who had taken a personal interest in my return and arrest, who had gone up in the world a great deal since. I thought it had been about extorting as high a price as possible, but he was there to protect his tame murderer who needed a scapegoat to take the blame for his unsanctioned activity.

'Very likely,' said Collier. 'As well most likely the head of this particular unit he is also Deputy Director of the Bureau itself. A very powerful man.'

'What about the men they sent last night?' asked Milady.

'We Bertie'd all three of them early this morning,' I said, grimacing inwardly slightly at the memory of holding the corpses' heads still while Patience dealt with each in turn. 'The Whitechapel tour guide was a fellow called Evan Hughes; he served in the Army for a few years before he was discharged for drunkenness and misconduct towards a superior officer. The other two were cousins. Both served time in prison for assault and aggravated burglary and were jointly arrested for the murder of a shopkeeper but released due to lack of evidence. Unofficial notes on their file linked them to a protection racket run by a gang in Hoxton.'

'Nasty,' said Church. 'We were lucky.'

Milady's voice was suddenly raised. 'Three men broke into our supposedly secret headquarters, killed a potentially valuable source of information and a member of our staff and you think we were lucky?'

Church seemed unfazed by the tone of her voice. 'I just meant, ma'am, we were lucky Sterling was there. Patience wouldn't be alive if she'd been on her own.'

'Nor would Carlton Gardens be intact,' added Collier. 'One of the men had an incendiary device with him. Their original intention in going down to the basement was undoubtedly to start a fire which would cover their tracks and destroy any evidence we had collected. Such a shame you couldn't have taken your friend Hughes alive, Sterling.'

'It is,' I agreed.

'Still,' Collier said, 'when I spoke to her, Patience was clear enough that you had no option but to kill him.'

'I did manage to speak to Hughes briefly and confirmed that, like Harris, Hughes had no idea who was hiring him. Similarly, he received his orders by telegram. I mentioned Leonora Mills and Harris's names, but it was clear he didn't know them.' I looked at Collier. 'I am sorry there wasn't more before he died but, given how the three of them were armed, I just couldn't take any chance.'

'Ah yes. Very modern, fully automatic, all three silenced,' said Collier. Not readily available to your average burglar, ex-army or not.'

'Is it possible that they were provided by K17?' I asked.

'Possibly,' said Collier. 'We shall have to see.'

'How is Patience?' asked Milady, the ire smoothed from her voice.

'She seems alright, considering what happened,' I said. 'She's young, pretty tough. I think she'll be fine for now. We should keep an eye on her, though.'

'Mr Church?' Milady again.

'I'd agree. As Sterling says, she seems alright. But it takes people in different ways, killing a man,' said Church. 'Assuming that's her first of course,' he added wryly. 'I wouldn't be too sure with her.'

'Church, really,' said Milady, frowning slightly at him. 'Where is she now?'

'Back at Carlton Gardens,' said Church, 'working on a location for K17. There was some sort of automated security on her engine that means when they traced us, she traced them. Apparently. When we left, she was confident she could get an exact address. There's a couple of Jays keeping an eye on her.'

Milady nodded slowly. 'What about our operations? Mr Collier?'

'Mac is supervising the clear-up. Once that has been completed to my satisfaction, we'll bring in the other staff and begin packing.' Collier's tone was calm and matter of fact, as if he were talking about a morning of tidying up after a party rather than the removal of bodies. 'The new office will be up and running the day after tomorrow. Things won't be as complete as I would like them, our signals capability will be limited, ma'am, but it should be good enough for now.'

'Excellent, Mr Collier, let me know as soon as my office is ready. Now what about Wallis?'

The Jays had arrived the night before, just as Patience predicted, and while one of them stayed with her, I had gone around with the rest of them as they cleared the house. We had found Wallis lying in the briefing room, blood soaked into the carpet around him. It would have been quick.

'Yes. Poor fellow,' said Collier, still in the easy tone of a man with a short list of errands to complete before lunchtime. 'We'll arrange for his death to have taken place elsewhere and elsewise. When the details are tied up, I'll contact his parents.'

Milady nodded. 'Good.' She was still for a moment or two, eyes narrowed in soundless calculation. 'How did they find us?'

'Our best guess is that it started with the calls that Harris made,' said Church. 'We think that he used a speech code when he called his handler to let them know he was speaking under duress.'

'Nigh impossible to catch, unfortunately,' cut in Collier. 'It could be as simple as leaving out a word or using a prearranged greeting to start off the call.' He smiled apologetically.

'It shouldn't have mattered in any case,' said Church. 'We had a set-up that ran our lines out through a public telephone in Piccadilly which Patience swore would have been enough to keep out your average tapper. Turns out they were smarter than we thought. Patience thinks they traced the call to the telephone box, worked out the trick Patience was using and then set up a trace in the local exchange so that next time we dialled out they could find us. We found an anonymous telegram like the ones that Harris mentioned on one of the killers telling them to go to a pub near Piccadilly and wait for a call. It was timed yesterday afternoon, not long after Harris made his calls.'

'Patience was working on the photos from Richardson's camera yesterday afternoon,' I said, 'so there was nothing for them to go on for a while, but she would have shown up when she was searching on-wire last night. And it wouldn't have mattered how much she covered her tracks at the other end because all they were interested in was the line that came into the phone box. As soon as it was used again, they got a fix on the address and called in their hired killers.'

Milady didn't reply immediately. When she spoke it was with a thoughtful tone. 'So after your little fracas on the train they knew you were more than a pair of countryside lawyers, and Patience's telephonic arrangement and our address would have given them a sense of our resources.' She paused again. 'Yet, in spite of that, or perhaps because of that, they acted without hesitation to eradicate our investigation, without any care of who we were.'

'Because it didn't matter,' I said. 'The only thing that counted was what we knew or what we suspected; that eight years ago they organised the murder of five prostitutes so that they could harvest their organs. If that got out, they would be finished, the Bureau would suddenly be put under the spotlight, severely reined in, perhaps even closed down and with elections next year it would certainly bring down the government.'

'But why not simply arrest us?' asked Milady. 'Trump up some charge of engine crime? The Bureau, especially their counter-espionage division, have carte blanche when it comes to protecting technology. They could have played the national security card and had us off to Millbank before you could say habeas corpus.'

'Because of who the patient is,' I said, my voice a little louder than I had intended. Seeing that card on the board in my mind's eye, I added, 'I was thinking someone rich, well resourced but seriously ill and willing to try anything. A wealthy industrialist perhaps.' I took a deep breath. 'But a private individual wouldn't bother setting up a government team, in the middle of the Bureau no less. He might bribe someone on the inside, but he'd hire his own private team to run it.' I took another breath. The fire was fading to be replaced by a sort of light-headed nausea. The other three looked at me, Milady cold, Collier mildly puzzled, Church grim.

'I think only a government conspiracy would be housed wholly in the government, would be cleaning up their tracks from the inside.' Another breath because it was getting harder now as the face that should be on that card swam into focus.

'And what stakes are big enough to set up a conspiracy like this inside the most paranoid part of the most suspiciously watchful organisation in the country?' I asked. 'I mean, who would you bribe, threaten and serially murder for without question?' I left the question hanging in the air. I looked at the others. Collier's face was pale, a look of shock creeping onto the placid visage. Church's jaw was tight as he stared at the floor between his feet. Only Milady seemed unfazed by what I had said, her face blank, eyes sharp.

'Say it.' Milady, voice level.

A last breath before the world changed, before I made the four of us the most dangerous people in England. 'Victoria,' I said, voice wavering. I swallowed. 'It's the Queen.'

No one said anything for a moment. Then Milady muttered

something loudly in a language that I didn't understand, though Church's snapped his head to look at her, a slight blush creeping up his neck.

Collier face by comparison was bloodless. 'I. That is. Ah.' He stopped, speechless, and hung his head slowly down till his chin rested on his chest.

'She was ill about ten years ago,' said Church. His voice was flat, steady. He looked around at us. 'Do you remember they almost had to call off the banquet for her jubilee?' Collier nodded and Church continued. 'Said it was the strain of too many public appointments. A year later she's no better, some of the papers start talking about abdication when, what do you know, while the Ripper's playing merry havoc in Whitechapel, she pops off for an extended break in Balmoral. Suddenly she's right as rain and the papers are full of the good news. Never mind the bread riots or the Ripper because the Queen is well again and all's right with the world. A testament to her hardy constitution.'

'It probably was in part,' I said, 'I imagine you would have to be hardy to survive an organ transplant.

'My God,' said Collier. 'If this got out it would mean abdication.'

'Abdication?' exclaimed Milady. 'The government would collapse and with Gordon as Prime Minister anything would be possible. Riots. Revolution. It could be the end of the monarchy altogether.'

'It would be all the Confederate States would need to finally make a play for Canada,' I said. 'With the Boers and the Zulus both flaring up again, the army would be stretched beyond the point of capability. It doesn't take much imagination to see that we would only need one or two other colonies to see an opportunity to rebel and the Empire would be in serious, possibly irreversible danger.'

'And some people would go to any lengths to preserve the Empire,' said Milady. 'Murder would barely register. Terror, mayhem, disorder at certain levels would be tolerated.'

We sat in silence again for a few moments, the weight of the truth pinning us down.

Church spoke first. 'So. What now?'

'The directive remains extant,' said Collier, pronouncing each word slowly and carefully. 'We identify those involved in the conspiracy and discreetly remove them from circulation. Which means the personnel in K17 and those they engaged to carry out the acts.'

'Did you know,' asked Milady, 'one of the reasons given for Sir Anthony Willard's knighthood was his charity work with the poor of the East End?' Church looked up at her as she continued. 'Yes, you wouldn't think it to meet him, but he very generously ran a free clinic for women who couldn't afford medical care. More than a few prostitutes were numbered among his patients. I remember them making a point of it at the unveiling of his new wing. Apparently they were tested for all sorts of things.'

She said it casually, as if the connection had suddenly occurred to her, but I wondered if that were really the case. It made me think of the way when I was young, my father would sometimes sit with my brothers and I, lay out a chess puzzle from a vast book and pretend ignorance of the answer so that we would see it for ourselves and win the prize of his hearty congratulations.

'Miss Green has been befriending his assistant and so may be able to shed some light on his current activities,' said Collier, the life beginning to come back into his tone. 'I will check on her progress.'

'And put a couple of Jays on him so we can pick him up when we need to,' said Church. 'We need to get after our friend from Preston, the pilot and whoever else she was working with.' He stood up and stretched out his shoulders. 'Sterling and I should get back and see if Patience has found anything. And we need to trace the other figure in the photos we got from Richardson. Sir Anthony might have been the one doing the surgery but there was someone else there as well.'

'One to cut them and one to mask his work,' I said, repeating the words that Richardson had said to us in his dressing room.

'That's it,' said Church, 'some lunatic who didn't mind hacking women about.'

A flash then in my mind: sheets soaked scarlet, a tiny broken form curled amongst them, its face battered in. 'Someone like that might be locked away by now,' I said, 'in gaol if not in Bedlam.'

'That may be the case, Sterling,' said Milady. 'He may be dead for all we know.' The amber in her eyes glinted. 'But until we know for certain let's leave him on the list, shall we?'

A knock at the door made us look round. It opened and Milady's bodyguard leaned inside. 'Ma'am. Patience is here. She says she has found them.'

18. Trip

I froze.

Around me the Jays did the same, instantly paused in mid-movement; their heads were moving slightly, each man tracking around him, gun up and aimed.

By the house, Church was motionless, door handle held in mid turn, head turned towards me. Slowly, ever so slowly, he brought his other arm up away from the door and waved it towards us. The meaning was clear: move back. The Jays obeyed instantly, shifting positions in a quick burst of steady and near-silent movement and settling into whatever cover they could find. They all wore dark blue police uniforms surmounted by black, state-of-the-art bulletproof waistcoats. All carried automatic weapons of a similar kind to those carried by the men who had attacked the Map Room. I caught the eye of one of them who was crouched next to a small statue of the Venus de Milo, the upper part of this version augmented, no doubt for the sake of decency, with a strategically placed garland of flowers. The Jay next to her raised his eyebrows, tilted his head at the statue and gave me a quick grin, conscious of the incongruity of the situation. I slowly backed along the path, pistol in hand. Glancing backwards I saw that, just beyond the

239

white gateposts at the end of the driveway, our driver – whose name I had discovered was Donaldson – was still standing by the van in his postman's uniform, smoking a cigarette in the unhurried style of a man without a care in the world.

I looked back to Church, who was, if anything, moving even more slowly as he rotated the door handle gently back to its resting position. This done, he stepped back from the door in a series of slow, careful steps, back down the garden path towards me. As he got closer I saw that, despite the sharpness of the air, several small beads of perspiration had formed across his forehead.

'There's a bomb rigged to the door,' he said in a low voice.

We'd travelled here in the back of a Royal Mail van, a brand new petrol-engined model, red paint gleaming, metal grill and headlights polished to a shine. Church and Patience had been up front in the cabin with Donaldson while I had ridden in the back with half a dozen Jays, including Mac, and a variety of equipment holders that put me in mind of cricket bags. It had taken the best part of an hour to drive from Regent Street down to Sydenham in south London, and an irresistible combination of military habit and tiredness meant I had slipped into a refreshingly dreamless sleep before we'd gone across the Thames.

The van was still by the time I had been nudged into wakefulness by a smirking Jay.

'Good kip, boss?' he had asked.

'Ideal,' I had replied, my head heavy with the grogginess of briefly snatched sleep. The ratcheting clicks of weapons being checked and readied had echoed around the van as I had shrugged myself into the ballistic protection waistcoat I was handed and belted on a side-holster and the boxy Colt self-loader that fitted neatly inside.

Two of the Jays had stayed in the back of the van. Mac

and four others checked in with Church briefly, then slipped through the gate and fanned out across the front garden of a large, suburban villa. The house looked recently built. Its imposing, red-brick form, gravelled driveway and carefully tended front garden spoke of pride and confidence in the face of any comparison with its fellows on either side. There were wheel marks in the driveway but no motor carriage and, as we had advanced, I had seen no sign of curiosity from behind the latticed windows, no residents glaring at the armed men not quite managing to avoid the rose beds.

'How do you know?' I asked, in the same low voice that Church had spoken in.

'Handle feels off, a little too heavy when I turned it,' Church replied. He looked at me. 'You any good with explosives?'

'Just basic training,' I said. 'You know, stay away from them.'

'Right,' he said. 'Mac!' he called over to the figure crouched near the gatepost, who stood up and walked across to us, eyes glancing past us to the house as he did, his weapon held at the ready.

'Problem?' asked Mac.

'I think the front door is booby-trapped. Any of your boys good with explosives?'

'Kelly knows his stuff.' Mac signalled to the Jay crouching next to Venus. The man darted across the lawn, keeping low to the ground.

'What is it, Sarge?' he asked Mac.

'Mr Church needs to borrow you, Kelly. There's a bomb rigged to the front door. You've volunteered to help him defuse it.'

Kelly gave a wry smile at the news. 'Right you are,' he said.

'With me, Kelly. You too, Sterling. Keep an eye on things, Mac,' said Church and walked back towards the house with

Kelly and myself in tow while Mac moved over to where Kelly had been next to the statue.

'Kelly?' asked Church, receiving a silent and minimal nod by way of reply. 'The door's rigged, could be an anti-personnel mine, could be something heftier. We need to get inside, find out what we're dealing with and clear it as soon as possible so we can search the place.'

'Yes, boss,' came the response.

'Let's take a look around the outside. Sterling, you too.' I followed along behind the two of them, Church gestured me off to the left of the house while he and Kelly moved to the right-hand side where an offshoot of the front path continued through a bright green wooden gate to the rear of the house. I looked over the two windows that I passed. Both were covered on the inside by white wooden shutters, though, leaning on the brickwork around the frame, I was able to catch small glimpses of the rooms through the small slits between them. As best as I could see there were no sign of any explosive devices attached to the windows, or on the doors to the rooms. Mahogany surfaces and the glint of cut glass made the one nearest the door a dining room while shelves of books and paperwork in the narrower room next to it seemed to suggest a study of some sort.

I followed the edge of the lawn round the house and down the side where the way was blocked by the same high wall that stretched between both sides of the house and the white, flat-rendered wall that separated this garden from its neighbours on either side. The only window I could see at ground floor level was a narrow, horizontal oblong at about head height. Probably the WC, I thought.

Suddenly I saw hands grip the top of the wall in front of me and Kelly quickly and silently heaved himself over to sit on top of the wall. Then, reaching down, he pulled Church up to join him and the two of them dropped to the lawn in front of me.

'Anything?' Church asked.

'Nothing on the windows themselves, as far as I could see,' I said.

'Same here,' said Church. 'But we saw what looked like a pressure plate inside one of the windows at the back. We have to assume there may be others. Could be just an alarm system. Or maybe the whole house is rigged to blow.' He paused and stabbed a finger at Kelly. 'So we'll need to keep an eye out when we go in.'

Kelly nodded soberly.

'The two of us will go in through the dining room,' said Church. 'I'll crack the window. Kelly, you'll go in first, clear the space under the window, then I'll follow you in and we'll clear the room first, then the hall to the door. We defuse if we can, detour round if we can't. I think we're looking at a couple of tripwires rather than the whole house but you never know. Sterling, you'd better wait by the van. Wait until I signal you that it's clear then come in. Tell Mac and his boys to stay outside and keep back from the house.'

'Got you. I'll let Mac know,' I replied, and walked over to where Mac was still in position. 'We'll go in once Church and Kelly have given things the once-over. Stand fast for now but stay back from the house and stay out of sight.'

'Understood,' replied Mac. He attracted the attention of his men, raised his arm and signalled them with a few clipped movements, receiving a nod from each man in acknowledgement.

Suddenly I heard a voice call out from the street. I walked across the gate to see a small, sombrely dressed and perfectly coiffured septuagenarian walking out from a gate further down the road. Behind her walked a housemaid carrying a tray of white mugs that steamed in the cold air.

I walked through to meet the new arrivals, Donaldson looking over at me with a look of gratitude as I did so. 'Can I help you, madam?' I asked, as the woman and her maid got closer.

'You can indeed, young man. But first, given the briskness of the weather today, I wondered if you and your men would like a cup of tea?' Her voice was a little unsteady with age at the edges but this did nothing to lessen the overall tone of confidence that she exuded.

'My men?'

'Yes indeed. Your good self, this charming gentlemen who has failed to extinguish his cigarette in the presence of a lady and, of course, the three more that are crouching in the garden behind the hedge. I wasn't sure if you had any more lurking in the van so I brought a few extra. Perhaps you could whistle or signal them in some way? The tea won't stay hot for long in this weather. If it would be easier I could ask Louisa to take the tray round to them?'

'That really won't be necessary, madam,' I replied, feeling like a man stepping outside his front door equipped for a light drizzle and finding himself confronted with a hurricane and for the briefest of moments defusing explosives seemed like it may have been the easier option. Next to me, meanwhile, Donaldson was hurriedly stamping the cigarette out under his shoe and pulling himself to silent attention. 'Why doesn't your girl put the tray on the bonnet there and we'll help ourselves?'

'Very well,' she replied. 'Louisa, why don't you do as he says, then run along back to the house and fetch my shawl for me would you?'

'Yes, Mrs Edwards,' said the girl with the tray nervously. She pulled her gaze away from the holstered pistol at my side and carefully placed the tea on the bonnet of the van before giving a small curtsey and half walking, half running down the road to a house further down and on the other side of the road.

'Now then,' continued Mrs Edwards in the same confident

tone, 'you really ought to tell me who you are, don't you think? I might otherwise draw all sorts of erroneous conclusions, particularly given those other two fellows of yours who seem to have disappeared inside the house. Completely illegally, I might add.'

Struggling slightly to reassert control in the face of her combination of gentility and inquisition, I reached under the bulletproof waistcoat into my pocket and pulled out my Special Branch ID. 'My name is Detective Superintendent Sterling, madam. We are investigating the illegal activity which we think was perpetrated from this address.'

She stared carefully at the identity card for a few seconds. 'Yes,' she said, her tone giving the impression she had reserved judgement on my legitimacy to the title, 'I supposed it would be something like that. Well Detective Superintendent, are you at liberty to tell me the nature of this illegal activity?'

I slipped the ID back into my pocket. 'I am afraid not, madam. It's a question of National Security.'

'Yes, I'm sure,' she replied. 'No doubt this explains why you felt the need to bring a small army along with you this morning.' She pointed at the tray. 'Look, why don't you ask your man here to hand these round. I am sure that your men would hate to waste it.'

I nodded at Donaldson, who grabbed up three of the mugs and took them into the garden.

'Now then,' the old lady said, 'what would you like to know about Mr Baxter?'

'Mr Baxter?' I said. 'Our understanding is that the house belongs to a young woman, a Miss Mills.' I described K17's tapper to her.

'Oh that's his niece, Katie. Such a lovely girl. Always brings him flowers when she visits. No, I'll think you'll find that the house belongs to Mr Baxter.'

'Has he lived here long?' I asked.

'He arrived just after myself and my late husband. We were the first to move in. It was, let me see, the January of '89 just after the houses were finished and Mr Baxter moved in a few months after that.'

'And could you tell me what line Mr Baxter was in, Mrs Edwards?'

'Oh he was retired because of ill health. He used to be a scientist for the government, apparently, in quite a senior position, but he was involved in some sort of accident and they pensioned him off. Hence him being able to afford to live here.'

'Could you describe him for me?'

'Small,' she said, 'only a few inches taller than me. Somewhat paunchy but sprightly in his step. Short grey hair, no beard. Younger than he looked. He had a tattoo. Is that helpful? I saw it on his arm once when he was gardening. It was of a bird of sorts clutching what looked like a wheel.'

'So you knew him very well?' I asked.

'Oh no, not really,' she replied. 'He kept himself to himself. And no wonder, the poor man,' she said, sadly. 'you could see that they had tried to mend his injuries but you could still see the scars on his face.' She shook her head. 'He was quite a lonely man, I thought, Detective Superintendent. He hardly ever left the house at all. He always had his groceries delivered and had very few visitors apart from his niece. He adored his roses. I don't think he could really have been involved in any sort of treasonous plot or whatever other sort of wrongdoing you suspect him of. And there is certainly no need for you to be armed. A less violent man I can't imagine.'

'Well Mrs Edwards, experience has taught us that we need to be careful in cases like this. This,' I patted my gun, 'is really here for our protection. And yours of course,' I added.

At which point the front door exploded.

I grabbed Mrs Edwards, my back to the house, and dropped us both to the ground, relaxing my grip as the sounds of clattering debris subsided.

'Well,' said Mrs Edwards as the explosion faded. 'I'm not sure this is entirely appropriate, Superintendent.'

I moved away from her. A quick glance up and down showed me she was uninjured, and, despite her levity, shocked. I stood and gently lifted her up, steadied her against the bonnet of the van.

I saw Patience leap up in her seat in the cab, pale faced and wide eyed, so I left Mrs Edwards leaning against there and pulled open the door. 'Stay with her.' I pointed at Mrs Edwards. Patience nodded, dazed, and began to climb down out of the cab. 'And don't move!' I shouted, though I could barely hear my own voice through the ringing in my ears.

The front of the house was a mass of white smoke. Two more Jays came running from the back of the van. I beckoned them to stop and, pointing at Patience and Mrs Edwards, I shouted, 'Look after them. Keep people back.' They both nodded and dashed off past me. The smoke was thinning slightly as I walked through the open gate, blown open, though still on its hinges. Mac was standing over the body of one of his men, lying halfway down the path, coated with a mixture of dirt and blood. Another was being helped up by his comrade from where he lay by the hedge, hands on his ears as he tried to clear the noise from his head. The front door was gone, replaced by a haphazard scattering of wood and metal debris, some of which was embedded in the side of the man that Mac was tending to.

'Mac,' I shouted. Laid my hand on his shoulder in case he didn't hear. He looked up at me, dazed. He shook his head then nodded, let the soldier down gently to the ground and stood. 'Move him to the van if you can. Keep everyone back. If the police turn up, keep them out. If they get shirty send for me.'

'Sir.'

I clapped him on the shoulder again and took a look at the man on the floor. He looked like he was breathing, just, but his breath was flecked with blood. Trusting Mac to be the best judge of how to look after his men, I walked through the smoke into the house. Once past the doorway it was surprisingly damage free though the air was thick with dust and fragments of glass and china littered the floor from a broken display cabinet on one side of the hallway.

'It was a shaped charge.' Church, shouting from where he stood in a doorway off the hall. He looked uninjured.

'What?' I shouted back.

'It blew the door out.'

'What happened?' I shouted.

'Bastards had wired in a hidden trigger. We both missed it.'

'Are you okay?'

Church nodded. 'I'm fine.' As he spoke Kelly pulled himself through the doorway opposite. Both of them looked bruised and grazed but didn't seem to be otherwise injured.

'Kelly!' I shouted. He looked at me, trying to focus. 'Go and help Mac. You've got a man down out there.' Kelly nodded and headed out through the wreck of the doorway.

'Is this all of it?' I asked Church.

He nodded. 'This was it, nothing else.' He was wheezing as he spoke and paused for a moment to cough loudly before he continued. 'We searched all the rooms down here. There's an engine upstairs. We need to get Patience in here. See what she can find.'

'Are you sure it's safe?'

'It is now.' He coughed. 'I'll go and get her and check on the others.'

'Tell her I'll wait here. Have you called Collier?'

Church nodded. 'The telephone was still okay. He's coming

himself with another squad of Jays. I told him to get an ambulance over here as well.'

'There's neighbour out there, Mrs Edwards,' I said. 'Sharp as anything. Make sure she gets home okay. And get someone to question her about the man who lived here. I think it was our pilot.'

Church nodded again and walked unsteadily down the hallway, kicking debris out of his way. Somewhere in the distance I heard the faint wail of a siren. There was shouting outside as the first onlookers arrived and were told to stay back. I looked around at the hallway and the spread of haphazard destruction. Nearer the blast the patterned tiles were scorched and broken, while further back they were unscathed. Only a few of the banister posts on the wooden stairs were split while beyond them the display cabinet's contents were almost completely disintegrated and near the door an oil painting of naval battle scene was merely hanging slightly askew. I straightened it, the crunch of glass under my feet as I stepped back to judge it level.

'Up a bit on the right.'

Patience stood in the doorway, hunched into a too-large black overcoat. I nudged the picture lightly.

'Perfect. Shame you can't do the same with the garden, eh?' She walked towards the stairs. 'Upstairs, Church said the engine was.'

'Is he alright out there?'

Patience stopped and looked back from halfway up the first flight. 'Church? He's surrounded by chaos, barking orders at men with guns. He thinks it's Christmas come early.' She turned the corner and walked up the next set of steps. 'Come on.'

I followed her up the stairs to first floor where a thick bundle of wiring ran along the bottom of the wall and disappeared through a doorway into one of the rooms. Patience ran ahead and disappeared inside. I heard a whoop of delight from the room and followed her in to see her caressing a large, covered engine that stretched across the width of the room, half blocking the windows at the end. 'This is amazing!' she said.

'What is?' I asked.

'This engine. It's brand new, top-of-the-line equipment. I've been asking for one for ages but Collier just kept telling me to make do. Look at it!' she turned round, her face bright with excitement. '800 kilodrum mill. Electric memory. Hi-speed data cylinders.'

'Good?' I ventured.

'Sterling, this is choice.' She pulled the cover off the engine, threw it on the floor and started flicking switches. The engine whirred into life, cylinders humming up to speed and, deep within its caged form, cogs whirred and span. The tiny squares of the screen rippled into life as strings of numbers and letters stuttered upwards. Patience pulled out a wheeled piano stool that was tucked under the desk and sat down. She held her hands a few inches above the keyboard for a moment, pausing like a concert pianist, then began to tap away.

I heard footsteps in the corridor outside and my gun was in my hand as I turned to face the door.

'Thought I'd find you in here.' Church was breathing more easily but his voice still sounded ragged.

'How are things outside?' I asked.

'Under control. Couple of uniforms just turned up, full of vim and outrage, why weren't they told etcetera etcetera. I flashed the badge which shut them up, but I hope Collier turns up before their Inspector does.'

'How is Mac's team?'

'Few scrapes and scratches for most of us. Coulter was nearest the door so he's the worst. Mac bandaged him up and we're waiting for the ambulance. Should be okay.' He took a long breath and looked at me. 'I should have seen that second trigger.'

'What happened?'

'We were all pleased with ourselves, Kelly and me. We knew what we were dealing with. They'd wired three anti-personnel charges together, then set them all facing outwards. Should have been easy to disconnect and disarm but they'd hidden a tamper switch in there. Kelly cut the first one and the whole lot went off. Luckily the blast on those things is designed to go forward so the two of us were pretty unscathed.' He shook his head. 'I should have seen it.'

'Maybe,' I said. 'Maybe not. Either way, let's debrief later. Focus on finding them. What have you got, Patience?'

'Nothing.'

'What do you mean, nothing?' Church said. He and I walked over to stand behind Patience, looking at the screen.

'I mean it's blank, they cleared it out before they left. Overpunched the cards, cleared the memory and wiped the cylinders.' She tilted her head back to look up at us. 'Sorry.'

'Did you say that you thought the pilot was here?' Church asked me, as Patience got off the chair and had a look around the engine.

'Did you meet Mrs Edwards?'

'I did. Wily old bird,' said Church.

'Her description of the chap who lived here, Baxter, matches the airship pilot who worked for K17. She told me about a tattoo that he had. Royal Aerial Navy.'

'You sure?'

'Positive,' I said, briefly remembering my brother Gus unveiling an identical tattoo after a drunken night in Hong Kong. 'She said he'd been here since early '89.' Patience was back in her chair now, reaching underneath the engine for something.

'The year after the Ripper murders,' said Church. 'They paid him off, hid him here. But why not just kill him.'

'In case they needed him again?' I guessed. 'I read some of the papers on organ transplants that Green got hold of. Even when the process is successful it only lasts for a few years. Seven years is the record. So even now they might decide to keep him alive.'

'But where? That's the problem,' said Church. 'Added to which, when I spoke to Collier just now he told me that the bloke running K17, Fuller was his name?'

'Sebastian Fuller,' I recalled.

'Well they sent a couple of Jays round to see him this morning but he'd gone. Wife had no idea where, only that he'd packed a suitcase.'

'So we're in the dark again.'

'Au contraire,' said Patience. 'Because luckily for you, I'm on hand to save the day. Again.' She spun her chair round, pointed at the screen with one hand and with the other typed out a rapid sequence of letters. 'Voila.' The page suddenly filled with information.

'I thought you said that it was empty,' I said.

'I did say that,' she replied. 'And that's what it looked like. What it was arranged to look like. Old tapper trick called drum-splitting. You section off part of the engine.'

'Like a false bottom in a drawer?' asked Church.

'Yes, I suppose so, a bit like a false bottom in a drawer. I mean, not really, but close enough.' She was hurriedly typing as she spoke now. Next to the engine a printing machine came to life and started its slow journey back and forth along the paper.

'So why would they have one?' I asked.

'I think their tapper put it there for us to find,' she said.

'Leonora's throwing her boss overboard,' said Church.

'What information is there?' I asked.

'It looks like telegrams, telephone call logs, telemessage transcripts. Thousands of them.'

'Can you tell if she made a copy?'

'Erm. Wait a sec.' The screen rippled and another set of data took its place. 'Yes!' Patience exclaimed. 'How did you know?'

'It's insurance. She's sending us a message,' I said. 'This will stay secret as long as we go after her boss and leave her alone. What's the most recent document?'

The screen rippled again. 'Rather dull really,' said Patience. 'It's a telegram requesting the use of a private room in an inn somewhere called Warehorne.' Patience read some more. 'It says to take the train to Ashford?' She pronounced the name uncertainly as if half-doubting its existence and the need to ever visit it. She tapped through the document. 'The booking is in the name of Sebastian Fuller.'

'What the hell is he doing down in Kent?' asked Church.

'He's leaving the country,' I said. 'And he's got his own insurance with him.'

'But where's he off to?' asked Church.

'Well,' I said, 'where would he find an easy, no-questions-asked market for secret information that would bring down the Queen, the British government and possibly the Empire?'

Church stared at me for a moment, then his face suddenly darkened in grim realisation. 'He's selling us out to the French.'

19. Local

We made slow going on our way out of London so that, by the time we got near the village, a clear night was beginning to fall across the countryside, the air sharpening with the promise of frost. We had left the mail van behind for Collier to take care of, one of the many incongruous additions to suburban London that he was using his skills to smooth away. Instead we were driving in a large motor car, a sort of half-sized coach that reminded me a little of the military transports that we used to sometimes be carted around in in Canada, though a much more civilian version thereof, with sleeker lines and a finer finish. There was plenty of room inside for me, Church, Mac and the three Jays who, least affected by the blast, were coming with us. Besides the seating there was a rear luggage compartment that now held a number of plain wooden crates along with the kit from the van, hurriedly ferried across while Collier ran interference. A local inspector had arrived just after Collier had, keen to reassert his authority, and a semblance of normal life, on his patch. Thanks to Collier's unmistakable aura of senior officialdom, and some suitably heavy name-dropping, we slipped away without a problem.

One of the Jays, a short, wiry fellow called Curtis, drove us.

He was out of uniform now and dressed instead, like the rest of them, in more casual, dark-hued clothes of the sort that a workman might wear. It was odd, I thought, but in some way changing out of police uniforms had made them seem more, rather than less, professional.

No one had talked about what happened in Sydenham on our way down to Kent. The Jays sat in the back of our vehicle in patient silence, with the occasional burst of low-toned conversation. They seemed to have put earlier events out of their mind for now, focusing on what might be waiting for us when we arrived at our destination. Church hadn't mentioned the bomb again and, as I didn't feel that there was much to say that we hadn't already said, I didn't bring it up. Instead, once we had left the final outskirts of London behind and were well into the Kentish countryside, we talked through ideas of how K17 might have functioned and discussed Fuller's motives for defecting.

France had had a reputation for espionage for as long as I could remember but under Napoleon V the craft of spying in the New French Empire had been elevated to a new level. An ex-military officer, of no relation to the Bonapartes but wisely seeing the advantage in taking their name, this Napoleon sought to rekindle the grand idea of empire-building possessed by the first of his name but with one key difference. While the race to colonise Africa was being fiercely contested by the other European powers, Napoleon V chose not to take part. Instead, the old Republic's Committee of General Security was reinstated with a new brief; to focus on the on-wire world of engines, telecommunications and data and to make it theirs. The result was that, though possessing a smaller empire geographically than the other major powers, its reach in the realm of information ensured that France punched well above its weight when it came to influence and intrigue. Paris became the pre-eminent location for the purchase and trading of secrets, and gained the reputation of being the sort of place where pretty much anything or anyone was available for sale. A senior agent like Fuller, with what he knew of the Bureau of Engine Security and its systems, would hold a high value in the Parisian spy markets. In addition, his knowledge of K17, and the proof that he carried with him in the shape of the missing airship pilot, would, if played well, assure him a new place of honour within the intricate pantheon of French espionage.

'He might decide to aim higher, of course,' I said.

'What do you mean?' asked Church.

'Well, as I understand it, France isn't the only purchaser of information to ply its trade in Paris,' I replied. 'So if Fuller was feeling particularly confident he might decide to cut out the middle man, as they say, and go directly to one of the other major powers. Prussia, for instance, or the Confederate States.'

Church nodded. 'Dangerous though, as an independent. You would have to put the word out in such a way that avoided tipping off the Security Committee. They really hate people going behind their back. And if he went to the Americans, they might grass him up to the French anyway.'

'So why take the risk?' I asked.

'Because he worked out who we are,' he said.

'That's what I've been thinking,' I replied. 'It's the only reason that makes sense. If he thought that we were reporters or even private investigators of some kind, he would have simply trumped up some charges and arrested us. Who knows about the Map Room?'

'There's a minister that oversees us,' said Church, 'at barge-pole's length of course. But no one else at cabinet level, not even the prime minister, knows any details in case we do something terrible,' he rubbed the flat of his palm across his stubbled chin, 'without a good enough reason.'

'But people have heard of you?' I asked

He shook his head. 'Had you? We tend to keep ourselves to ourselves. Some people in the business might guess that something like us exists, and they might have heard rumours about what we've done, but it's in everyone's interests not to guess too hard otherwise they wouldn't get to act all shocked and deny all knowledge when something like this morning happens.'

'I think someone like Fuller would make it his business to know who else might be operating in his arena,' I said. 'Even if he didn't know the name, he may have formed an idea of the kind of organisation you are. Then after last night, he and his tapper do some rapid adding up and come up with an answer they don't like. They check all the obvious suspects, MO5 and so on, but you and I aren't listed anywhere so that leaves only one other organisation, which, rumour says, doesn't play by the rules and isn't shy of expedient and robust problem solving.' I paused. 'So Fuller tells her to destroy all the evidence that's on their engine and, while she is doing that, he'll take care of the physical evidence.'

'And instead, they both betray each other,' said Church.

'Exactly. She disappears and Fuller makes a dash for France,' I said.

'Makes me wonder what other cleaning up he has stopped to do on the way,' said Church, 'or asked her to do? Maybe get rid of the two that actually carried out the crimes, the surgeon and the lunatic they used to cover up his work?'

'They might be dead already,' I said, seeing Edgar in my mind, blood on his chest and surprise on his face as he pawed at the air on the platform at Waterloo.

'They might be. It will have slowed him down though, so we might be still in with a chance of catching him,' Church said.

As we were talking we turned off what in my head I had been thinking of as a narrow country lane, which I now realised was a capacious thoroughfare compared to what we now found ourselves driving down. 'Here you are, boss,' said Curtis, deftly avoiding a tree trunk that jutted into the road, 'we just passed the sign for Warehorne.'

'Right, slow down and pull over before we get to the pub,' said Church. Behind us the other Jays started gathering their gear. 'What's it called again?' he asked me.

'The Woolpack Inn,' I replied.

'Right,' said Church, remembering.

'All we like sheep have gone astray,' I sang quietly. 'Church looked at me as if I'd gone mad. '*Messiah*,' I said. He stared at me blankly. 'Handel?' I added.

'If you say so,' he said. 'Any good is it?'

'That does seem to be the generally held opinion,' I said. Church made no reply.

We came to a halt at a point where the lane widened and where we could leave the van concealed under a cluster of trees. We all got out, and Mac set Curtis and another Jay to stay with the vehicle, though to bring it up quickly if they heard any kind of trouble. Church and I then walked towards the village while Mac and the Jay he had brought along, a hard-faced Scot called Baker, flanked out wide in front of us and on either side of the road They were in the same ballistic waist-coats they had worn in Sydenham but instead of automatic rifles they were both carrying squat, black pistols fitted with large silencers. Their dark clothing, gloves and blackened faces meant that, even in the full moon that shone down out of a clear sky, I kept losing sight of them. Church and I by contrast were dressed in suits, coats and hats as we walked down the road, our pistols holstered out of sight.

The lane curved slowly round to the left and as we walked

on a little further an inn came into view, its windows glowing with light and warmth. A pair of old-fashioned lanterns mounted on posts lit either end of the pub's driveway where it swung in from the road. It was an old building, perhaps a few hundred years in age but it was well cared for, with whitewashed walls and no sign of the disrepair that I might have expected from a pub in such a remote location. Not quite opposite the pub was an even older church, sitting on higher ground that rose gently away from the road that we were walking along. Again, the church was well looked after, its low wall and grounds well maintained, with a small flock of sheep grazing amongst the gravestones. It struck me that, though remote and small, Warehorne wasn't quite the down-at-heel hamlet that I had first imagined it would be. Beyond the church I could make out a small cluster of cottages strung out along one side the road while opposite them were a few grander houses, though none sizable enough to be that of the local landowner.

As we drew level with the pub we could make out its sign in the moonlight and the horse struggling beneath a load of white bales told us that we were in the right place. Now that we were close enough we could hear the noise of conversation and laughter from within and, under it, the sound of music.

'Hold on, Sterling. How do you want to play this?' asked Church as we reached the door to the pub.

'You're Arthur, I'm Ralph and our motor carriage has broken down. Let's take it from there and see how we go,' I said.

'Sounds like a plan.'

Church pulled the door open and stepped aside to let me go in first.

Inside was a porch and a second door which I walked through into the welcome warmth of the public bar. It was a large room, plainly furnished but homely with some nice photographic prints of country life hung on the walls. The room was lit by gas lamps around the walls and the low red glow of a large inglenook fireplace that took up almost the entire left wall of the room. Next to this fire sat a trio of men in tweed trousers of varying degrees of sophistication, their matching coats hanging up on a row of pegs nearby. Two more patrons stood next to the finely carved, dark wooden bar, one a younger man in relatively well-turned-out business attire, the other much older, with a red-faced complexion set off by a startlingly overgrown set of white whiskers.

On the other side of the bar a tall but elderly barman was carefully pulling a pint, which I rather imagined may have been the focus on attention for at least one of them until we walked in. At this precise moment, however, all five customers were looking in our direction with guarded expectation and not a little suspicion, as if judging what level of unwelcoming manner to reward us with. I walked up to the bar while Church closed the door behind us and came to stand slightly to one side of me, towards the trio by the fire.

'Good evening,' I said, as cheerily as I could.

The man standing nearest to me, he of the white whiskers, took a deep drink from a pint glass of something pale and murky that may have been cider. As if acting on a signal, the rest did likewise, all in silence, and for a brief moment I entertained the idea of trying out French to see if that would make any difference. For a few moments the only sound in the room was provided by a cylinder player tinkling its way through a jaunty, music hall tune on a low table by the windows.

'Good evening gentlemen!' The barman, having finished pouring the pint which he placed in front of one of the men, now turned his attention to us. 'There's nothing hot till six o'clock if that's what you're after but there's mutton that I could use for sandwiches. Or maybe some hot cider to warm away the cold?' His accent was softly burred, slightly like the accent of a West Countryman, though less strident and with the slightest trace of London woven through it.

'Well a drink sounds like a brilliant idea, doesn't it Arthur?' I said to Church.

'Always does to me,' he replied, beaming at the room in a cheerily convincing way. 'I'll have a pint of ale along with a wee dram of something, as those Scottish laddies say.'

'Same for me, barman,' I said. 'And while you're doing that could you think of somewhere nearby where we can have our car repaired?'

The barman looked up, paused with his hand on the beer pump. 'Ashford would be closest, wouldn't it lads?'

At this point, our attentive audience, whose intent scrutiny of the two of us had shown no sign of waning, replied to the barman by variously agreeing with his suggestion, puzzling loudly over possible alternatives, suggesting that we could try walking to Hamstreet, and, in the case of whiskers, proclaiming us bloody fools to break down with the weather the way it was.

'What's the problem with the car?' asked the office worker once his companions had had their turns. He was a youngish and thin-faced man who, unlike the others, sipped carefully at his pint rather than gulping it down as if for sustenance.

I smiled as I spoke to him. 'You know, I'm not sure. It's quite a new kind of car, some sort of combustion engine. I'm not really an expert you see.'

'It's not steam then?' asked the red-faced fellow, who in my head I had begun to think of as Rufus.

'No, it's not.'

'Or electric neither?' asked one of the men by the fire, about the age of Rufus but in better shape, thick armed and broad shouldered. Though dressed in fairly coarse tweed, he sported a rather thick and ornate gold watch chain. He took a few large gulps of the ale he was drinking, emptying his glass and holding it above his head to catch the barman's attention.

'No,' I said, 'it runs on petrol. Oh thank you,' I added as the barmen placed our drinks down on the bar. He pocketed the coins that I gave him and turned his attention to the man by the fire, taking his empty glass and beginning to refill it.

Church had thrown back his whisky while I was paying but waited for me to pick up my own pint then, with a quiet 'cheers', he took a sip of ale.

'Cheers,' I said.

'By the way, where are you off to?' asked the young man in the suit.

'On our way down to Rye,' I said. 'For a birthday party.'

'Bit of an odd way to come,' continued the young man.

'Now, now, young Matthew,' said the barman, handing Gold Chain's refilled glass back to him, 'let these gentlemen catch their breath.'

'It's okay,' I said. 'Actually we were stopping off along the way to pick up a couple of friends. Maybe you've run into them?

'Maybe,' said the barman, busying himself under the bar.

'There's two of them,' said Church, 'one's about Ralph's age, tall, well-dressed, short beard, name of Seb Fuller and the other one's older, shorter, balding, called Baxter.'

I took another drink. In the silence that followed Church's description, the only sound came from the player by the window, its finished cylinder spinning endlessly in silence, the needle jumping with a small click as it did so.

'Here,' said Rufus, indicating us with an unsteady wave of his glass. 'They're them.'

'Them who?' I asked, pint in hand.

'The ones we were warned about,' he continued, winking grandly at the barman. 'Foreigners.'

'I think there's some mistake,' I said, taking a sip of ale. 'Nothing foreign about us.'

'Oh I think we'll be the judge of that,' said the barman, straightening up from behind the bar and, as he did so, raising the shotgun that was in his hands and aiming it at the two of us. Rufus and the young man next to him stepped away from the bar, moving over into a doorway leading through into the other bar. The three by the fire, meanwhile, held us intently under what they surely imagined to be watchful observation. Church and I both raised our hands.

The barman spoke again. 'Check outside, Matthew.'

The young man strode over to the door and flung it open before walking outside and having a look round, then coming back in and closing it again. 'No one out there, George.'

'Good,' said the barman. Now bolt it shut and come back over here. Now you two gentlemen,' he continued, gesturing at us with the barrel of the gun, 'I'm going to have to ask you to stand very still while Matthew here calls the constable in Hamstreet.' He nodded behind him. 'Phone's in the other bar, Matt, the number for the constable is on the wall next to it.' The young man left his station by the door and walked through to the other bar.

'George is it?' I asked. The barman said nothing but he couldn't very well deny it. 'George. If you could let me reach into my pocket, I have some identification that I would like to show you.'

'Oh, going to try and tell us that you're police now are you?' asked Gold Chain. 'The Colonel said you would try and pass yourselves off as constables of some sort.'

'The Colonel?' asked Church. 'Which Colonel would that be?'

'Ha!' said Rufus from the doorway. 'Shows how much you know. His name isn't Fuller, it's McKindrey and he's a colonel in Army Intelligence.'

'He's been spying in France!' declared one of the mean by the fire.

'On Her Majesty's service!' added Rufus.

'Is that a fact?' asked Church.

'He told us that he was being followed by two men from a Foreign Power,' said George the barman while holding his shotgun steady and covering Church and myself with his aim.

'Did he say which one?' asked Church, barely containing his exasperation with the situation.

'The Prussians it was I thought,' said Rufus.

'No, no, it was the French,' said Gold Chain.

'All he said was European,' said George, seeming to become a little exasperated himself at the contributions of his clientele.

'Tell me, George. What's your opinion of young Matthew?'

'Why do you ask?' replied George, his eyes narrowed with suspicion.

'I mean,' I said, 'do you think he is a sharp enough young man?'

'He should be,' said Rufus, 'he's George's nephew.'

'He doesn't know what he's talking about,' said George.

'I see,' I said. 'Well then, I'd like you to be very calm and think very carefully what you do next, George.' I paused. 'Because by the time that you manage to flick your safety off, my man behind you will have shot Matthew through the head.'

Panic showed in the barman's eyes for a second, then he regained his composure. 'Will he now? You know, that trick was old when I was young so I think I'll just keep an eye on the two of you,' he said and smiled, confident in the knowledge that he had seen through me. 'Matthew,' he shouted. 'How's that phone call coming?'

And suddenly Mac was there, immediately behind the barman, pressing the gun to the back of his neck, causing most of the room, including the barman, to give a startled jump, and while I threw myself to the left, Church dived in to push the shotgun upwards so that the blast went into the ceiling. I bounced back off the wall next to the fireplace, dislodging a picture as I did, and looked around, drawing my revolver. The barman was kneeling down with his hands folded on his head, Mac covered him while Church, now holding the barman's shotgun, was telling the rest to do the same. The gold chain wearer by the fire looked as if he was going to try something while Church's attention was divided but he paused, half-risen from his stool, when he saw my pistol and sat slowly down again.

The other Jay, Baker, appeared in the doorway, pushing the barman's nephew in front of him and making him kneel down next to Rufus. Having done that, he stepped back a few yards from the pair and readied his weapon with a loud, mechanical click.

'Now then George,' I said, 'I am going to reach into my pocket and pull out my identification and prove to you that we are who we say we are.'

'You expect me to believe you're some sort of policemen after what you have just done,' said the barman. 'I don't think so.'

'It would be fake anyway. You're no policemen,' said Gold Chain from the fireplace. The men with him muttered their agreement.

'That's right,' said Rufus from where he was kneeling in the doorway and half leaning on a chair next to him, 'and those fellows are made up like dervishes! No Englishman would do such a thing!'

I sighed. 'Okay, have it your way,' I said, 'We are agents of a foreign power searching for Colonel McKindrey and if you don't tell us what we need to know, I will order my men to kill one of you every minute till we get what we want.' I turned my wrist and pushed back my sleeve with a flourish, displaying my watch for the benefit of all.

Church looked across at me and raised an eyebrow, sceptically. I shrugged by way of reply.

A silence slowly filled the bar while I ostentatiously watched the second hand on my watch.

The moment the minute was up I spoke: 'Alright men. Let's start with the boy.'

'A man came and took them outside,' said the barman. 'He looked official. I heard them say something about an airship.' He looked directly at me. 'You'll never catch them,' he added, defiantly.

'Tie them up,' I said, 'put the telephone out of action, and I'll get the car.' I unbolted the door, opened it and turned to face the room. 'Dankeschön meine Herren!' I said, and stepped as dramatically as I could into the night.

Behind me in the room I heard a triumphant 'Told you' before Church shouted them into silence.

20. Springheels

'What does it look like?' I called up.

'It's small. An aerial sloop maybe,' came the shouted reply from Church, standing on the flat top of a family memorial at the top of the slope. He was squinting into a pair of powerful nightscope binoculars. 'Looks like they're making straight for the coast.'

I turned to Mac, standing next to me. 'How fast do those things go?'

He thought for a moment. 'In this wind? Maybe fifteen knots.'

'We'll never catch it.'

'We've got some springheels with us,' Mac replied. 'Might do it. Curtis, get Garner and bring them up here.' Curtis headed back through the graveyard and vaulted over the low wall into the road where the car was parked.

Church dropped down from the memorial and stood looking over Baker's shoulder at the map spread out on its stone surface. 'How far away are they?'

'Looks like five-and-a-half, maybe six miles,' replied Baker. 'If they're doing fifteen knots they'll be over the coastline at

Dungeness in about...' he looked at the map, 'twenty minutes give or take.'

'And how long will it take us to catch them?' I asked.

The Jay looked at me. 'In springheels?' He smiled wryly, 'About twenty minutes, give or take.'

'Better get a move on then,' said Church as Curtis and Garner came up the path carrying a long wooden crate which they put down on the ground near us. Curtis dropped a crowbar on top before the two ran back to the car again. Church took the crowbar and prised off the lid. 'Baker,' he said, 'help Sterling get into these. Mac, let's get the rest of the kit.'

'These' turned out to be what looked like a metal set of legs, about four feet long and made of heavy brass. Visible within each leg was a mass of rugged looking gears while a central piston ending in a long, jointed foot protruded partially from the bottom. 'Right then,' said Baker, 'let's get you strapped in, boss.' He lifted out the first of them. 'Easier if you sit down.' He pointed to a nearby gravestone in the shape of a curved coffin lid. I sat down and waited while he guided my feet into the legs, then clicked home curved metal facings that wrapped securely around the bottom half of my legs. Once this was done he pulled me to my feet so that, now elevated by the mechanical extensions, I towered over him precariously, holding onto his shoulder for balance. 'One last thing, sir,' he said and reached down to the legs, tugged quickly at a metal ring on each of them that came away, bringing with it a long ripcord. Almost immediately the legs hissed into action, pistons extending them a few feet further, while around my legs I suddenly felt some sort of inflatable material expanding to hold them firmly in place and, in a few moments, I realised, balancing was no longer a problem. They must have been gyroscopically stabilised, I thought, as I tried a few tentative steps then stopped. I looked across the graveyard to where a small flock of sheep, wary of this intrusion into their normal routine, regarded me with mute disapproval.

'Best keep moving,' said Baker, looking up at me.

'Why?' I asked.

'Because the engine in the middle of them is chemical and it tends to overheat if you stand still for too long,' said Church putting down another of the crates.

'It blows up,' explained Baker cheerfully.

Curtis and Garner dropped down two more while Mac dropped down two of the large, black canvas bags that had been ferried across from the postal van. 'Baker,' he said, 'get one of the rockets out and give Sterling a quick run through.'

'Rockets?' I asked.

'Hale Mark Nines,' called Baker bending down to unzip one of the canvas bags and standing back up holding a dull grey metal tube, about four feet long and about ten inches wide, with a pistol grip about halfway down and a canvas carrying strap fixed along its length. Baker held it up to show me. 'Have you used one before?' I shook my head. 'You have to release the cover first.' He unclipped a metal cover from one end and, as he did so, a portion of barrel seemed to automatically extend itself several more inches. 'Then you flip up the sights,' he continued. 'Use them to aim. Lift up the trigger guard and you'll see two trigger buttons built into the handle.' I nodded as he showed me. 'The top trigger fires wire guided up to eight hundred yards; keep the target in the sights and the rocket will follow wherever you point. You'll get a warning bell when you're about to run out. Hold down both triggers for free fire which is good for about a thousand yards.' With some struggling he managed to clip the lid back on and pass it up to me. 'The warhead's high explosive, will go straight through anything less than three-inch armour.'

'Which that ship shouldn't have anyway,' said Church,

standing up now in his own pair of the mechanical legs. I saw that Mac was also fitting a pair as was the wiry Curtis. Baker carried on unpacking rocket tubes similar to the one that he had given me. Reminded by a growing warmth under my feet, I took a few steps across the grass to look from the top of the slope across the countryside that fell away below us. Off to my left a single narrow lane wandered out from the village and disappeared between a dark patchwork of fields studded intermittently by the shapes of farm buildings. At the very edge of the horizon I could just make out the slim shape of the airship, starkly silhouetted in the moonlight. Somewhere in the village behind me I heard a dog bark for a few seconds then fall silent.

I hoisted the rocket over my shoulder by the carrying strap. It was bearably uncomfortable in the way that I had learnt to associate with any item of equipment designed by the British Army for one man to carry. 'Something that small will be using hydrogen.'

'That's right,' said Church, walking in short, bouncing steps to come and stand next to me. He looked at me. 'It's your directive, Sterling. What do you want to do?'

I looked at Church for a moment, as we were joined by first Curtis and then Garner, each moving easily on their own springheels. Each of them had a rocket slung across his back.

'Let's bring it down,' I said, feeling for the top of my shoulder holster and making sure it was fastened securely.

And we set off.

I went over the graveyard's small wall with as much thought as I would normally give to stepping off a curb, the bouncing action in the springheels' pistons making it effortless. Church and the two Jays followed, all of us picking up speed as we went down the hill, each loping stride accompanied by a sharp pneumatic hiss. It felt less like running and more like flying. The combination of pell-mell speed and slow bounds made effortless by the machinery of the springheels was glorious and after only a few moments of this I found myself grinning like a delighted child.

We flashed past a sparse line of bare-branched trees that marked the boundary of the slope, variously leaping round or through their whipping branches and across the fields that lay on the other side. The ground there was softer, slowing us down enough that we spotted the canal before we dashed headlong into it. It looked too wide to jump even wearing the springheels and I was glad that Mac led us to the corner of the field and onto a lane running towards a small bridge.

We clattered noisily over it and found ourselves on the other side following the road past the yard of a small farmhouse, where a startled farmer stared at us, white faced, eyes wide in terror as we flew past, legs hissing and coats flapping behind us. Next to him a black collie crouched in confusion, crawling behind its master's legs where they were rooted to the spot. Beneath and around us the land flashed past as we sped along. We kept our course as straight as the land would permit us, while avoiding the marshier looking areas that increased in number the closer we got to the coast. Mac led the way, ranging ahead of the rest of us at times to scout out the land.

A few minutes later, Mac raised his right arm above his head and slowed his pace, turning his last few steps into a deft half-pirouette as he halted and waited for the rest of us to catch up.

'Village ahead,' said Mac as we reached him. 'Looks soft going either side so it's probably best to go straight, then use the road for a while before we head for the coast again.'

'Any sign of life?' asked Church.

'Everyone looks tucked up inside to me,' replied Mac.

'Fine. Let's cut through,' I said. 'As quick as we can.'

Mac took the lead again as we moved onto the road and followed it towards the crossroads where the village started. Moving quickly on the hard surface we picked up speed so that by the time we reached the first houses we were travelling down the main street faster, I'd wager, than anyone had ever done before. The village was too small for gas lamps and what little light there was came from the shuttered windows of houses and, as we came to the centre of the village, the cheery glow warmth of the pub. Mac was just past it and I was following on, the other two behind me, when the door suddenly flew open as I drew level, disgorging a handful of farm labourers, lost in cheerfully loud conversation and oblivious to their surroundings.

Moving too quickly to change direction, I simply leapt up and over them, landing my next step onto the roof of the pub's porch and then the roof of the pub itself, the springheels easily carrying me over and directly to the ground on the far side. I landed on both legs with a heavy thump that forced the pistons almost totally back into the frames of the legs and almost, but not quite, had me over. I recovered, though, and set off again, accelerating to catch up with the others and leaving the sounds of disbelief and astonishment in our wake.

We regrouped, a few hundred yards past the village, at another crossroads.

'Didn't take you for a hurdler,' said Church as I arrived.

'Nice one, boss,' said Curtis, smiling, 'Those yokels will still be scratching their heads at that a week from now.'

'Thanks,' I said. 'Okay, Mac, which way now?'

'We can't keep heading straight across country,' said Mac. 'It's getting marshier so we'll have to work our way back and forth a bit.'

'Maybe not,' I said.

'Why not?' asked Church.

By way of an answer I pointed down one arm of the crossroads, which was signposted towards Rye. Just along the road a red triangle was mounted on a post, and under it, a silhouette of a train with the letters LCDR.

'Because I think instead we might avail ourselves of the goodwill of the London, Chatham and Dover Railway,' I said, and set off down the road at a gentle, long-limbed trot. After a few hundred yards we came to a gated crossing point. I stepped over the gate and looked over in each direction but there was no sight or sound of a train along the tracks. Church stepped over and stood next to me. 'Branch line,' he said. 'Probably doesn't run at the weekend and in any case, we'll just have to keep an ear out, right Mac?'

'Right you are Mr Church. Curtis you get up front. I'll take the rear.' So saying, he bounded down the track for about 100 yards, then did the same sort of neat, balletic turn that he had when we stopped earlier and raised his hands, signalling us to set off.

There was enough room either side of the tracks for us to avoid the tricky surface of the sleepers as long as we kept in single file, spaced over a few hundred yards and each of us keeping an ear open for the sound of steam or whistle. We heard neither as we sped along, so Church's guess must have been right, and we saw little sign of life along the railway line as it took us deeper though brackish marshland. It briefly passed through the edge of another village as we got nearer the coast and then we were firmly into a barren coastline of coarse sand, dotted with short clumps of dune grass and shingle.

The only building I could see was the lighthouse, towards which the railway line seemed to be gently curving and to the right of which the airship was clearly aiming as it serenely carried Fuller and his treachery on towards the Channel. At its base I could clearly see the windows on the small cabin which looked less cramped than I might have imagined and, just faintly, I could hear the thrumming of its engines. We had made good ground on them and I was trying to estimate how much closer we would have to get in to be within range when, a few hundred or so yards ahead of me and Church, Curtis must have decided he was close enough. I slowed to a walk and watched him as I saw him go through the same quick motions that Baker had showed me back in the graveyard and bring the rocket up to his shoulder.

A second or so later there was a bang and a steady rush of noise as the rocket raced up towards the airship. Curtis must have been using the wire-guidance mechanism because I could see him making slight adjustments and the missile shifting as it flew so that, a second or so later, it had curved a parabola towards the cabin and was about to strike when suddenly an arc of explosions rang out directly in the rocket's path, detonating it some twenty or thirty yards short.

'Counter-rocket munitions,' I heard myself say, remembering my brother describing the German airship in Montreal airport. Hard on the heels of the explosion a stream of tracer fire hammered out from the back of the airship at the ground by the base of the rockets' launch. Moments later came the rattling sound of the machine-gun as it reached out across the sky and I saw Curtis go down next to the railway line and lie still.

I could hear the sound of Mac's springheels as he charged up the path behind us and it struck me that the three of us were clumping nicely for whoever was on the other side of the trigger up there when suddenly the tracer fire erupted again, only this time it was carving a path down the railway towards us.

'Scatter!' shouted Mac behind me but I was already moving, heading diagonally away from the track across the dunes, legs pumping as I forced every last ounce of power out of the springheels, Tracer bullets screamed through the air behind me, splintering railway sleepers, but I didn't look back, just kept running wide and trying to see what the airship was doing, whether he would keep heading straight or turn and try to finish us off. He turned and the night echoed with the sound of machine-gun fire for a few more seconds, the white streaks of tracer rounds eagerly reaching for targets. Then silence.

'Reloading!' I heard Church shout off to my right and seconds later saw another rocket whoosh up towards the airship as he or Mac tried their luck. They must have decided against staying in one place to guide it, just fired and run; it was close but still narrowly missed the rear of the airship and whistled off across the water. I kept moving, picking up speed as I left the dunes, and found myself running across a flat, open expanse of scrubland, as inviting a background for a machine-gunner as I could have found. He was still taking things personally, though, up there at the back of the airship and the next stream of tracer flashed down to the site of the second rocket launch before being walked back and forth in a pattern of short bursts.

I kept running forwards, trying to get closer to the airship while at the same time staying out of its gunner's eyeline. The lighthouse was in front of me and, as I ran, I saw another, similar shape in the darkness, though shorter, wider and unevenly edged. As I drew closer and my eyes grew used to it, I saw the geometric conundrum for what it was; a second, partially completed lighthouse surrounded by scaffolding. An idea forming in my mind, I ran harder.

A few hundred yards further on from the second launch, a third rocket streaked up towards the airship. This one was on target but, as with the first, a ripple of small explosions caught it before it reached the cabin. Once again a staccato burst of tracer fire probed the launch site.

Even as I got closer to the lighthouses, the airship was moving slowly away along the coastline, seemingly in no hurry to make a dash for the continent. They knew they were safe from attack, I guessed, but either wanted to make sure of it, or, if Fuller had told them who we were, were taking the opportunity to remove some opposition. Someone was still moving over there, either Mac or Church keen on keeping their attention away from me. Another burst of fire rattled out in response. I reached the scaffolding and kept moving, the springheels taking me quickly up the ramp that led up around the scaffolding of the new lighthouse until I reached the wooden platform at the top. From there I could see the top of the existing lighthouse, no more than twenty yards or so away and a few yards higher from where I stood.

I walked back to the far end of the wooden platform and sprinted along it, waiting till the last minute before I jumped, feeling as though I hung in the air for a brief moment of heart-stopping terror before slamming against the outside of the old lighthouse and sprawling on the metal walkway surrounding the light chamber at the top, the rocket in its case thumping painfully into the back of my head. I tried to get to my feet and realised that, choosing exactly this moment to run out of their energy, the springheels had become cumbersome weights again. I reached down and found the clips where Baker had fixed them, managing to unclip them both and extricate myself from the machinery. I stood up and unslung the rocket. I unclipped the rocket cover and hefted its weight on my shoulder.

About six or seven hundred yards away, and not much higher than I was now at the top of the lighthouse, the airship had slowed to a crawl and, confident in its superiority, was firing in short, controlled bursts into the darkness. I hoped that Mac and Church were still, somehow, alive down there.

I flicked up the trigger cover and looked through the sights at the airship, then lifted the rocket up to point at the blank sky above it and pressed the button. The rocket roared out of the cylinder and raced away up into the night sky. Lifting my eye away from the sights I held the trigger down and watched the rocket climb then, as the bell trilled to tell me that the wire was almost used up, I jerked the cylinder back down to point at the airship. In response the rocket dived straight down, exploding through the roof of the airship to set off an enormous explosion that ripped the airship apart and, for the briefest of moments, lit the beach up like day.

It took me a while to force an entry into the old lighthouse and make my way back down but when I reached the beach the flames were still burning.

21. Mapmaker

The tick of the clock on the mantelpiece had the tone that all clocks have in rooms where someone will be required to wait; a persistent, nagging reminder not just of time passed but of time lost. Aside from the clock's tick, the occasional scratch of the secretary's pen and the faint, almost inaudible murmur of city bustle from outside the window, the room was silent.

I had been listening to the clock for twenty-seven minutes.

The low, wooden table next to me was a rich, brown in colour. Its surface was inlaid with either 208 or 214 small wooden diamonds, depending on how one counted the half diamonds around the sides of the pattern. There was a bronze bust on a plinth by the door to the managing director's office, but from where I was sitting it was almost impossible to make out the features in any detail.

Apart from myself and the principal secretary, the only other person in the room was a serious-faced young woman whose name and role I could only guess at. She was in the same position that she had been when I arrived; head bowed, eyes intently scanning a thick sheaf of papers in front of her. Occasionally, with no pattern of regularity that I could discern, she would turn a page over onto the other side, place it upon a different pile and make a mark of some kind in a large binder next to her.

The secretary had received four telephone calls in the time that I had been sitting waiting. In each case his responses had been too brief and hushed to deduce the nature of the calls.

An electronic bell trilled briefly on the secretary's desk, to which he responded by lifting a handset and speaking into it in a low voice. Replacing the handset, he pushed back his chair and, gesturing to the door behind him, said, 'Viscount Millbrook will see you now, Mr Sterling.'

I stood, hoping that cramp hadn't set in and, as guided by the secretary and walking behind him, passed through into the office beyond the door.

'My Lord, this is Mr Sterling from the Royal Office of Topography & Survey.'

'How do you do Mr Sterling?' The man behind the desk was slim, a few years older than me. His grey hair was cut severely short, his clothing plain but impeccably tailored. The wide expanse of mahogany desk in front of him was as neatly ordered as he was. He came round the desk to greet me as he spoke, extended his hand.

'Lord Millbrook,' I said, exchanging a firm shake.

'Would you care for some refreshment?' he asked me, indicating one of the chairs on my side of the desk.

'A coffee would be lovely, thank you,' I replied.

'See to it, please, would you, Mr Longley?' Lord Millbrook walked back to his chair and sat down.

'Of course, my lord,' the secretary replied, giving a slight bow and exiting the room with quiet and practised ease.

I looked at Julius with grudging admiration as the secretary left. The last time that he had seen me was eight years ago, when I had been sitting in a stale and crumpled dinner suit, wearing handcuffs, and listening in shock as he explained why ten years' exile was the best offer I could expect. And yet, except for the briefest flash of recognition, he was exuding the calm and polite demeanour of a powerful and busy man facing an almost certainly unimportant visitor. There was a moment of silence before he spoke.

'When you weren't at the funeral, I rather assumed that common sense had prevailed and that you had given up on Augustus's ridiculous scheme. I see now, however, that I was being hopelessly optimistic.' He sighed briefly, a rare mannerism of his that was broadly equivalent to a shouted stream of curse-laden invective in most ordinary people.

'I suppose I should be glad to see you alive, Ti.' A name from our early childhood, before I had decided I preferred the less-mocked Charles to the cumbersome Tiberius.

I was silent.

'I went to Father and told him about your and Gus's inept scheme to bring you home, you know.'

'And he wouldn't hear of it, I expect,' I replied. 'I learnt well enough in Canada what he thought.'

'Of course,' Julius said, 'because he knew you were safe there. But of course, given the self-absorbed, fat-headed fool that you are, settled in your role of unforgiven exile, you never saw that. Poor little brother, so busy shouting angrily at the unfairness of the world around you that you ignore what is actually going on around you.' Another small sip. 'He would have given anything to have you there, at the end, but he knew you couldn't be and didn't blame you.'

'It doesn't sound much like him.'

'What happened to you changed him,' said Julius. He seemed about to say more but at that moment the door opened, and the secretary returned with a silver tray on which sat an exquisitely fine Wedgwood coffee set in purple and gold, the letters VR emblazoned in gold on the side.

'Thank you, Longley, we'll manage for ourselves,' said Julius as the secretary placed the tray down on the desk and reached for the handle of the coffee pot. Longley, though evidently surprised by this, did as he was told and left us alone once again. Julius poured two cups of coffee for us and handed mine across to me, rising briefly from his chair as he did.

Julius took a small, precise sip from his cup. When he spoke again it was in a more formal tone.

'Well. I dare say we could arrange for a discreet visit for you to pay your respects. Would I, however, be labouring under a vain expectation in imagining that you might be returning to Canada in the near future?'

'There's no need,' I replied.

'I most strongly disagree.'

'What I mean to say is,' enjoying the moment, 'I have been fully pardoned.'

He was silent for a moment. 'Is this anything to do with Edgar Huntingdon's death?' Julius paused. 'Was that you?'

'People do die in duels,' I said, 'but no, the pardon is nothing to do with that. Arranged in recognition for services rendered to the crown.'

An eyebrow went up at that, a well-worn Julius Maddox trademark. 'And may I ask the nature of these services?'

'You may,' I said. 'but I'm afraid I am not at liberty to say,' enjoying the almost-unique experience of being one up on him.

Julius lifted my visiting card from his desk. 'Though the use of a pseudonym is, shall we say, suggestive of their nature at the very least.'

I shrugged my shoulders and smiled. 'Given the line of work I'm not sure about that but at least you can stop worrying about the Maddox family name.'

He smiled back and something was reconnected in that

moment, something that had dropped away from us for a good few years.

He stood, then, the conversation evidently over. 'Mr Sterling.'

'My lord.' And I smiled at him as we shook hands. 'I will come down to Millbrook, discreetly, as you say.'

'I shall look forward to that,' he said.

'I suspect, however, that for the immediate future my travel plans may not allow it.'

'I see. As soon as you find it possible, do let me know and we can make the necessary arrangements.'

'I will.'

Our meeting was either precisely timed, or Julius had some way of signalling that it was over; the door opened, and his assistant came in to whisk me away from his office and out through the grand entrance hall of the building into the City.

A cab ride later I was tucked away with the rest of what I had come to think of as the 'team' in a corner of the restaurant in Fortnum & Mason. We were there, in Milady's words, 'to pat ourselves on the back and to tie up a few things'. Triple-tiered trays of delicate sandwiches and flamboyant pastries were arrayed across the table. At Milady's insistence, however, we were drinking champagne rather than tea.

'Well done all.' Milady had raised her glass in a toast, the rest of us joining her. 'To success.'

'Which you feel it was?' I asked.

'And you don't? Sterling, everything has played out most wonderfully. The Ripper conspiracy has been rooted out and destroyed, we have recovered details of a number of compromised officials and, best of all, the Bureau is to be subjected to an independent enquiry questioning the scope of its responsibilities.' She smiled. 'Mr Church, you seem unconvinced.'

Church put down his glass. 'I am,' he said, 'for two reasons. Namely, the surgeon and the killer.'

'Quite simply,' said Milady, 'it was as we suspected, Sir Anthony Willard was the surgeon, both at the scenes of the crimes and for the procedure itself.'

'So, are we arresting him, or will he be having an accident?' asked Church in the matter-of-fact the way that a tailor might ask about whether a suit was to be single or double-breasted.

'Neither,' replied Milady. 'We can be quite assured of Sir Anthony's silence and future cooperation, thanks to Miss Green's findings. Miss Green?'

'Milady. Yes, thanks to his assistant and a few local enquiries we have a more complete idea of Sir Anthony's Venetian connection. The picture you saw in his office, Sterling, was of a free clinic that Sir Anthony runs every summer for locals, especially women, who can't afford medical treatment. The clinic was only made possible in the first place with a large personal donation from Sir Anthony.'

'Assuaging his guilt?' I asked.

'We think so,' replied Green, 'and also slightly more than that.'

'What do you mean?' asked Church.

Milady gave a wicked little laugh. 'It seems that Sir Anthony took his charity to a very personal level.'

'He has another family there,' explained Green.

'And not just a mistress,' added Milady. 'The fool married her.'

'And so we'll take over from K17 in blackmailing him?' asked Church.

'But for the right reasons, Mr Church,' said Milady, 'which

makes all the difference, wouldn't you say?' She took a sip of champagne.

'And, of course, it leaves him at liberty to perform the operation again should the Queen sicken for a second time,' I said.

'Though condoning such a barbaric procedure would, of course, be something we would never dream of doing,' said Milady.

Church looked as unconvinced as I was. 'And what about the Ripper?' he asked.

'Well, I had a conversation with Sir Anthony himself and, thanks to his eager cooperation, we were able to identify the other man.' Milady paused. 'No one of interest, just someone they roped into the conspiracy. He was a desperate and inveterate gambler who originally carried out his role in return for a substantial payment, but it seemed that, once they started, he found a taste for the work and may have committed other murders of his own volition, as it were. A thoroughly despicable individual whom chance has already rewarded with the justice he deserves.'

'He's dead?' asked Church.

'That is correct,' said Milady.

'How did he die?' I said.

She looked straight at me. 'On a station platform, I believe. Some sort of accident.'

'Their tapper, this Miss Mills, is still abroad,' said Collier, 'but we have reason to believe that she will keep her silence in return for her freedom. We will keep a quiet eye out for her in the meantime. Isn't that right, Patience?'

'What? Yes,' said Patience, looking up from where she sat, carefully stacking three differently coloured macarons, one on top of the other. At Milady's insistence she had been forced to wear a dress for the occasion, a state of affairs which she seemed to have taken in good grace, the gaudily mismatched pair of gloves she was sporting the only obvious sign of rebellion. Collier waited expectantly for Patience to say a little more but, ignoring him, she smashed the three macarons flat into a single, multi-layered biscuit which she lifted up and from which she then took a large, less than ladylike bite.

'Well,' said Milady, 'rumours of Prussian agents abroad in the Kentish countryside notwithstanding, all has been brought to a successful conclusion and if the rest of you would excuse us, I would like a few moments of privacy with Mr Sterling.'

The others left us then, with handshakes from Collier and Green, a firm clasp on the shoulder from Church, and a sarcastically overwrought curtsey from Patience. I noticed that, while the others left, Collier loitered by the door.

It was then that Milady asked me whether I was thinking of staying on.

'I am,' I replied.

'Oh, I am pleased,' said Milady, refilling both our glasses. 'I think you'll make a marvellous field executive and, in fact, there's something that Mr Collier has in mind for you.'

'There was just one thing that I am curious about,' I said.

'What was that?' asked Milady.

'Why did you rescue me?'

'What do you mean?' she said.

'I mean, what made you take the risk?' I asked.

'Well, we knew who you were and your track record in Canada fitted the profile we look for in our operatives.'

'And I was in the country illegally and probably desperate enough to do whatever you asked of me?'

'That too.' Milady smiled and drank from her glass. 'Why do you ask?'

'Because I've been thinking about the attack on Carlton Gardens,' I said.

'What about it?'

'That it was too heavy-handed a way of dealing with a pair of lawyers and too careless if we were a government organisation. But it might make sense if they thought they were dealing with a lone armed man, a soldier perhaps.' I sipped my drink. 'Because I was wondering what if someone had told Sebastian Fuller who I really was? And that I was back in London, had already killed one half of his Ripper and was hell bent on finding him and punishing his betrayal. Under those circumstances Fuller might be tempted to act rashly way in the way that he did. But that would mean whoever told him would have had to have known who I was, why I was in Canada and to have at least suspected Fuller's involvement in the Ripper business from the start.'

Milady had been listening as I was speaking, face impassive, the socialite's sparkle slowly fading from her eyes.

'But if I knew or suspected Fuller was behind the Ripper,' she said, 'why not simply arrest him? I could make him tell me who the conspirators were, and have it all wrapped up much more simply and quietly.'

'Because that wouldn't have solved the other problem.'

'Which was?' The warmth was almost gone now.

'That the Bureau was getting too big for its boots and encroaching on everyone else's territory. Putting a stop to that would have benefitted from a much noisier and more disruptive approach, with any fallout laid at the Bureau's door,' I said. 'I dare say that quite a few of the other agencies are equally delighted with the idea of a formal review of the Bureau's activities and a curtailment of their power.'

'Well,' said Milady taking a sip of champagne, 'what a fascinating theory. That sort of imagination will serve you well in your work with us. The trick, of course, is to know when to let it run on and when to reign it in. Also, completely unrelated to any of this, I should remind you that your pardon is dependent on your position with us.'

No humanity left in the eyes then, just the cold calculation of a feline predator waiting curiously to see which way its prey is going to run.

I held her gaze. 'I understand.'

'Excellent,' said Milady, standing up. I did the same. 'I will so enjoy keeping you with us, Sterling.' She beckoned across the room at Collier, who walked over to us. Milady smiled. 'Mr Collier, Sterling is ready for his next directive I believe?' I nodded. 'Well, then, I shall leave you both to it. Do finish up the fizz, Sterling, it's a terribly good vintage.' And she walked lightly out through the restaurant, a fashionably dressed gentlewoman with not a care in the world.

Collier walked over to me. 'Agent Sterling. How pleasing to know that you will still be with us.' He handed me a thick envelope. 'What do you know about Constantinople?'

Acknowledgements

First off, a huge thank you to my parents for their encouragement throughout the writing of this book and for their belief in the idea that it would, really, really be published one day.

Added to this, a massive thanks to the family, friends, friends of friends, Twitter acquaintances and complete strangers whose backing turned this idea into a reality. And thanks to good friends and artistic geniuses Dan Simpson and Andrew Park for agreeing to create some fantastic rewards for backers.

A big thanks also to the team at Unbound, to Xander who gave the go-ahead in the first place and did a great job of keeping me on track throughout, and to my editors Craig and Andrew, who in the process of pushing me to write the best book possible have also helped me learn and improve as a writer.

My beta readers most certainly deserve a mention: Esme, Cassy, James, Steve, Sian, Andrew, Anthony, Dan, my brother Jeremy and my father. Their tireless enthusiasm, questions, suggestions, comments and far greater levels of grammatical awareness than mine were invaluable in making this happen. In addition, my brother's encyclopaedic historical knowledge was vital in helping me to create the alternative timeline of Sterling's world. Thanks also to Isha and Eugenie for their professional feedback early on in the process which was so incredibly helpful.

Finally, the fact that this book ever made it past the third chapter, and every chapter along the way, is down to my own personal test-reader, editor, advisor and the person who patiently disagreed with my consistently pessimistic view of my writing, my very kind and very lovely wife, Mary Ann.

Unbound is the world's first crowdfunding publisher, established in 2011.

We believe that wonderful things can happen when you clear a path for people who share a passion. That's why we've built a platform that brings together readers and authors to crowdfund books they believe in – and give fresh ideas that don't fit the traditional mould the chance they deserve.

This book is in your hands because readers made it possible. Everyone who pledged their support is listed at the front of the book and below. Join them by visiting unbound.com and supporting a book today.

Conrad Ash
Peter W. Blumbach
Nick Breeze
Ian Bridgeman
Helen Brocklebank
H

David Heilbron
John Key
Dan Kieran
Christopher Kraken
Rupert Lang
John Mitchinson
Rhel ná DecVandé
Carlo Navato
Notink Notlnk
Justin Pollard
Ian Sanderson
Sara Shinton
R Trowbridge
Craig Vaughton